THE PRODIGY

GREATNESS HAS A PRICE

A. L. CAMPBELL

Tim,

Thank you for supporting me. Sorry I
don't have any pictures for you this
time. Maybe next time!

5-17-12

A. L. Campbell

By A. L. Campbell
www.theprodigybook.com

Published by Rustic Wood Publishing
P O Box 391521,
Snellville, GA 30039

ISBN: 978-0-9849265-0-3

Library of Congress Control Number:
2011962972

Printed in the United States of America

This is a work of fiction. Names, characters, places, and incidents either are the product of the author's imagination or are used fictitiously, and any resemblance to actual persons, living or dead, businesses, companies, events, or locales in entirely coincidental.

While the author has made every effort to provide accurate telephone numbers and Internet addresses at the time of publication, neither the publisher nor the author assumes any responsibility for errors, or changes that occur after publication. Further, the publisher does not have any control over and does not assume any responsibility for author or third party websites or their content.

Dedicated to my mentor and friend's late wife Barbara Burdette and the millions of fans around the world who absolutely love the sport of football and wonder what the future of the sport will look like.

ACKNOWLEDGMENTS

Thank you to my family and friends for supporting me with this novel from day one. I wish to express special gratitude to the cover models (left to right) Chris De Ved, Tamsyn Solomon, and Dwayne Johnson. They were an awesome group to work with.

Thank you to Green Island Entertainment for producing such wonderful photography of the cover models. I'd also like to acknowledge my editor Annette for her hard work in helping me make this a truly sensational read.

Last, but not least, I want to send a special thank you to my wonderful son and beautiful wife for encouraging me to believe in myself and the work I produce.

The Prodigy
Greatness has a price.

We invite you to continue your experience and stay updated
on the author's activities with The Prodigy at our website:

theprodigybook.com

Please like "The Prodigy Book" on Facebook

PREFACE

I wrote this book because American Football is the most profit-able sport in the world, according to Forbes.com, and the money continues to pile up year after year. We simply love the sport and can't get enough of it. Regardless of the numerous black eyes the sport receives in the news headlines from various scandals rang-ing from alleged illegal compensation, rumored back room deals, and unscrupulous acts that end up on police reports, we all remain continuously loyal with our wallets and our viewership. Given the sport's current culture from high school to college to the pros, what will become of football ten, twenty, or even thirty years from now? I wanted to take readers on a journey to where we are headed at our current pace.

I simply didn't want to write just another story about football that only fans of the sport would enjoy. I felt compelled to dive deep into the life of the greatest athlete the world has ever seen and examine how he would handle falling in love for the first time, dealing with people who have their own agendas, and, of course, living in the spotlight of the entire multimedia universe before leaving high school and after.

There is indeed something that everyone will take away from "The Prodigy". Greatness does come with a price.

CONTENTS

PROLOGUE

August 2051

My old friend Carlos won two tickets behind the dugout, including airfare, to see his beloved Los Angeles Dodgers play at home against the Angels. At first, I didn't want to go when he asked. After all, who wants to see baseball? He never missed a televised Dodgers game for as long as I had known him, and I didn't want to ruin his excitement. I reluctantly accepted his all-expense paid, one-day trip, even though he blew off several of my invitations to watch football at my house when the Dodgers were playing.

I still can't believe he won. I have listened to that sports talk radio station for 25 years trying to win tickets to a football game, and I never even made it through on the phone. Sometimes life just isn't fair.

We landed at LAX at 2:15 p.m. on Friday afternoon. I didn't want to be a total mooch, so I split the cab fare to Dodger Stadium with Carlos. The cab ride lasted 30 minutes or so. Traffic congestion increased the closer we got to the stadium so we asked the cab driver to drop us off three blocks away from the entrance. "All these people are here just to watch a freaking baseball game?" I thought.

Carlos and I exited the cab and began our short journey toward the stadium. We passed a couple of hotels and other businesses during our walk. Carlos turned an eight minute walk into a 45 minute nightmare, considering the fact that he had to stop at every other vendor on the way and decide whether he wanted a t-shirt or not. After he decided on a shirt, he had to try to negotiate for a better price. The poor vendor felt sorry for us old guys and gave him a senior discount. I think Carlos just wore him down. Apparently, the vendor didn't think it was that important to argue over a $2 souvenir.

The short but long walk turned out to be quite an ordeal for my frail legs. I didn't have the stamina that I had back in my better days.

The Dodgers beat the Angels 4-3 in the longest three hours of my life, but Carlos could not have been more elated. Wearing a new long-sleeve shirt over his faded, wrinkled Dodgers t-shirt, Carlos left the stadium on a natural high.

At 7:40 p.m., the streets in Dodgertown, California, bustled with activity after the game. We headed back in the direction we had come in hopes of getting a cab so we could make our 11:45 p.m. flight back to Phoenix. We thought we would have better luck hailing a cab if we walked a little further from the stadium exit.

While Carlos and I were walking by the Farley Hotel, I thought I heard someone call out for help. I looked around but saw nothing. I asked Carlos, "Did you hear that?"

"Hear what?" Carlos responded.

"Someone yelled 'help'."

Carlos flagged a cab that was just pulling up to the curb. "Nothing's going on around here except people trying to go home. If someone in this crowd is calling for help, they won't be getting it from either one of us. We're outta here!"

In actuality, we could have witnessed quite another scene if we had only looked up to the 23rd floor balcony of the Farley Hotel. Derrick Wright dangled upside down from Suite 2308. Two, tall, muscular men wearing dark suits held each one of Derrick's ankles, preventing him from plummeting to his death on the sidewalk below. The loud music from the bachelor party directly above in Suite 2408 drowned out his tears and cries for help. The music, along with the exotic dancers, kept the attention of all the men throwing crumpled money at their feet. The only reason Derrick was still breathing was because the men's boss had not given the order to release him, which normally would have happened without hesitation. Rick Dorset stood about 15 feet away from the action, barely visible in the dimly lit suite, allowing Derrick's fear to set in before continuing the conversation he began with him moments earlier. Rick stepped out of the darkness onto the balcony so Derrick could hear his every word.

"Derrick, I don't think you understand me perfectly clear. I hope that you can understand me now that you have gotten a little air. Your parents have already spent the money I gave them, so there is no such thing as turning back at this point. Commitments have been finalized. You'll complete your obligation to me. Do we understand each other now?"

"Yes, yes. Pull me up. Pull me up!" Derrick pleaded.

"If we have to have this conversation again, I won't be so nice. You're lucky I've been seeing a therapist for the last few weeks. Pull this little punk up before someone sees us," he told the men before heading toward the door alone.

The brutes slowly collected the teen from his 23-story nightmare. Once Derrick's feet made contact with the balcony floor, he collapsed to a seated position with his back to the stone balcony wall. The henchmen could smell the foul stench coming from Derrick's freshly soiled jeans. They followed Rick out the door laughing over another successful intimidation session and leaving the teenager soaking in humiliation and an unpleasant aroma.

* * *

Traffic began to pick up as everyone started their Saturday morning routines. I was still somewhat exhausted from the late flight home last night. While I listened to my favorite sports talk radio station again hoping I could win something for once, all of a sudden, a breaking news announcement interrupted the commentators' analysis and interviews from last night's Dodgers game.

"Number one ranked high school running back Derrick Wright held a press conference this morning announcing his decision to stay close to home and play for the University of Southern California Archers. This news shocked most sports fans due to widespread rumors that the five-star athlete made a verbal commitment to a school in Texas. "Now back to your regularly scheduled program."

"I guess all the so-called insider predictions were wrong," I thought. All the sports analysts had been saying for weeks that the kid was going to Texas where he'd fill a much-needed slot.

Once I arrived at Green Acres Cemetery, I parked near my destination so that I only had a short walk. My legs were still sore from walking to that darn Dodgers game yesterday. I locked the doors and maneuvered through the maze of weathered headstones. I tried not to read the many stone tablets aligned row by row with forgotten lives lying down below.

A stark reminder of despair and death, the cemetery is adjacent to a field filled with hope and life. The little league football teams for 8-year-olds held normal fall games just like they did last year when I visited the cemetery and the year before that. I could hear the hopeful parents cheering their little ones on in the distance. "Good job, Aaron." "Way to go, Thomas." Maybe some of them were hoping that their sons would be playing in front of a national audience one day.

I visit this cemetery once every year during football season to stare at a particular tombstone with which I had become quite familiar. Every year I try not to cry, but every year I fail. I mused, "Why did it have to be this way? Why do I still feel responsible for this? That cold box below would be empty if it wasn't for me." For years I have dealt with this burden, and I don't see it going away during my lifetime. Maybe I'll be lucky and not have to wait too much longer. Maybe I'll be in a cold, dark box very soon, and this pain will finally end.

The wind carried my tears toward the left side of my face. I was grateful because they dried faster that way. Standing there for nearly an hour, I must have lost track of time. Realizing that my daughter, Michelle, and her husband, Roy, would be dropping my grandson off at my house pretty soon, I began walking toward my truck.

* * *

Right after I pulled in my driveway and started to exit my truck, my daughter pulled in behind me and almost immediately began her questions.

"Dad, why didn't you answer your phone?" Michelle asked. "I tried to call and let you know we were on our way. I was starting to get worried. Where were you?"

"I was out running errands and didn't hear it. You know I can't figure out how to work those new phones half the time," I said without looking her in the eye and instead focusing on my grandson, Tyler. "You know my hearing isn't so good anymore." I lied to my daughter because I didn't want her to get started on me again.

"Did you have a safe trip to L.A. yesterday? I know you were looking forward to the game."

I could hear the sarcasm in her voice. "It went as expected," I said, just glad she changed the subject.

Tyler reluctantly grabbed his things from his mother's car and headed in the house. He hardly looked at me, but I could still see the frown on his face. Tyler was very much against a 13-year-old being looked after, especially by his grandfather. He thought he was old enough to stay at home alone.

I shook my son-in-law's hand and hugged my daughter before they drove off to celebrate their 15th wedding anniversary. They planned to pick Tyler up later that evening after dark. No matter his disposition, I relished the thought of spending an entire day with my grandson.

When I walked in the house, Tyler already had his video game system wirelessly accessed with the big screen monitor in the living room. He sat on the sofa, activating some kind of college football game. After cycling through the team options for several minutes, he finally settled on one.

When I asked him why he chose that team, he said, "They have the best quarterback in the universe."

I chuckled at Tyler's statement because I was familiar with the young quarterback. I disappeared into the attic for a few minutes and then returned with a scrapbook full of old newspaper clippings and pictures. I sat down on the sofa next to Tyler and flipped the book open to the first page. "Your generation has no idea what a great quarterback is," I said proudly. "Turn that game off and listen carefully, as I tell you the story of the greatest quarterback that ever played the game."

CHAPTER 1
FIRST DAY AT OAKRIDGE

August 2018

"**M**iles, are you up?" yelled his mother, Melissa, from the kitchen. "I don't want you to be late on your first day."

"Yes," replied Miles in a low voice. He wasn't at all in the mood for loud noises; but it wasn't for the typical reason teenagers usually don't like loud noises early in the morning. Miles hadn't stayed up late the night before partying, playing or hanging out with friends. Instead, the 14-year-old hardly got any rest because he was nervous about his first day at a new school. He spent the night thinking of all sorts of scenarios in which he was either rejected or accepted by the other kids.

Miles was an extremely intelligent young man, so his fears had nothing to do with academic ability. In fact, he was such a gifted student that his grades earned him a grant to attend the prestigious, private institution of learning known as Oakridge Academy, a school normally attended by the children of the wealthiest members of Scottsdale, Arizona, or elite athletes. Miles was neither. One could only say that fate played a role in him getting the opportunity to attend Oakridge.

Melissa worked at a high-end department store in Scottsdale's Fashion Square Mall. She served extremely wealthy regular customers who ranged from professional athletes to state politicians. Melissa often bragged to her regulars about Miles and how well he performed in school. One day she was assisting Arlene Goldstein, whose husband owned Joseph Goldstein Jewelers, a custom design jewelry store in Scottsdale, and once again commented on Miles' academic achievements at his public school. Melissa continued to explain how she wished she could afford to enroll him in a prestigious private high school for the next year. Mrs. Goldstein, having grown fond of Melissa and her service over the years, mentioned that she was on the board at Oakridge Academy. She explained that the school created a grant program with limited access for the area's brightest, underprivileged academic achievers.

Mrs. Goldstein proudly told Melissa that the program was her idea because she wanted "to help smart, deserving kids." She detailed the application process to Melissa, excitedly writing down every word of information. Melissa learned that all tuition and book fees would be covered under this grant as long as the student maintained at least a 3.0 grade point average. Melissa was overwhelmed with joy and could not wait to get home to tell Miles. She felt like that day, almost six months ago, was the first day of his journey to a promising professional career.

Emerging from his room, Miles wore dark brown leather dress shoes, khaki slacks, and a short-sleeve, yellow polo shirt with an embroidered school crest on the left. The ensemble comprised standard attire for all male freshmen at Oakridge. The only exception was on game days when plain clothes featuring the school colors of blue and red were permitted. Miles appeared ready for his first day at Oakridge. He walked into the kitchen to find his mother and Aunt Evelyn already seated at the table. Melissa was dressed and ready to drive Miles to school, while his aunt was still in her favorite brown robe sipping on her favorite Columbian brew of coffee.

Miles and Melissa lived with her sister Evelyn ever since Miles came into this world. His mom could not afford a decent place in a safe neighborhood on her income. Evelyn didn't mind because she lived alone and liked having company. Evelyn was an emergency room physician assistant at Tempe Saint Luke Hospital. She worked long hours and found comfort in knowing relatives occupied her home, especially when she worked third shift.

Miles hooked one strap of his backpack over the upper edge of a kitchen table chair before sitting down to join his mother and aunt at the table. He did not walk into a kitchen with the smell of eggs, bacon, or toast filling the air. Just like every morning as far back as Miles could remember, his mother had her special nutrient-enriched smoothie waiting for Miles in a glass in front of his chair at the table. Evelyn sat at the table sipping from her usual black coffee mug while reading the news on her I-Pad. She watched Miles drink his breakfast as she had every school morning as far back as she could remember, but she had to say something that morning.

"It should be a crime to feed a teenage boy such tasteless crap for breakfast, especially today."

Melissa rolled her eyes but didn't comment. For the average teenager, the mere smell of the concoction would cause vomiting. When Melissa learned she was pregnant with Miles, she committed to raising a healthy child. For years, Melissa studied the benefits of herbs and other plants, such as kelp. She was convinced her nutritional diet plan made her look 10 years younger. She also took credit for Miles' academic achievements, claiming the supplements and liquids kept his mind sharp and focused, enhancing memorization. There was little room to argue with her, after taking one look at Miles. Did he have any signs of popular teenage acne? No. As a matter of fact, finding any 14-year-old with better looking skin, teeth, or hair proved challenging. If questioned, Evelyn would have trouble remembering the last time he fell ill. He had gone his whole life without catching as much as a cold.

Standing nearly 6 feet tall and weighing 170 pounds, Miles' sandy hair and deep blue eyes were somewhat of a stark contrast to his pale skin. He was above average height for his age. Solely based on his physical stature, most assumed he was some sort of athlete. However, as long as his mother had any say, he would not participate in activities that would expose him to any type of harm or injury, such as sports.

His mother introduced him to her workout routine when he turned 13. It entailed a combination of yoga and light weight training. Miles resisted at first, but he took a liking to it once he began to notice the results while staring into the bathroom mirror. He even started jogging to increase his cardio endurance.

Because Melissa wanted her son to grow up strong and healthy, she didn't mind spending extra money on totally organic groceries. Miles was worth it, she thought. Melissa loved knowing that her son avoided consuming all the toxins that food producers exposed society to in processed foods and some fresh vegetation. She felt that she made a statement to the world in her own little way. Evelyn wanted no part of the "garbage" they consumed daily. She was fine with taking in all the toxins she could, and her appearance indicated that she did just that. Even though Melissa and Evelyn shared similar looks, no one ever confused the two. Evelyn was about 40 pounds overweight and clearly would never fit into her high school prom dress again without some major lifestyle changes. Melissa garnered most of the male attention when they were out in public together.

"Just continue to do what you have been doing your whole life; just be yourself," said Melissa, who noticed her son's constant shuffling in his seat.

"Yeah, just stay out of the way of those trust fund babies, and you will be fine," mumbled his aunt in her usual cynical tone. She never had a problem telling anyone exactly what she thought.

Miles sat staring blankly at the remnants of his drink. He knew that it was easy being himself at his old school were everyone came from middle class backgrounds and had a lot in common, but this school was different. He felt that these wealthy kids would take one look at him and know that he was not one of them. He was sure he would spend the next four years of high school without any friends. Still, he tried to bury those thoughts in the back of his mind and to focus on the potential this opportunity offered. Miles, like his mother, knew that if he graduated from Oakridge Academy, he would have his choice of universities to pursue his dream of becoming a doctor. Miles knew he had to figure out a way to channel any apprehension or negative thoughts into a four-year plan of motivation.

* * *

Twenty minutes after leaving home, Melissa dropped off Miles in the Oakridge Academy student parking lot. Miles exited his mom's blue 2012 Honda sedan and pulled his backpack over his right shoulder after retrieving it from the back seat.

"Have fun, I love you, and remember what I said," Melissa encouraged Miles.

Miles waved goodbye and began walking toward the school entrance. He immediately began to realize the world he was venturing into as he walked up the sidewalk. He saw several students exiting their vehicles. They paid no attention to the new guy heading in the same direction. The students were either engaged in conversation with each other or chattering away on their satellite phones gripped firmly to their chins. A stranger to the campus may have thought he or she was at a car show. Miles passed several new Mercedes and BMW models. He saw a few Bentleys, as well as one Ferrari. The list of expensive cars went on and on. Miles knew immediately he wasn't at his old, run down public school anymore. Franklin High didn't have new paint on the walls or freshly buffed floors, but he liked his old school nonetheless. Miles didn't even mind traveling through the metal detectors every morning. He began to miss his old friends even more at that moment.

Armed with a map, Miles followed the directions he printed out the night before. He hardly noticed the students, wearing similar khaki bottoms and yellow tops, zooming past him due to his slow, listless pace. After maneuvering through the maze of hallways and sea of yellow and brown garments, the map eventually led him to the new student orientation room where several newcomers were already seated. Miles spotted a seat in the back and slowly made his way toward it, trying not to make eye contact with any of the other students. This proved unnecessary because nearly every student was busy texting or having a conversation on satellite phones at every turn. They wouldn't have noticed the president of the United States if he entered with a full security detail. Miles finally made it to the empty desk and pulled out an e-note pad to record important information he might learn during the orientation. He didn't want to have to ask anyone any questions, which would force him to make eye contact with or speak to strangers.

Out of nowhere, a male student sitting two rows in front of Miles turned around toward him and said, "You must be one of the charity cases?"

"Excuse me?"

"I can tell because you're not wearing a designer polo shirt with the matching backpack like these other rich simpletons in this room. That can only mean you are a jock with a killer jump shot or you're a genius like me, here on an academic grant."

Miles took a moment to examine his inquisitor before responding. The nearly 5-foot-6-inch young man with pale, white skin and dark, thick hair was in bad need of a haircut. He had a slim frame accompanied by a slender, oval shaped face. Weighing only 135 pounds, no one would ever mistake him for a jock.

"And who are you again?" Miles asked.

"I'm sorry. How rude of me," he said. "The honorable Andrew Myers." Andrew extended his hand to greet Miles.

"Miles Starr, and I guess I am one of the charity cases here on an academic grant," he said while shaking Andrew's hand.

Andrew told Miles not to worry about the free education they'd receive because they were giving the academy something in return. He explained that a large percentage of the student body would never seek real jobs in their lifetimes, so excelling academically was not a high priority. Oakridge offered grants to students with above average IQs to increase the academy's SAT scores, average GPA scores, athletic win records, and professional success stories. Andrew said increasing the numbers in each category fostered an image of exceptional educational standards. Doing so guaranteed continued funding from generous, wealthy donors and parents. "Plus, they look charitable as heck," he added.

After the bell rang, the moderator began to welcome the freshmen to their new institution of learning, but only after making several attempts to get the majority to relinquish use of their satellite phones. Eventually they did. For the next 20 minutes, she went through a bunch of routine rules and expectations. The students looked bored up until the orientation finally ended. When asked if anyone had any questions, the students simply remained quiet, looking around and hoping no one would say anything. Finally, someone asked, "Are we done yet?"

Afterward, Miles collected his things and headed toward the classroom exit to find his first class. Andrew walked with Miles down the hallway. He rambled for a minute until indicating that he would continue their conversation at lunch. Andrew took the fact that Miles didn't dismiss him as an invitation to continue his monologue over a meal.

* * *

The lunchtime bell rang as an overwhelmed Miles headed to the cafeteria, where he eventually found a small table where he could eat alone. He was relieved to get a break after being bombarded with information ever since his first class. He felt like his brain had grown in the last 3 hours. He sat down for a few seconds before Andrew flopped down in the seat across from him. Miles quietly began to retrieve the healthy lunch his mother prepared. As soon as Andrew saw what Miles was eating he said, "What the hell is that shit?"

"This is called a vegetable smoothie with wheat grass" said Miles, trying to explain what it was and what benefits it had on the body. "I drink this every day for a breakfast or lunch meal replacement."

All Andrew heard was "blah...blah...blah." He made a weird face before biting into the chili cheese dog he purchased a few moments before. Andrew enjoyed his heart-stopping meal so much that he failed to realize some chili had taken an interest in his shirt. Not wanting to interrupt Andrew's obvious enjoyment, Miles didn't mention the new shade of red added to his new friend's yellow polo shirt.

While still devouring his chili cheese dog, Andrew shared news he learned about the school since they spoke earlier. "Did you know that the daughter of a United States Senator goes to school here? And did you know that the son of CEO James Garrett goes here? I hear this school gets millions of dollars in donations from people like that every year."

"The Virtual Tech James Garrett?" Miles questioned.

"No wonder they can afford to sponsor us little people to come here. Our tuition is peanuts compared to this school's operating budget," Andrew claimed with an amazed look on his face. Miles just listened attentively as Andrew gave detail after detail about Oakridge Academy's faculty, students, and their parents.

Miles finally asked, "How did you find out all this?"

"Well, if you haven't noticed already, I like to talk. Believe it or not, so do a lot of other people."

Miles asked Andrew about him introducing himself as the "Honorable Andrew Myers."

"I plan to be a judge one day, and I'll bang my gavel all over whosoever shall enter into my courtroom."

Miles grinned at Andrew's obvious attempt at humor. He realized he was dealing with a true free spirit.

The loud tone signaled the end of lunch period. The pair gathered their belongings and headed off to their next destinations. As Miles was about to exit the cafeteria, he couldn't help but notice the help wanted announcement scrolling across the school news monitor up by the doorway. He stopped to input the information in his e-note pad while Andrew continued on to class. Ever since Miles learned of Arizona's law allowing 14-year-olds to work a couple of hours a day with a parent's permission, he wanted to find a part time job. His mother wouldn't hear of it. She felt it would interfere with his studies, but Miles wanted things and didn't want to burden his mother with the cost because he knew she didn't make much money in her retail position. However, he figured she would likely approve of him working at school instead of some off-site location. If not, he flirted with the idea of forging her name and telling her he was staying after school to study in the media center. That was wishful thinking, though, because Miles had never lied to his mother about anything. They shared open and candid discussions on all topics. That was one of the reasons they had such a great mother-son relationship.

Melissa anxiously awaited her son's emergence from a small crowd of students, obviously freshmen, at the student pickup area at the side of the building, next to the gym. No sooner than Miles opened the car door, Melissa began asking questions about his day. To her disappointment, Miles didn't say much on the drive home. He gave the shortest answers possible, hoping she would stop and he could instead devise a strategy to get a job at school, maintain his grades, and satisfy his mother while fitting in with the rich kids with whom he had absolutely nothing in common.

"Everything was fine," he reassured her several times.

"Well, you don't act like it."

"Mom, everything was great. I guess I'm just tired."

Miles couldn't focus on answering his mother's questions, and she eventually realized it. Melissa understood that her son needed time to adjust to his new environment, so she stopped with the questions, and they both enjoyed a quiet ride home.

CHAPTER 2
MR. SOMERS

August 2018

Two weeks into his new educational surroundings as a freshman at Oakridge Academy, Miles felt comfortable enough with his ability to handle his class workload to inquire about the job opportunity he saw on the first day of school. The posting instructed applicants to report to the custodial office and to ask for Mr. Somers. Miles waited until the end of the school day, at 3:15, to head down to the custodial office. Earlier, he asked his mother to pick him up an hour past his normal time so he could inquire about the opening, which was fine by her considering her fluctuating work schedule.

Miles approached the location while using his map as a guide. He had never been to that side of the campus, so the map came in handy. The main office was open, so he just walked in. Miles immediately noticed an open door to his left with a small sign above it that read: "Pete Somers, Head Custodian."

He continued in the direction of his obvious destination. Miles peeked inside and raised his right hand to knock on the door but stopped short. He didn't want to interrupt the man he came to see just yet. Miles took a moment to observe Mr. Somers, a middle-aged man with thinning hair. He sat with his back to the door behind a metal desk sparsely decorated except for a family portrait. It was obviously a picture of Mr. Somers, his wife, and young daughter. Miles thought it odd that Mr. Somers and his wife wore dressy, picture worthy clothing, but the daughter wore a football jersey in the photo.

At the moment, Mr. Somers was heavily engaged with his satellite phone and appeared to be changing his fantasy football lineup.

Miles could tell because Mr. Somers read the names of professional football players aloud. He leaned back in the chair with his legs crossed and raised the device in the air out in front of him.

Miles waited but soon realized the man was not going to notice his guest's arrival. "KNOCK..KNOCK!" said Miles, finally making an effort to get Mr. Somers' attention.

The startled gentleman sat upright in the chair and spun around. "Can I help you, young man?"

Miles completely entered the office. He responded, "I sure hope so. I'm looking for Mr. Somers."

The sandy-haired, 5-foot-8-inch man looked up to make eye contact with the towering young man. "I'm Mr. Somers, and you are?" Mr. Somers stood behind the desk. He had a neatly trimmed executive style cut to complement his one piece, black janitorial uniform.

Miles extended his right hand for a formal introduction and uttered, "Miles Starr, sir! I'm here to inquire about the job announcement I saw a couple of weeks ago."

"Well I'll be damned. I didn't expect anyone to respond to that. I've posted that bulletin every year for the last 5 years, and you're the first person to ever actually show up. The types of kids that attend Oakridge don't have a problem making money, if you catch my drift, son. Cleaning toilets and sweeping floors around here won't actually gain you any Facebook friends or Twitter followers, which is what you kids seem to live for these days."

"I really could use the money, and I'm not afraid of hard work," said Miles. "I've never had a formal job before in my life other than keeping my room clean and helping out around the house."

Somers told Miles that the school constructed a new state-of-the-art athletic training complex that needed someone to keep it looking good. "It isn't a big enough responsibility to hire another full-time employee."

"I think I'm the right man for this job, Mr. Somers. I won't disappoint you."

Somers retrieved a job application from his filing cabinet for Miles. "Be sure to list any emergency contacts. I need to know who to call in case you inhale too much cleaning fluid and pass out or something."

Miles put his backpack on the floor, pulled out a chair in front of Somers' desk, sat down, and completed the application. Somers asked Miles if he could work a couple of hours a day after school. He also warned Miles that occasional Saturday work would be required, but Miles didn't mind at all. Miles simply saw an opportunity to make additional money.

When Miles handed the application back to Mr. Somers, he immediately noticed that he and Miles lived in the same neighborhood. He then asked Miles how he got to and from school.

"My mom picks me up and drops me off every day," said Miles. "She doesn't mind, though, because she worries about me so much." Miles was embarrassed to mention the fact that his mother wasn't always on time.

"You seem like a nice, well-mannered, young man. I think you are going to work out just fine."

Somers felt like he and Miles were cut from the same cloth. He was not a wealthy man, but he was surrounded by money every day at work. In his eyes, Miles was like a much taller version of himself. He told Miles that he could start the following day.

"Thanks so much for the opportunity," said Miles, shaking Somers' hand once again across the desk. He exited the office and then headed to the pick-up area. Surprisingly, his mother was already waiting in the car with her satellite phone playing Sudoku, her favorite game for passing the time.

Miles entered the passenger side of the car with a huge smile on his face. His mother knew why she was picking him up late, so there was no need to ask him how the job inquiry went. She merely put the car in drive and drove them home with a slight smile on her face as well. Melissa was glad to see her son happy about something at his new school, but she had her reservations about Miles' first job.

* * *

Convincing his mother was no easy task. After repeated begging and using his Aunt Evelyn as a character reference, Miles finally convinced his mother to sign off on him working a couple of hours a day after school. Eventually, she reluctantly gave in with only one stipulation. She said he would have to keep his work hours within the legal limit, and she made him promise it wouldn't affect his grades. "That sounds like two stipulations," Miles thought. He said nothing and remained glad that she was willing to sign the work permit.

Miles knew the job would have no effect on his grades, but he still promised her. Accepting the position was mutually beneficial considering how Melissa had to negotiate with her boss to leave early to pick up Miles on time right after school. On days when the store was busy, Miles was sometimes forced to wait alone in the parking lot. Other students, including freshman, carpooled with friends. He didn't know anyone well enough yet to even consider asking for a ride.

CHAPTER 3
THE NEW COMPLEX

September 2018

Miles reported to Mr. Somers' office the next day after his last class to begin his new job. Mr. Somers greeted Miles and gave him a black, one-piece janitorial uniform that zipped up in the front. After Miles changed clothes, they both walked toward the new athletic training complex.

On their walk over, Mr. Somers handed Miles a key card and told him it would work on any door in the complex. Mr. Somers used the three-minute walk to inform Miles of some of his daily duties as a new employee, which mostly included sweeping, mopping, vacuuming, and taking out the trash.

While walking toward the complex, Miles also observed the immaculate landscaping and concrete designs decorating the front of the new 100,000-square-foot, multi-level megaplex. Oakridge's heavily manicured property full of colorful plant life and golf course style lawns put many college campuses to shame. The cobblestone walkway leading up to the main entrance of the brick building featured a 30-foot-wide, circular water fountain as its centerpiece. A 10-foot long, 4-foot high marble wildcat peered out the center of the fountain, standing on all fours with water shooting from its mouth into the surrounding pond. The statue was a huge statement toward the enormous future expectations of the Oakridge athletic programs. Miles soon found out why the expectations had become so high.

Mr. Somers stopped in front of the main entrance doorway and glanced at Miles. Then, he cleared his throat and glanced at the key card access slot. It took Miles a few seconds before he realized that

Mr. Somers wanted him to use his new key card to open the door for the both of them.

When the door swung open and Miles walked in, he could not believe his eyes. It was the most beautiful and chilling site he had ever seen. It was like he had been transported to another world where technology was the basis for most everything. The front door led them immediately into the athletic lounge area, which was divided into two areas on either side of the main doors. The school colors of red and blue adorned the carpet at the entrance, and the scent echoed the smell of new carpet and fresh paint. A huge wildcat emblem, the school mascot, was sewn into the carpet, mimicking the statue outside. The walls were painted red on one side of the room and blue on the other. Oak and cherry wood chairs and tables were scattered throughout the main social area. Touch screen 3D monitors hung everywhere. Students could also use the monitors as computers to surf the Web, check e-mail, initiate video calls, and just about anything else a young teen wanted to do. Students were so engrossed in their gadgets that they barely noticed Miles and Mr. Somers walking past them.

After leaving the lounge area, the building turned into a maze of hallways, doorways, and rooms. The expansive complex had different wings for each sport. All the coaches for each sport had offices in the complex. The football program occupied the largest section of the building. Football, by far, was the most popular sport at Oakridge and brought in the most revenue. Mr. Somers explained to Miles that a parent of one of the students was the CEO of Virtual Tech, the largest technology company in the world. His company donated this first-of-its-kind facility to the academy. It was sort of like a sports testing facility. If the sporting performance improved at Oakridge, Virtual Tech could use the school's success as a marketing tool for college and professional sports of all kinds around the world.

Mr. Somers was smiling with satisfaction the whole time they walked through the building because he took pride in being able to work around such high-tech, expensive equipment. He took Miles to almost every location in the building and continued to explain what his responsibilities were during his two-hour work period after school every evening. However, Miles could hardly pay attention to what Mr. Somers said due to his overwhelming fascination with everything within the complex walls. Mr. Somers took him into one of the shower rooms and showed him the completely voice-activated temperature control system. The lights came on automatically when they walked through the doorway. Miles later learned that solar panels on the roof of the complex provided 50 percent of the power. Virtual Tech not only wanted to be the world's leader in new age technology, but the company also prided itself on being environmentally conscious.

"Go over there and stand by that shower head but not directly in front of it," suggested Mr. Somers.

Miles complied immediately.

"Now say, 'warm water on.'"

"Warm water on," Miles commanded, anxiously awaiting the forthcoming water.

Instantly, a stream of water began flowing from the shower near Miles' feet. Miles hopped out of the way before his shoes got wet, but he extended his hand and felt the water temperature. The water was warm.

"Now keep repeating the word warmer and keep your hand under the water," Mr. Somers instructed.

"Warmer, warmer, warmer...Ouch, hot, hot, hot," Miles repeated before yanking his hand from the unbearable water temperature."

Somers laughed and tossed Miles a fresh hand towel to dry his hand before leaving the shower room.

The lights turned off automatically when they exited.

Mr. Somers continued his tour of the facility with Miles, but nothing could have prepared Miles for the first major stop of the tour. Mr. Somers normally saved the best for last, but he couldn't resist showing Miles the football wing of the complex. It was empty at the time because the football team was practicing outside in preparation for the first game of the season that coming Friday. Mr. Somers took Miles into what appeared to be some type of control room with a large glass window in front of where most of the chairs in the room had been placed. On the other side of the window was a huge chamber with green colored walls. It looked something like a small warehouse.

"What is this room for?" Miles asked.

"I was hoping you would ask. This is what is called a HSC, a Holographic Simulation Chamber."

Mr. Somers was a huge sports fan, but nothing compared to his love of football. Miles could not help noticing the grin on Mr. Somers' face grew when they entered the football HSC. As if a different spirit had overcome him, he explained to Miles that the quarterback is the key element of any football team. "If you can't score points, you can't win. And if you can't throw the ball, you won't score points. I could have been a great quarterback back in my day if I had been given a chance," said Mr. Somers enthusiastically, abandoning his lecture on Miles' job responsibilities.

"The quarterback goes into the HSC behind this glass and puts on that white football helmet over there that has the black visor," explained Mr. Somers. "He sees a full-length football field and feels high-grade synthetic turf under his feet. He hears simulated sounds from other players and screaming fans through a next-generation, surround-sound speaker system. Hell, the chamber can even simulate weather conditions. A hydrokinetic turbine simulates the wind conditions. This thing even simulates rain or snow through an irrigation system installed somewhere in the ceiling."

The standard size football helmet had a solid outer shell with a layer of shock-absorbent padding inside, but the innovation was the black visor attached to the facemask that allowed the quarterback to see the simulated game. While looking through the visor on the helmet, the quarterback saw his offensive line, his backs and receivers, the defensive players, and even fans in the stands. When the ball was hiked to the quarterback, it looked like real live action on a real football field.

In fact, everything was simulated with the exception of the football. The football used in the chamber looked and felt just like a normal football even though it had microchips sewn into the threading. The quarterback received the football from the center on the offensive line that appeared as a holographic image from one of two ways.

Mr. Somers continued, "The quarterback steps behind the center's holograph to receive the football or stands back in the shotgun formation. Either way, that mechanical arm you see in there delivers the football to the quarterback when he says 'hike'. It's like the quarterback walks into an alternate universe.

"During a simulation, the holographic receivers appear to go out for passes, and the quarterback actually throws the football."

To the naked eye from behind the glass, the football simply hit the green wall of the chamber. If the quarterback threw the ball accurately, he saw a completed pass and then either the receiver got tackled or a dashed for the end zone. The coaches saw a completed pass on the huge monitors mounted in the control room seeing what the quarterback saw. The chamber recorded the throwing motion, velocity, accuracy, as well as many other significant features needed to develop a quarterback's throwing ability.

"One other thing the HSC helps a quarterback develop, which is probably the most important skill of them all, is timing. During the simulation, if the defensive holographic players get to the quarterback before he throws the ball, the trainee sees a red text message scroll across the visor and hears the message read aloud in the chamber through the surround-sound speaker system. It says, 'You have just been sacked.'" Mr. Somers didn't leave out any details.

The chamber was designed to help a quarterback work on mechanics while simulating environments or conditions that couldn't be duplicated during practice outside. The goal was to prepare the quarterback for any and every game situation while testing and improving his skills.

Miles asked, "What situations can't be duplicated at practice?"

"You can't duplicate the crowd intensity and noise during an away game on a 4th and long play with nine seconds left on the clock when your team is down by six points in the fourth quarter. The only way to mentally prepare for that scenario is to actually be put in that situation. No one knows how they would respond to that level of pressure until they are actually put in that position. The HSC comes as close as possible to creating that scenario and preparing a player to handle it. There are no screaming fans at practice. Even if they did allow some local fans to attend practice, they won't be yelling the obscenities you hear during an away game."

The control room technology displayed completion percentages based on the likelihood the receiver or back would catch the thrown pass. The computer printed out a summary of results for each participant. The data was automatically uploaded to Virtual Tech for analysis of the player and equipment.

Virtual Tech stood to make a fortune if the technology could deliver on what most football teams needed most: elimination of the skill gap in the first and second string players in key positions, namely the quarterback. The problem was exacerbated during regular practice, when the starting quarterback got most of the snaps and all of them during a game. What happens when the starting quarterback goes down? The inexperienced back up is then thrown in the game and everyone hopes for the best. The HSC was designed to equalize skill levels on a team. The technology created game-like situations so that the real game would not rattle the nerves of a less-experienced quarterback, or it could help develop rookie talent faster in the event the starting quarterback sustained an injury. The chamber could also keep the starting quarterback's skills sharp during the off-season.

"No college or professional teams have this technology yet, but they will if evidence proves that the HSC creates a better quarterback," Mr. Somers explained.

By that time, Miles couldn't believe what he was seeing or hearing. He thought the HSC was like a video game but only 100 times better.

"Miles, similar chambers are set up in the basketball, baseball, golf, and every other sport wing in the complex. Virtual Tech is allowing our school to test the HSCs so they can have an inexpensive real life trial of the technology."

Next, Mr. Somers took Miles to the basketball wing, where there was a similar HSC setup. The basketball looked, felt, and weighed the same as a real ball, but it actually had a real basketball goal and court, unlike the football chamber. The basketball HSC technology worked the same as for football. The trainee would wear special goggles that simulated defenders on the court, teammates setting picks, the fans, and any other game attributes. When the trainee took a jump shot or free throw, the computer analyzed the player's form for each attempt. The analysis told the trainee if the form in his or her wrist was off or not and what adjustments needed to be made. Just like the football HSC, the system was designed to help the players perfect their mechanics in a game-like environment, therefore, increasing results during actual games.

The HSC chambers were all designed with basically the same technology. If a player wanted to perfect his batting average, he would spend a couple of hours a day in the baseball HSC. If golfers wanted to perfect their swing, they would spend time in the golfing

HSC. Miles, extremely, overcome with joy and excitement, could hardly stop smiling. Never dreaming he would be working around such amazing technology, Miles was glad he took the initiative to inquire about the job.

"Miles, I'm not going to walk you through every inch of this building, but you can follow the signs and use this," said Mr. Somers, handing him a small handheld electronic locator device that had electronic sketches of the entire building loaded on it.

"With this device, I'll know exactly where you are at any time while you're in the building, and you can learn your way around a little quicker. Also, if I need you to take care of something, I'll send you instructions on this device. It clips onto your uniform right there on your left side."

Miles took the device and examined it curiously before clipping it onto his uniform.

"Just remember not to take this home. It needs to be charged in my office at the end of your work day. If you lose it, I'll have to take it out of your pay."

Miles raised his head, widened his eyes and began to wonder aloud, "How much does this device cost?"

"You don't want to know. Virtual Tech provided a few of them with the building."

Once Mr. Somers finished showing Miles everything he needed to do and in what order the tasks needed to be done, they walked back out the main entrance and headed for the school building. As soon as the door shut behind them, Mr. Somers turned to Miles and said, "Under no circumstances whatsoever are you ever allowed to touch anything in the training HSCs. Those computers are worth more than both of our lives combined."

For a moment, Miles just stood there taking notice of the seriousness of Mr. Somers' tone.

"You have my word sir. I won't touch a thing that I'm not supposed to."

Mr. Somers ushered Miles into the gymnasium in a separate building to help him finish setting up for the pep rally at the end of the week. The Wildcats were about to open the football season that Friday. This year, the team had high expectations for a successful season, just like the previous one and the one before that. Despite boosters pouring tons of money into the various sports programs, Oakridge Academy was not known for its dominant athletic achievements. The HSCs were supposed to help change all that.

As the Christmas holiday season approached, Melissa's work schedule at the department store became more hectic, so Miles waited up until 6 p.m. sometimes for his mother to arrive. Miles could have watched or even participated in one of the many after school activities, but he sat in the pick-up area trying to finish his homework. He promised his mother that his work schedule and responsibilities wouldn't interfere with his grades. While beginning his drive home one afternoon, Mr. Somers noticed Miles sitting on the steps. He stopped the car and waited with him. Soon this became his routine, waiting with Miles whenever his mother ran late.

One day, Mr. Somers asked Melissa if Miles could ride home with him every day instead of waiting. "It just doesn't make any sense for you to have to drive all the way over here and miss time from work when we are going in the same direction," Mr. Somers stated.

"I don't want my son to be a burden on anyone. We'll be just fine. Thank you, though," Melissa responded.

The next day Melissa was over an hour late when a delivery truck made an unscheduled, late drop-off at the store. She arrived at Oakridge Academy to find Miles and Mr. Somers laughing and talking about next year's football season. Melissa asked, "Is your offer for taking Miles home still on the table?"

"Without question," said Mr. Somers.

From that day forward, Mr. Somers drove Miles home after work each day, and soon he started bringing him to school also.

CHAPTER 4
SENIOR YEAR BEGINS

September 2021

At the ripe age of 17, Miles began his senior year at Oakridge Academy. He had grown 4 inches taller since his freshman year and now stood 6 feet 4 inches and weighed 195 pounds. Miles took advantage of his unrestricted access to the training complex and hit the weights religiously when he wasn't working or studying. His percentage of body fat was less than 2 percent, and his muscle tone was extremely developed by then. He had rippled abdominal muscles and well-formed biceps.

People who didn't know Miles mistook him for an athlete, not the academian he was. Tall and handsome, he started getting more stares from several of the young divas at Oakridge Academy. While many of the girls may have been interested, most would not allow that information to be made public. Wealthy female students at Oakridge considered dabbling outside of their social circle social suicide. After all, who was Miles in the grand scheme of things?

Miles was not the type of flashy, popular guy who most girls at Oakridge would have normally been drawn to. He wasn't a big time athlete. He had no parents with an important last name. Despite his better-than-average looks and chiseled athletic physique, Miles wasn't bothered much by his invisibility. He was sort of shy although not in a geeky way. His only concerns with his social life centered on relationships with his best friend, Andrew, and his only female friend, Christine. Currently, he focused mainly on his grades and mastering the next level of his solo athletic training in the weight room.

Andrew, on the other hand, remained a social butterfly who still maintained a high GPA. He knew everyone and everyone knew him. His career plan, becoming a judge, had not changed over the last three years. He still referred to himself as the "Honorable Andrew Myers" when introduced. However, no one ever called him that.

Christine Boozer was a 16-year-old junior who befriended Andrew and Miles two years prior. Truthfully, Christine took every opportunity possible to be in Miles' company. She would never reveal how she really felt about him to anyone, not even Andrew. Miles didn't have a clue about her feelings, but Andrew was not fooled. Perhaps if Christine were as beautiful as some of the other girls at Oakridge, maybe Miles would have noticed her shallow advances over the last two years. Her dark framed glasses didn't help her sex appeal either.

She was fortunate enough to attend the school on a grant, the same way Miles and Andrew did. At 5 feet 6 inches, she was almost one foot shorter than Miles, and her petite frame barely matched his girth. She wanted to be a biologist and ended up taking some of the same advanced science courses that Miles had already completed. Andrew speculated that she took those classes so that when she asked Miles to tutor her last year the request seemed completely innocent, even though she didn't need any help at all, given her 3.9 GPA.

* * *

Miles outperformed his expectations at Oakridge up to that point. One of the top candidates for valedictorian, all of his teachers adored him. Several universities around the country offered him full academic scholarships. Miles knew, like his mother, exceptional grades and a degree from Oakridge would put him in the driver's seat in the college selection process. They both set a goal three years ago and Miles was right where he expected to be. Miles planned to attend a four-year university and then head straight to medical school. Miles' mother had all but made him an expert on keeping the body healthy, and he enjoyed helping people. Thus, he decided what better way to help people than to heal them as a doctor. Besides, his favorite subjects in school were biology and science.

That year, Miles saved up enough money from working to purchase a used hybrid. Mr. Somers helped him find the small car, which had become inexpensive since most automakers used hydrogen cells to power newer models. He no longer needed to ride with Mr. Somers, although he missed the life lessons his boss and now mentor shared with him during their drive to and from school. Since Miles' father was not around and he lived with two women, he enjoyed those brief periods of male bonding.

Miles developed a deep level of love and respect for Mr. Somers. He often sought his council for important decisions. Once he asked him what medical school he should consider. Of course, Mr. Somers, who went to a technical school, couldn't provide much help in that regard. Still, Miles felt he needed to share in this important decision, as he had in most everything else. Mr. Somers had not only shared advice with Miles, he also shared his family. Miles had enjoyed several meals and televised football games with Mr. Somers, his wife, Diana, and their 10-year-old daughter, Squirt, who couldn't wait to outgrow the nickname. Mr. Somers treated Miles like a son. In fact, most students assumed that Miles was the janitor's son who attended school for free as a perk. That assumption didn't help his social life.

* * *

Most of the buzz around school was due to the season-opening home football game at Oakridge later that night. The opponent, the Sand Hill Coyotes, would offer no easy win. The Wildcats considered winning a must if they had any hopes of obtaining a state title. The Coyotes won two state titles in the last six years, and they were very well coached, executing almost flawless plays. Everyone knew the Wildcats were favored to win the state championship that year due to last season's performances by heavily-recruited QB Matt Barkley and receiver Shawn Wells.

After cycling through last season's highlights and big plays, mostly by Matt and Shawn, the gigantic 3D billboard at the school's main entrance announced the big game. Between video conferencing on their satellite phones and reading the billboard, the students miraculously avoided any accidents while driving into the parking lot. The billboard was another generous donation by Virtual Tech, evidenced by the "Donated by Virtual Tech" inscription at the top of the billboard.

When the bell rang, Miles headed to the gymnasium with all the other students and faculty for the pep rally. The school always hosted a pep rally on the Friday of every home game. All the players wore game jerseys. The bleachers were filled with a sea of the red and blue everyday attire, which was permitted on pep rally days. The school relaxed its uniform policy on rally days and those days only at that time. Some students even spray painted their hair or painted their faces red and blue. Miles' only preparation for the pep rally was helping Mr. Somers and other staff setup a 4-foot platform in the middle of the gymnasium floor with a podium.

During the pep rallies, Miles, Christine, and Andrew always sat together. Whoever arrived first would save seats for the other two. Due to Miles' height, shorter students sitting behind him would often stand because he blocked their views. Sometimes when he stood near the platform, people would mistake him for one of the football players minus a jersey, which he thoroughly enjoyed. Leaving Andrew alone, Christine would go stand next to Miles on occasion. Each time, a faculty member would ask her to return to her seat.

While the cheerleaders lead the chants as the school's starting offensive and defensive players were introduced, Andrew took that time to tell Miles and Christine that he wanted to be the president of the Oakridge Future Business Leaders of America Association. "I have to come up with a brilliant business plan in order to be considered for president, and I don't have any ideas. I need some leadership experience to brighten up my college applications."

"I'm sure something will come up," Miles reassured Andrew. "You always seem to land on your feet."

"Yeah, something will come up," said Christine, just repeating what Miles said.

Miles tried to hide his annoyance when she copied his words. Andrew smirked as an obvious sign of disdain.

"Can I get a lift to the game tonight?" asked Andrew while they sat in the stands among a tsunami of screaming students. Andrew volunteered to be the videographer for all the football games that year as an added attempt to pad his college application with volunteer experience. Andrew knew Miles was going to all the game because he'd become a sports junky thanks to Mr. Somers, who never missed an Oakridge home game or any of his favorite college and professional teams' televised games, for that matter.

"Sure," said Miles.

"I need to be there early, so can you get me at 6?"

"Yes, and anything else, your honor?"

"That'll be it for now unless your codefendant wants to add anything else," said Andrew, staring at Christine.

"I'm not sure if I'm going," said Christine, hoping to get a reaction from Miles. Once she saw his blank expression, unwilling to inquire about her possible absence, she said, "Julie's coming by my house to study for awhile, so I'll probably just go with her."

"That's fine," said Andrew, answering for himself and Miles.

Before meeting Mr. Somers, Miles wasn't much of a sports fan, but Mr. Somers really helped motivate Miles' interest in football. He started attending Oakridge home games with Mr. Somers and his daughter shortly after beginning to work for him. In fact, Miles' visits to Mr. Somers' home to watch sports on the weekend with him and Squirt became a routine during his junior year. Squirt sat on the couch with them wearing the same jersey she wore in the photo in Mr. Somers' office. His infatuation with football had infected her too.

Mr. Somers once compared the description of a quarterback leading 10 players down the field to the end zone to a conductor leading an orchestra. When Miles heard that, he became intrigued with not only the sport of football, but also the quarterback position itself. One day when they were talking about football, Mr. Somers admitted to Miles that he never played football in high school.

"They wouldn't let me play. Coach said I was too puny and would get hurt out there. He offered to let me get the team's water, so I accepted just to be around the players. I've always loved the game ever since my father took me to my first high school game when I was only 6 years old."

Mr. Somers proudly displayed the 8-inch little league football trophy in his living room from when he was 8 years old. He never told Miles that he, along with the rest of his teammates back then, earned the small token for participation only.

Somers admitted to Miles privately one day that although he loved his daughter without question, he had always hoped for a son, who would be an athlete or, at least, share his love for sports.

Diana, his wife, said she was done having children after having so much difficulty delivering Squirt, who was a breech birth. Although Mr. Somers wanted to be the father on the sideline at his son's football practice, Squirt would have to do. Mr. Somers played football, soccer, and basketball with her since she was 4, so she became a tomboy at an early age.

Right after Miles agreed to pick up Andrew before the game, Coach Burdette stood at the podium and began to announce the two remaining starting players, the stars, QB Matt Barkley and receiver Shawn Wells. He liked saving the best for last. Anyone who drove by Oakridge would recognize those two on sight due to the 100 foot images of them draped on the side of the athletic complex. They could be seen from at least a mile away. Mr. Somers followed orders to install lights to highlight the billboard-sized images from the ground up.

The students rose to their feet and cheered louder for those two than they did for the rest of the team combined. Several of the females in attendance, including teachers, clapped and screamed, "I love you Shawn," when his name was called. Shawn's entrance brought both excitement and angst. Some female students looked around to notice other girls clapping with extra enthusiasm and then gave them evil glares while rolling their eyes. They each felt slightly insulted from other females giving so much attention to someone with whom they each felt a small claim. One could say that was the result of Shawn being Shawn, the ultimate lady's man, womanizer, Casanova, and on and on. If it weren't for Sam, Shawn would have had sole ownership of the title "champion of the ladies."

"Sam" was short for Samantha. Sam was a lesbian and Oakridge's senior star female basketball player, standing 6 feet 4 inches. She had Shawn's swagger but in a female body. If Shawn and Sam were characters in a comic book, they would be considered arch enemies. Sam was the only person who could get under Shawn's skin, as they each would try to upset the other by bragging about how many women they had. It was some sort of game between the two of them that began three years prior during Shawn's freshman year. Then, Sam allegedly became romantically involved with a young lady Shawn really liked. He took the betrayal to heart. Everyone said Shawn changed after that ordeal, creating the ultimate player both on and off the field. He never fell for anyone again in high school.

Coach Burdette allowed each of the two high school stars to say a few words to excite the crowd even more. Looking like a Ken Doll, Matt simply said, "How are my Wildcats feeling today? Is everyone excited about beating the hell out of some Coyotes tonight?" The crowd responded to every word with ear-shattering cheers. One or two of the students even shed tears as Matt continued to speak. Football always seemed to generate those kinds of reactions.

"I want to see all of you at the stadium tonight cheering even louder than you are right now. Now, I'll turn it over to my number one target. The man who never drops a pass...the number one receiver in the nation...many of you know him as S-Dub...Ladies and gentleman, I give you Shawn Wells."

Some of the players started calling Shawn "S-Dub" last year, and the moniker sort of stuck with him. Shawn shimmied towards the podium. Matt handed the microphone to Shawn, who remained silent. He nodded his head up and down and licked his lips while waiting for the yelling and screaming to lower in intensity. Shawn lived for attention. He lived for those moments. He loved being in the spotlight while he continued licking his lips, his signature sign of sexuality. Shawn knew the girls loved it when he did that. He was a modern day LL Cool J, but taller.

"I don't have much to say, but my abs would like to say a few words," said Shawn. He then immediately took off his jersey, revealing his bare chest and held the microphone to his stomach as if inviting his mid-section to read a prepared speech. The gymnasium morphed into an oasis of female hands reaching out toward Shawn's body from the stands. As if he was just within 2 inches of their outstretched arms, the girls kept reaching harder and harder. The commotion was so loud and mind numbing that people in Phoenix probably heard the teenage noise squad in Scottsdale. Every female with a satellite phone in her possession began snapping multiple photos of Shawn with his shirt off. The photos were immediately uploaded, posted and shared online.

Shawn, 210 pounds and 6 feet 6 inches of pure lean ebony dominance, rippled with muscles from head to toe. Biceps, triceps, and all the other ceps; he had them all. His shiny, platinum necklace dangled onto his chest with an even shinier cross hanging from it. With the exception of select female students and possibly some teachers – based on some unsubstantiated rumors – people normally didn't see Shawn at school or practice without a shirt. He kept his tattoo-laden arms, back, and chest covered for the most part by wearing long-sleeve uniform shirts all year while at school.

Tattoos were not a common adornment at Oakridge, but Coach Burdette's players were allowed more leeway. He asked for special privileges before accepting the head coaching job at Oakridge, and since the chairman of the board was a huge football fan, his conditions were granted. Even if Coach Burdette had not taken steps to shield Shawn from any scrutiny, his father, Mark, would have. Mark was a well-known and respected member of the Scottsdale community, not to mention a major school donor.

In anticipation of his little stunt, Shawn looked as if he had covered his upper body with baby oil for added effect. He remained near the podium, as the pep rally officially started. Coach Burdette spoke into the microphone, but no one could hear him let alone themselves think due to the enormous amount of excitement still being generated from Shawn removing his number 80 jersey. Some female and even male students stretched out their hands as if attempting to rub Shawn's abs. Meanwhile, he stood there with his white million-dollar smile and glistening, brown skin. Shawn winked in Sam's direction. She just returned a small grin, trying not to appear too pissed off from Shawn's antics. A minute later, she finally gave in to her anguish and saluted Shawn by extended her middle finger high above her head assuring that he would see it.

All the local sports writers in Scottsdale and Phoenix predicted Oakridge as contenders for the state high school football title solely based on the expectations of Matt and Shawn. Both were heavily sought after by all the major college football contenders. In fact, several college scouts were rumored to be attending the game that night.

Miles picked up Andrew about an hour before the game. Once they arrived at the stadium, Andrew went to set up the recording equipment near the stadium press box, and Miles joined Mr. Somers and Squirt in the stands at their usual location, one row up from the 50-yard line. Christine was already there anxiously waiting to sit next to Miles. Even though they were early and had good seats, it didn't take long for the stands to fill. With the team's predicted success, no one wanted to miss a second of the game highlights that were destined to take place on the grid iron during the season. The band played fight songs while the cheerleaders hyped up the crowd. Fans carried popcorn, hotdogs, and soft drinks to their seats. You could practically smell the sensation of football season beginning in the air. The weather was perfect on that September evening, with a temperature of 78 degrees.

Like every home and away game over the last three years, Shawn had his own private section of fans basically comprised of about 20 teenage girls. They started a Shawn Wells fan club, which had its own website. They all wore his number 80 jersey and never missed watching him play – home or away. They didn't give a damn whether the team won or lost as long as they got to watch their idol perform. Their screams rang above the crowd in stands whenever Shawn caught a pass or scored a touchdown. Shawn loved every second of it, and he rewarded his following by pointing in their direction after making a big play. Matt had several of Oakridge's finest screaming for him as well, but it was nothing close to how the ladies felt about Shawn.

His swagger was something underclassmen admired and tried to duplicate. If Shawn made up a name for girls like "sweet potato," for example, you would hear stories about some lame freshman walking up to a hot girl and saying, "What's up my sweet potato?" You sure are looking right out of the oven today." The stories typically ended with the hot girl and her friends laughing the embarrassed young man out of their presence.

The Wildcats exited the tunnel, tore through a red and blue banner the cheerleaders held, and sprinted to the sideline from a cloud of manufactured smoke. It was quite an intimidating scene for the youngest newcomers in the stadium. Shawn looked like the gladiator that he was in a crisp, blue, red, and white uniform. You could always pick him out of a crowd of players by looking for the dark visor on his helmet. It hid the warrior-like aggression embedded in his eyes.

Finally, the head official blew his whistle to signal the kickoff. Oakridge won the coin toss and elected to receive the ball first. The kicker for the Coyotes signaled his team to get ready as he planted his right shoe just under the center of the football. The football sailed through the back of the end zone from the strong leg of the kicker. The official placed the ball on the Wildcat 20-yard line.

Coach Burdette finished giving his pre-snap speech to the offense before they hustled onto the field. Matt walked up behind the center and lowered his body to receive the snap from the center.

"Blue 41, Red 46, ready, set, hike."

Once he felt the ball firmly in his hand, Matt turned to the left and handed the ball off to the running back, Brian Collier, for a hard fought 2-yard gain. Coach Burdette called the next play into Matt's helmet earpiece, and then the Wildcats broke the huddle. Matt settled under the center once again. When the ball was hiked, Matt handed the ball off to Brian for a 7-yard run to the left. The situation was third down and only 1 yard for a first and ten on the Wildcat 29-yard line.

When the ball was hiked this time, Matt stepped back as if to hand the ball off to the running back for the short 1-yard run for the first down. That was a play action fake hand off to the running back. Instead, Matt took five steps back and threw a flawless right-handed spiraling pass to find Shawn Wells in perfect stride all alone for a 71-yard touchdown pass. He pointed in the direction of his fan club while he crossed the goal line.

Shawn's small fan club went berserk along with the rest of the Wildcat fans. The Wildcats scored first and completed the 7 - 0 lead with the extra point. The Coyotes didn't take long to respond. They evened the score up seven plays later with a 30-yard touchdown run by their running back after obtaining great field position from the kickoff.

As the game went on, neither team's defense created a turnover or forced the other team to punt more than a couple of possessions. It became more and more evident that the team with the ball last would probably win.

The game was tied 35 to 35 in the fourth quarter with only 19 seconds left on the clock. The Wildcats had a first down on the Coyote 49-yard line and no time outs left. The Coyotes were only sending three players after the quarterback and playing the rest of their defenders deep in the secondary so the Wildcats couldn't complete any huge passes down field. If necessary, the Coyotes were hoping to force the game into overtime.

Coach Burdette figured they could run about two more plays before the clock expired. He had no faith in his freshman field goal kicker and wasn't about to leave the game in his hands. He signaled the play to Matt from the sideline and verbalized it in Matt's earpiece. The Wildcats broke the huddle into a shotgun formation triple receiver right line up with one receiver to the left. Shawn was the middle receiver spread out to the right. The center hiked the ball to Matt and the offensive linemen just let the three defenders run by toward Matt. Shawn stepped backwards away from the line and raised his hands to receive the ball from Matt. The offensive linemen ran in Shawn's direction as Matt backed away from the speedy defensive linemen. Matt tossed the ball to Shawn to complete the screen pass to his favorite target. As soon as Matt released the ball, two 250-pound defensive linemen pounded him onto the ground. Meanwhile, Shawn followed his beefy offensive linemen and three other blockers down the field for a 49-yard touchdown pass.

The Wildcat faithful and players jumped up and down with joy in celebration until they noticed Matt rolling around on the ground in the backfield. The crowd hushed, only letting out whispers of concern and showing worry on their faces. Coach Burdette jogged onto the field to help his trainers assess Matt's injury.

"Are you OK, son? Where does it hurt? Don't move. Try to remain still." Coach Burdette and the trainers instructed and questioned Matt all at once.

They could barely hear the responses of the teary-eyed star. Matt just held his right arm in extreme pain while rolling on the turf. Eventually, an electric medical cart rolled onto the field to retrieve Matt. The Wildcat fans and some of the Coyote fans erupted in applause when Matt rolled off the field toward the Wildcat locker room.

Still, eight seconds remained on the clock to end the game. The Wildcats lined up and squib kicked the football in an attempt to run out the clock. A Coyote player scooped the football, ran a few yards and attempted a lateral pass to another player. The football fumbled to the ground and was recovered by a Wildcat player. The game was over.

Oakridge fans and players celebrated the victory in the stands and on the field, but everyone was still more concerned about their star QB. Coach Burdette briefly shook hands with the opposing coaching staff in the middle of the field before jogging off to go check on Matt, who was awaiting an ambulance to be taken to the hospital.

Mr. Somers, Squirt, and the rest of the fans headed to their vehicles to leave the stadium. Miles waited on Andrew to finish wrapping up his video duties so he could drive him home. Christine wanted to wait with him but had to leave with her ride home, a classmate named Julie Rivera.

Coach Burdette arrived at the hospital and received upsetting news from the attending physician: Matt had a broken arm and fractured ribs. He was done for the season. Coach Burdette walked into the hospital room where Matt rested. His parents waited by his side.

"Hello, Mr. Barkley. Ma'am," Coach Burdette removed his Oakridge cap while shaking hands with Matt's father and nodding his head to acknowledge his mother respectfully.

"Hello, Coach, and thanks for coming. We'll give you a moment with Matt," said Matt's father. He had to pry his wife's hand from Matt's bedside railing in order to get her to leave the room with him. Tearful, she left reluctantly.

"Hey, Coach," Matt said in a weak voice.

Coach Burdette could tell the pain killers had started working. "You played a hell-of-a game, son. I'm proud of you. We sure showed those Coyotes how to play real football tonight."

"Yeah, Coach. We showed 'em."

Everyone knew that Coach Burdette was never one to show emotion in public or to engage in much small talk. The fact that he even came to the hospital was a huge accomplishment, but he had to know what the future of his team's season was going to look like or he would not have been able to sleep that night.

Coach Burdette struggled to find words to fill the discommodious silence in between the sentences. As luck would have it, help was about to walk in the room to rescue him from the awkwardness.

A nurse came in and said, "I have to take him to get fitted for his cast."

Matt's eyes stretched in anxious anticipation. The medication couldn't block the dreaded thought of wearing a cast for several months.

Coach Burdette said goodbye to everyone before heading home. He called his assistant coaches during the drive and told them the normally scheduled coaches meeting on Saturday morning was cancelled. He didn't see the point in planning for the next game without his star QB. He was in a near panic, knowing his two freshmen backup quarterbacks, Paul Knox and Reggie Brown, were nowhere near ready to command an offense and lead the team to the projected success for the remainder of the season. Since they were only freshmen, they had only recorded about 10 hours combined in the HSC. It took Matt almost a whole season during his freshman year as a back-up to show signs of improvement on the field. He wished that Virtual Tech's technology could magically transform a rookie's skills into a veteran's overnight, but that simply was not possible. Without Matt on the field, Coach Burdette thought it would take a miracle to finish the season with a decent record and a championship was completely out of the equation.

Of the two, Paul was better at throwing the ball. The problem was Paul's height, only 5 feet 5 inches, which made it impossible for him to see over Oakridge's greater than 6 feet tall, on average, offensive linemen. Reggie possessed a flaw as well. He knew the playbook. He knew how to read defensive schemes. He answered all of Coach Burdette's situational questions correctly. His only problem was that nervousness led to stuttering. He would gather the players in a huddle at practice to call a play. They would wait for a while, trying to comprehend what Reggie was saying. "Tri... Tri...Tri...Triple Right Phoe....Phoe....Phoe....Phoenix Sunset... Dou...Dou....Dou...Dou....Double Action On Thr...Thr....Thr..Three."

Shawn and the other players struggled to keep a straight face in the huddle. Who could blame them? Reggie's unsteady cadence utterly distracted and broke up the offense's rhythm. Strangely enough, Reggie's voice immediately returned to normal as soon as he left the practice field.

Coach Burdette knew he had what seemed to be an insurmountable problem. Unable to settle his nerves, he slept restlessly that night.

CHAPTER 5
THE MYSTERY

September 2021

Coach Burdette drove to the athlete's complex the next morning to think about how he could salvage the season without Matt. As he walked down the main hallway of the football wing, the coach noticed the exterior light of the HSC room was on, indicating someone was in the room. He thought, "Why would anyone be in there on a Saturday?" All of his players and coaches had instructions to either rest or take the day off. Coach Burdette walked toward the entrance of the HSC room with eager anticipation. He thought someone must have simply left on a switch.

Coach Burdette edged closer and closer to the door and extended his right arm to open the door. Just as he was about to twist the door handle, Miles opened the door and left the room with his trash cart.

"Oh, hey, Coach. I didn't think anyone was here this morning."

Still looking a little startled by Miles' abrupt exit, Coach Burdette responded, "That's quite alright, Miles. I was just here doing some thinking."

"Yeah, tough break with what happened to Matt," said Miles with sincere concern in his voice.

Coach Burdette simply nodded and didn't seem interested in much small talk, so Miles added, "Enjoy the rest of your day." With that, he rolled his trash cart down the hall and disappeared around the corner.

Coach Burdette didn't really want to go sit in his office, so he thought the HSC room was as good a place as any to collect his thoughts. He walked into the control room and sat down in a chair. Knowing he was alone he folded his arms, leaned over to rest his elbows on his lap, and allowed his forehead to hang over his knees. He wept in the silence of the control room. No one would have ever believed that the tough-as-nails, old school football coach was actually crying.

He lamented that he could seemingly never catch a break. Throughout his coaching career every time he put together a winning team, the injury bug would strike and derail his plans. Coach Burdette groomed Matt from his freshman year and this was to be the year all that hard work concluded with a championship. It just wasn't fair. He continued on for about a minute before rising and drying his eyes on his shirt sleeve. While doing so, he noticed a simulator result summary on the printer. Picking it up, he said, "Holy Shit."

The sheet read a perfect score in all categories, 100 percent in pass accuracy, completions, throwing technique, ball velocity, and everything else. Coach knew that on Matt Barkley's best day, his total high score was only around 77 percent. The numbers in his hands were impossible. He figured it was one of the players trying to play a joke or something was wrong with the HSCs calibration. There had to be some mistake or malfunction. Still, he wanted to ask Miles if he saw anyone else in the building that morning because the time on the printout read 10 minutes before the current time on his wristwatch.

Burdette used the P.A. system to call Miles back to the football HSC control room. He waited a few minutes, but Miles never showed. Coach Burdette went looking for him. He was nowhere to be found. Coach Burdette figured he would ask him at school on Monday before practice. He didn't really see any urgency in contacting Mr. Somers about someone playing with the equipment because he thought the results were inaccurate anyway. Furthermore, he figured that even the best QB in the professional league couldn't score a perfect score in the simulation room. He carried the paper printout back to his office and put it on his desk.

* * *

On Monday before practice, while the players were getting dressed in their pads and cleats, Coach Burdette looked for Miles around the complex but didn't see him anywhere. He was running out of time because he had to join his players on the practice field soon. Coach Burdette quickly went back to his office and called Mr. Somers' office to locate Miles. Mr. Somers answered the phone and told the coach that Miles asked for a few days off to work on a class project. Coach Burdette asked if he knew Miles' home address.

Somers thought it to be odd that the football coach was looking for Miles. "Is there something wrong, Coach? Has Miles done something that I need to be aware of?"

"No, No. It's nothing like that Somers. Miles is getting some information I asked for. I was just following up."

Now relieved, Mr. Somers gave the coach Miles' address. Coach Burdette wrote it down on a Post-It Note and put it in his pocket for later. He thanked Mr. Somers for his help and ended the call. A few minutes later, Coach Burdette was blowing his whistle on the practice field, signifying that practice had started for the players.

Coach Burdette experienced the most frustrating practice in years. He couldn't figure out which was worse, listening to Reggie fumble through the play calls or watching Paul's low passes getting batted down. After one fumbled play near the end of practice, he turned about as red as the t-shirt he wore that day.

After ending the grueling afternoon practice, Coach Burdette went directly to his truck and programmed the address Mr. Somers had given him into his satellite phone. He was headed toward Miles' home.

Coach Burdette pulled his truck into the driveway, walked up to the front door, and rang the doorbell once with the expectation that someone was at home. Evelyn opened the door. "Can I help you?" she asked while immediately checking for a wedding ring on Coach Burdette, which was not present.

"Yes, I'm Coach Burdette, the head coach of the Oakridge Academy football team. I was wondering if I could speak to Miles."

"He went to the store for me, but he should be back shortly. You are welcome to wait inside for him." He agreed and walked inside. Evelyn offered Coach Burdette a seat and something to drink. To her surprise and satisfaction, he accepted both.

Evelyn went to the kitchen at the rear of the house to retrieve the water and to fix a snack for her waiting guest. Even though Coach Burdette didn't ask for anything to eat, she emerged from the kitchen with a wooden tray carrying a bottle of water and some freshly baked cookies she had put in the oven prior to his arrival.

"Here is something I put together for you quickly. Hope you like it." Once she handed him the wooden tray, she sat down next to him on the sofa, which was a little too close for comfort as far as Coach Burdette was concerned. He tried to ignore her awkward behavior by avoiding eye contact. Being a curious person or some might say nosey, Evelyn asked why he wanted to speak with Miles.

"He's never played football in his life, so why do you need to talk to him? My sister, his mother, would have a heart attack if Miles were playing something as violent as football. She hates it when he only watches the games at Mr. Somers' house. Me, I just like looking at those men in those tight pants, if you know what I mean," Evelyn rambled on.

So ready to change the subject, Coach Burdette pulled out the printout he found in the HSC room and showed it to Evelyn. He said, "I was wondering if Miles knew who this belonged to."

Evelyn took the paper from Coach Burdette. "100 percent. Oakridge has some really smart students. Miles is really smart too. He makes good grades like this all the time. He isn't modest about them, though. He wants to make sure his mother and I see them, so he posts them on the walls in his room. Would you like to see them?" As usual, she continued saying way more than she should have.

Coach Burdette ignored the fact that she was talking about classroom grades because he was more interested in something else. "I bet Miles got his intelligence from you and his mother," he said, humoring her as he followed her to Miles' bedroom. What the coach saw once he walked in forced his eyes open wide along with his mouth. He dropped the printout on the floor.

Meanwhile, Miles was at Price-Mart on the supplement aisle looking for some kelp. He and his mother were out of their supply at home, so he promised to pick up some that evening. Miles retrieved the item from the shelf and started walking down the aisle toward a register. His satellite phone alerted him indicating he had a text message. He knew it was from either Christine or Andrew since they were the only ones who sent him text messages on a regular basis. Miles reached in his pocket, pulled out the device, and started to read the text from Andrew while he continued to walk without paying attention to his surroundings. All of a sudden, Miles walked into the rear end of a teenage girl bending over to retrieve an item from a bottom shelf.

"Hey, watch where you put that thing. Can I at least get dinner and a movie first?" questioned the young lady who immediately stood up and faced Miles.

Her beauty took him instantly, causing time to pause as he studied her face then her tanned body and finally her mouth. Everything she was saying was in slow motion. He didn't understand a word at the time but could only imagine what she was saying. He heard her paying him flattering comments and he responded in kind. Of course, there were plenty of stunningly gorgeous girls at Oakridge Academy, but none of them had ever made Miles feel what he was feeling at that very moment. He literally became aroused and unaware of the bulge in his shorts growing the more he smelled her sweet fragrance. Miles was completely ignorant of his body's instant change while being mesmerized by the young lady's long dark hair and smooth full lips that decorated her oval shaped face. Her eyelashes were long and curly, forcing attention to her sparkling brown eyes. Every feature of her body complemented something else, making it impossible not to stare at something about her. Her tight blue jean shorts defined her curvy, taut physique. The shorts went well with her black sandals and matching spaghetti string black top that exposed her toned midriff.

Miles finally came out of his trance when she snapped her fingers twice saying, "Hey, wake up." The attractive young lady was above average height for a 17-year-old female standing at 5 feet 10 inches. She rose up slightly on her French-manicured toes to wave her hands in front of Miles' face as she spoke.

"I am so sorry," Miles pleaded. "Please forgive me. I didn't see you."

"Yeah, yeah, I bet you say that all the time." The young lady continued to pretend to give Miles a hard time.

At that point, the level of Miles' back pedaling amused her. She wanted to have some more fun with Miles but decided he had apologized enough. "Okay, okay. I get it."

"My name is Miles," he said waiting for her to introduce herself. She said nothing.

He began to plead again. "Aren't you going to tell me your name now?" He wanted to prolong the conversation and to keep inhaling the wonderful berry fragrance she wore. He had to hear her sweet voice for a while longer.

"Why should I tell you my name? I don't know you. You could be some kind of teenage serial killer for all I know." She joked playfully with a smile on her face. She had perfect, white teeth, but at that point, Miles was focused on her sweet sound voice and the way words flowed off those full lips. She finally revealed her name: Sage.

"That sounds beautiful." Miles had never really flirted with a girl before that day, but there was something magical about her that he could not explain. He knew he had to talk to her as long as she would allow him to.

"Well, it was nice bumping into you, Miles. Same time, next week?"

Miles had no idea where his next statement came from. "How can I get in contact with you," Miles said, as pleading became his new art form.

"If it is meant to be, you'll see me again," she said. Before walking off, she added, "It was nice meeting you and your friend. I see that he likes me too." She pointed at Miles' mid-section bulge, which was trying to evacuate his khaki shorts.

Now really embarrassed, Miles covered his midsection with both hands while listening to Sage giggle as she walked away. Miles' spontaneous response was typically reserved for watching nude flicks online while alone in his room.

Sage represented the first time he became aroused while looking at a fully dressed female. She didn't let Miles know it, but she was very attracted to him as well. She had to play it cool because of what her mother had taught her. "Never seem too eager when dealing with a man. Never appear more interested in him than he is in you. Your number one goal when dealing with men is to always be pursued and never be the pursuer. The relationship works out better that way," explained Victoria, Sage's mother, before she began dating.

Miles was extremely excited by the conversation he just had with what he thought was the most enticing girl he had ever seen. He couldn't wait to text Andrew about his encounter with the mysterious Sage. While still in the store, Miles updated his Facebook status about his encounter with just a few words. "Today is a great day. Just saw one of the finest girls I've ever seen in my life. Hope to see her again real soon."

I didn't take long for Christine to read Miles' updated status and post her own update.

"Why does life have to suck so much sometimes?" Her status read.

Miles could not get Sage's sweet smell or the image of her lips out of his head. They were the only things overpowering the sight of Sage's sparkling eyes. With Sage still on his mind, Miles picked up a magazine he had absolutely no interest in to conceal his mid-section as he continued to the register to purchase his item.

As Miles drove home, he was unaware of the upcoming en-counter that would temporarily relieve the thoughts of Sage. Miles drove down the street approaching his house and noticed what appeared to be Coach Burdette's truck in his driveway. He imme-diately began to feel the same anxiety he felt on Saturday when he unexpectedly ran into the coach at the training complex. Miles slowed down to delay his arrival. With hesitation, he wondered what kind of conversation awaited him beyond the front door of his home.

Miles entered the living room to find his Aunt Evelyn and Coach Burdette having a pleasant conversation. By pleasant, this meant Evelyn did most of the talking. Coach did most of the listening.

"You're finally home. This nice man has been here about 10 minutes waiting on you," Evelyn informed Miles as if he was un-aware of Coach Burdette's presence.

"Can you give us a few minutes?" Coach Burdette requested of Evelyn.

She left the room but not before giving Coach Burdette a se-ductive look and her best catwalk. In complete silence, Miles sat down on the couch across from the coach. Coach Burdette pulled out the printout from Saturday and asked Miles point blank if he was responsible for the score on the paper.

"Before you answer, please know that I was in your room and saw all the score summary printouts for all the different sports."

"Yes. But let me explain..."

"No need to explain," interrupted by Coach Burdette. "You know that equipment is for players and coaches only. That equipment is extremely expensive. You could have damaged it and cost the school thousands of dollars for repairs." Coach Burdette explained with as serious a look as he could gather, but he really didn't care about any of that.

Miles looked depleted. "Please don't report me to the school, sir. I will do anything. My whole future depends on me graduating from Oakridge. I'll do anything, Coach. Please. Anything." Miles continued his begging in similar fashion to the begging that began at Price-Mart earlier with Sage.

"Well, it just so happens that my quarterback is out for the season. If you would be willing to try out for the position, I'll be willing to forget all about this major infraction," said Coach Burdette cunningly.

Without hesitation, Miles immediately agreed to his terms. He was not about to throw three years of hard work away and ruin his chances of becoming a doctor. Coach Burdette could have asked him to do just about anything, and Miles would have agreed. Miles then thought about Mr. Somers and his current commitments after school. "I have to work after school. How am I going to be able to make it to practice and work?"

"Somers and I are old friends," Burdette reassured him. "I'll call him as soon as I leave and take care of everything. Don't you worry. I'll even try to figure out a way to make sure you earn the same amount of money you were earning on that job."

Miles was curious on how that was possible, but he was in no position to question anything. Coach Burdette told him to meet him in the equipment room at 2:30 p.m. sharp the next day. Miles had to be fitted with shoulder pads, helmets, cleats, and all the other accessories to play football. Miles gladly acknowledged his instructions, and the coach headed toward the front door to leave. "Wait here, I have something you're gonna need." He briefly went to his truck and then came back to the door with an electronic playbook.

"This gadget will show you the play calls and a virtual simulation of how they are executed. You should be familiar with all of them, since the same plays are loaded into the HSC. I only run about 20 different plays. They are mostly five receiver spreads in shotgun formation. I expect you to know them all by tomorrow afternoon. Pay attention to the routes of each receiver." Before he left, he yelled goodbye to Evelyn, who was still in another room. Evelyn ran out to get one last glimpse of the coach before he left. She was too late.

Miles placed his back against the door and let out a sigh of relief. He felt as if he had dodged a bullet. The next test was convincing his mother to allow him to play a game she was so adamantly against. He knew he wasn't ready to lay the news on her right away. He figured he would delay it until he came up with just the right words or until he actually made the team, if that occurred. How could he tell her the truth? Miles mumbled possible scenarios of how a conversation with his mother might go down. "Hey, mom, I played with some equipment that costs tens of millions of dollars and now I have to play high school football if I still want to be a doctor."

"Yeah, right," he thought. "That would have gone over really well."

Chapter 6
THE NEW GUY

September 2021

On Tuesday afternoon, Miles waited in the equipment room at 2:30 sharp, just like the coach instructed. Coach Burdette walked in a few minutes later. He sized Miles for shoulder pads, helmet, practice pants, football cleats, and a red quarterback practice jersey. Only quarterbacks were allowed to wear red jerseys during practice. It indicated that they were not to be tackled for any reason to avoid injury.

Miles asked Coach Burdette, "What number will I be wearing?"

"Do you have a preference?"

Miles thought for a second. He started to remember his mother showing him a picture of his father wearing a high school football jersey with the number 1. He thought wearing that number would be a way of honoring his father's athleticism.

"If one is available, I want it."

"None of the other players have that number, so I'll order your game jerseys in the morning. They should be delivered by Friday morning, giving us plenty of time before the game."

Miles smiled with amusement at the thought of having something specially made just for him.

"Coach.....I have one more request. Can I have one of those dark visors on my helmet, just like the one Shawn wears? I want to look just as intimidating as Shawn."

Coach Burdette let out an unpleasant sigh and hesitated before finally retrieving the type of helmet Miles requested. Miles quickly dressed in his new attire before heading out the door with Coach Burdette.

Coach Burdette walked Miles down to the practice field where several players were tossing passes to one another, holding private conversations, or trying to get a glance at the cheerleaders practicing on the next field over. Coach Burdette blew his whistle and told all the players to gather round. Many of them motioned toward their coach wondering why in the hell the cleaning boy was wearing a practice uniform, and more importantly, why the red quarterback jersey? They mumbled amongst themselves before getting within proximity of Coach Burdette's ears. Shawn didn't say a word. He just headed toward his coach to see what was up. Shawn was all business when he put on his football uniform, aside from him showing off in front of his female fans during the game.

"Now listen up. I'm sure all of you have heard by now that Matt is done for the season. All of you know with the talent we have on this team, we have a legitimate shot at the state title this year. With Matt gone, we are going to have to be more creative with our strategy to keep that goal alive. I think most of you know Miles."

"Coach, isn't he the guy that cleans shit out of the toilets," one player asked?

Some players started to chuckle at the comment before Coach Burdette blew his whistle again to silence them. He did not look pleased. Still, some players were looking at Shawn to get his reaction since he was now the lone leader of the team. Shawn said or motioned nothing, even though he was wondering what the hell Coach Burdette was thinking. The assistant coaches were wondering the same thing. This was news to them as well, but they wouldn't dare question their commander and chief.

Coach Burdette continued his speech. "I have been working with Miles in the HSC chamber all summer long."

Miles raised his eyebrows in confusion along with the other players and coaches. He knew that hadn't taken place. Neither the players nor assistant coaches had knowledge of them doing so either. What Coach Burdette suggested was, in fact, illegal. High school coaches could only have limited contact with players in the off-season, and that certainly didn't include training of any kind. No coach or player questioned the comment, though.

"He has shown some promise, and in light of our current predicament, we are going to give him some reps with the first string offense."

Andrew and Reggie looked at each other very disappointed. They were completely taken off guard. Each of them had been texting and tweeting all weekend long, claiming one of them was going to be the next starting QB at Oakridge. They split time with the first string offense the day before at practice, which reinforced their optimism. Coach Burdette continued his announcement.

"I don't want any of you giving him a hard time. He has a lot of plays and technique to learn before our game on Friday. If I even so much as hear about anyone on this team giving Miles a hard time, that person will be running every single day after practice until I get tired. Does everyone understand me?"

"Sir, yes sir," they all responded in unison.

"I can't hear you," Coach Burdette barked.

"Sir, yes sir."

"Now line up for stretching," he said before blowing his whistle a third time.

After the players finished stretching, Coach Burdette asked Miles if he studied and memorized the playbook.

"Yes, sir. I have it all stored upstairs." He pointed at his head.

"Well, we're about to find out." Doubt echoed in Coach Burdette's voice.

Coach Burdette told the starting offense to huddle up on the practice field. He told Miles to huddle up with them. He put his headset on and said, "Testing, testing. Can you hear me, Miles?"

Miles nodded back to Coach Burdette on the sideline, indicating that he heard him loud and clear through the earpiece in his helmet. Coach Burdette then called the play into his headset. He wanted to keep it simple just to get Miles comfortable with the offense. Miles listened attentively and called the play in the huddle.

After calling the play twice in the huddle, Miles backed away to get in position. He never really made direct eye contact with anyone. Although still unsure about the whole new quarterback thing, Shawn complied. He jogged to his position out to the far right. Miles got into shotgun formation behind the center and scanned the field. There were no defenders present because Coach Burdette wasn't ready for Miles to get reps against the starting defense just yet. He wanted to see his timing and footwork in the pocket.

"Ready.....Set.....Hut....Hut," Miles shouted in his new made up, deep voice.

The center hiked the football to Miles. Miles held the football up to his right ear, with a firm grip in his right hand, before launching a perfect 40-yard spiral to Shawn, who was in perfect stride down field. Shawn made an easy one-handed grab before coming to a full stop and then jogging back to the huddle. The players, assistant coaches, and Shawn were in complete shock. They all started clapping but wondering if it was beginner's luck.

Coach Burdette smiled and thought the pass looked good, but he wasn't convinced just yet. He called the next play, and everyone was in position once again. Once the ball was hiked, Miles threw another perfect pass down field to Shawn, then another and another and another. After several more plays, the entire team and coaching staff started to believe in Miles' abilities. Shawn even started to high five Miles when he returned to the huddle after a successful play. This display of sportsmanship or approval from Shawn was the only acknowledgement the other players needed to fully accept Miles as a new teammate. With that, Miles' confidence shot through the roof. He felt better and better about his ability with each completion.

After nearly an hour, Coach Burdette had seen enough easy plays without any defensive pressure. He was ready to turn up the heat.

"Let's see if that equipment is worth all that dang blasted money," Coach Burdette whispered to another coach.

He instructed the defensive coordinator to get his first string defense to line up against the offense and go full speed. Coach Burdette wasn't in the mood for any half-assed effort at practice. He wanted to see how Miles handled the pressure. He needed to be reassured that he hadn't made a mistake by bringing Miles onto his practice field.

"All right defense, I wanna see everybody going balls to the wall. I need to see what I'm working with here. If I see anyone slacking, you know what comes next."

Although it wasn't necessary, Coach Burdette used his skill of intimidation on his players. The defensive players were anxious to show up the rookie. They boasted about making an interception or getting in Miles' face before he could release the ball. They were not allowed to hit him, of course. Hitting the quarterback at practice would earn a player some extra sprints after practice and a firm seat on Coach Burdette's bad side for an indefinite period of time. No player wanted to be on Coach Burdette's bad side – nobody dared.

The offense lined up once again, but this time with the defense intact. The same occurred, however. Miles completed pass after pass after pass. He even connected with a few receivers other than Shawn, so Shawn could take a breather in between plays. The defensive coordinator was signaling some pretty complex blitz packages against Miles, but they all failed. In fact, the coordinator started to get pissed off with his defensive players. He started yelling at his linebackers and linemen about not putting pressure on Miles.

Even when a defender was about to make believe tackle Miles with a two-handed touch to indicate a sack, Miles made some nifty moves to avoid the defender and complete a perfect pass just outside the defender's reach. Coach Burdette could not figure out how Miles was avoiding defenders even from the blind side. It was like Miles had some type of sixth sense and could just feel the pressure coming from behind him. Coach Burdette was impressed.

"That HSC is worth every penny," Coach Burdette mumbled to himself. He attributed Miles' ability to the advancements of technology.

The practices continued in much the same manner on Wednesday and Thursday. Miles still didn't have to tell his mother where he was just yet because practice was during the same time that he would normally be working for Mr. Somers. Speaking of Mr. Somers, Miles noticed his mentor standing off in the distance watching him practice every day that week. Mr. Somers would only watch for a few plays. When Miles would look up after initially seeing him at the start of practice, Mr. Somers would be gone within the first 30 minutes. It was like he vanished. Mr. Somers only wanted to get a glance of the young man who was like a son to him playing the game he loved. It was during those short moments that Mr. Somers really regretted not making his old high school football team.

* * *

Miles hardly slept on Thursday night before game day. He had never been more nervous. He wasn't even that nervous on his first day at Oakridge. Since Wednesday, Andrew had been giving him a hard time once buzz started going around about the new quarterback at Oakridge. "Don't go out there and wimp out," Andrew chided. "Make sure you throw the ball to the right color jersey."

Andrew couldn't help himself. He pretended to be puzzled by why everyone was talking about Miles' new role although he constantly told students and staff about it.

Miles' jersey arrived on Thursday evening, and Coach Burdette was waiting for him in the student parking lot that Friday morning to hand it to him personally. Miles didn't take long to remove his yellow shirt on the spot so he could model the magnificent piece of threading. For baring his chest, he received a few whistles of gratitude from a group female students walking by and even one guy attempting to mock the girls. Miles pulled the jersey over his head and pushed his arms through the sleeves. He thanked Coach Burdette and headed for the hallways with a huge grin.

Miles felt 10 feet tall walking through the hallway with his last name, Starr, heavily embroidered on the back of his jersey. A couple of female "jock sniffers" spoke to Miles while passing him in the hallway that morning. "Good luck, Miles. We'll be cheering for you," one of them said while giggling with her friend.

In genuine gratitude and awe, Miles turned to watch them walk away. He silently uttered the word "WOW," as he watched their perfect rear ends moving down the hallway in tight blue jeans and t-shirts with the school colors. Soon afterward, Andrew and Christine joined Miles while he walked down the hallway. Andrew appeared to be more excited about Miles' new gig than even Miles himself.

"Man, this is going to be so awesome. Everyone at school is talking about the game tonight, and this new guy playing quarterback that is supposed to be so good. They want to know everything about him. What are his hobbies? Does he have a girlfriend? Does he watch American Idol?"

"American Idol," Miles asked?

"Hell, I don't know, man. These girls are crazy. Don't ask me. All I know is, if you put on a good show at Canyon Creek tonight against the Iguanas, you will have every girl, and probably some guys, at this school lining up to give you some..."

"Andrew!" Christine interrupted.

"Watch your mouth, man," Miles added.

"Don't hate the player; hate the game," Andrew said confidently while popping his collar. "I'm just telling it like it is. Anyway, I need you to play well tonight. I got a little something planned. You may have given me an idea for a business plan."

Miles didn't even want to know what he was talking about, and he didn't really care.

* * *

The final bell of the day rang, and the football team loaded onto their state-of-the-art, automatic fuel-reusable bus. The boosters would have nothing but the best for Oakridge. The Wildcats climbed into the Virtual Tech designed buses that came fully equipped with flat screen monitors, surround sound, wireless signals, and just about every other technological amenity.

While boarding the bus, Miles saw Andrew loading his video equipment in the cargo space on the side of the bus. Before he could ask Andrew anything, Miles heard Coach Burdette yelling, "Miles, over here, son." He wanted Miles to sit with him to discuss the game plan during the brief 30 minute ride to Canyon Creek High School.

"The team's secondary isn't that good, and they are playing several inexperienced defenders because of injuries. You and Shawn should have a field day. So, don't mess around. I want to put this team away early so we can get the hell out of there."

Miles looked surprisingly calm at that point, especially considering the fact that he had never played organized sports in his life and his nerves were a mess earlier that day. Because he had never had to perform in front of a crowd before, Miles didn't know how he was supposed to feel.

The buses pulled up next to the stadium at Canyon Creek High School about two hours before kickoff. None of the fans had arrived yet since it was so early. A few Canyon Creek employees were walking around the stadium making final preparations before the game started. Meanwhile, the players exited the buses and headed straight for the field to do their routine field walk. This was like some spiritual ritual so the players could "become one with the field" or something like that, as far as Miles could remember.

Shawn went to the home team end zone and sat Indian style while listening to his iPod. The other players knew not to disturb him during his private time before every game. Apparently, he was getting acquainted with the area on the field where he would be spending most of the game. After the walk, the players headed to the locker room to change into their uniforms.

Miles entered the locker room and noticed the equipment crew had every player's locker and uniform laid out in order by jersey number. Since Miles was number one, his locker was the first one to the left. He started to get chills when he saw his own personal little space. It belonged to no one but him for the next five hours or so. Even with the novelty of his situation, he was still fairly calm at that point.

The Wildcats were soon dressed in their white pants with red trim, accompanied by their blue jerseys with red trim. The team helmets were blue with a red O on each side. By 6:20, they were prepared for battle. The team reentered the field to begin their pregame warm-up drills. Only a few fans sat in the home and visitor sides of the stadium by then, still an hour away from the 7:30 kickoff. Shawn's fan club was in full affect once again. Every time he took the field, Shawn always smiled and blew a kiss at them after licking his lips, of course. The girls would eat it up, responding with squeals and applause. He lived for those moments. He didn't joke around during the game, but he had to acknowledge his ladies for their loyal support and making the trip to the away game.

Miles was still feeling good. He went through the warm up drills flawlessly. He looked like a sharp veteran quarterback during the warm-up drills. The Wildcats finished the drills and headed back to the locker room with still about 30 minutes left to kickoff.

Miles noticed Shawn kneeling down in front of his locker as if he was praying. As Miles listened to his words, he began to further understand why Shawn was such a fearless competitor. "Yea, tho I walk on the field in the shadow of death. I shall fear no defender, for he cannot cover me."

Miles thought it was a beautiful football version of the Lord's Prayer. After waiting on Shawn to finish, Coach Burdette had the team kneel down in a circle around him while he stood in the middle of the locker room giving his pregame speech. Most of the seniors had it memorized because it had never changed. "Go out and give 110% effort. We are champions, so let's go out there and prove it. The only one that can beat us is us."

Coach Burdette sprinkled the players closest to him with saliva during his speech. It hurled from his mouth with every word. It was his version of an unintentional baptism. While everyone else appeared somewhat unfazed, Miles was listening attentively since the speech had never fallen on his ears before. The only other thing that got Miles' attention at the time was the stomping and yelling of the hysterical fans above them because the visitor's locker room was below the home team's seating areas. That noise in conjunction with the home team band playing began to unravel Miles a bit. Sure, the HSC chamber had noise, but that was through speakers. It was no comparison to the riot that was taking place just a few feet above the locker room ceiling. Virtual Tech's technology was good but not good enough to imitate those situations exactly. The fans were forcing chips of paint off the ceiling in the visitor's locker room.

By that time, Coach Burdette raised his right hand above himself to signify to the players to rise up and reach for his hand. He said, "Wildcats on 3...1, 2, 3...WILDCATS!"

Coach Burdette led the team down the tunnel leading to the field. Shawn was behind Coach Burdette and then Miles. Miles caught a glimpse of Shawn pulling his platinum cross from under his shoulder pads and kissing it before stuffing it back against his chest. Miles figured it must be another pregame ritual of Shawn's.

The Oakridge band had formed a path for the players to run onto the field. In front of the two lines the band formed, cheerleaders held up a paper banner for the players to burst through just outside the portal. Miles had seen the team do this many times when he was just a spectator.

Coach Burdette burst through the banner first, and the band began playing the school fight song when Coach Burdette led the Wildcats to their sideline. Shawn ran to the sideline jumping 2 to 3 feet in the air, getting himself pumped up. Everyone could see the veins pulsating up his arms and calves, which he wanted to display. He had to put on a show for his ladies and any college scouts in attendance. Still, Shawn wasn't worried about getting a scholarship offer to college. Wherever his dad wanted him to go play football, he was going and with a full scholarship. His dad had the kind of connections that afforded him the luxury of not compromising.

Miles headed to the sideline and stood next to the coach, not really sure where he was supposed to stand. He initially became nervous from the noise he heard in the locker room, but once the home team ran on the field and the fans erupted on their feet in cheers his nerves really got to him. Butterflies had a Super Bowl party in his stomach. He felt a sudden urge to vomit, and did do so just a little but swallowed it before it came out of his mouth. The HSC could not have prepared him for the energy flowing from the stands. Some Iguana fans had their faces painted and were yelling obscenities at Oakridge. Miles heard one opposing player call him out by his jersey number. The fans did everything legally possible to get under the new Wildcat player's skin.

While Miles was on the sideline trying to keep from vomiting in front of everyone, Shawn was at mid-field with two other seniors for the coin toss. Andrew was in a booth upstairs preparing to record the events that were about to unfold. Oakridge won the toss and elected to go on offense first. The Wildcat offense would start on their 20-yard line. Once Miles jogged onto the field with the starting offense, Coach Burdette broadcast the play in his helmet earpiece. The offense set up on the line of scrimmage in shotgun formation with five receivers as the Iguana defense got ready for the upcoming play.

When the ball was hiked to Miles, he immediately looked for Shawn. He threw a right-handed spiral into double coverage that was picked off and run back for a touchdown. The Canyon Creek fans exploded with joy and celebration. The Wildcats hustled off the field to get ready to get the ball back. Coach Burdette said nothing to Miles, but Shawn sneered at him while they were both standing near each other on the sideline.

Andrew was in the booth talking to himself and shaking his head. "Miles, what are you doing?"

The score was now 7-0 Canyon Creek. The Wildcats scrambled back onto the field to try to even things up. Miles got the offense set to run their second play of the game. The snap..... the pass.....the second interception for a touchdown return thrown by Miles. It was like the exact same play all over again. The home crowd cheered while the Wildcat fans started booing and demanded Coach Burdette to put Paul or Reggie in the game. When Miles went to the sideline this time, Coach Burdette took him to sit down with him on the bench. Miles was sure that was where he would be parked for the rest of the game.

"Miles, you're too tense. Relax. This is no different from the HSC room. Just close your eyes."

Miles closed his eyes.

"Imagine you are in the HSC chamber putting on that helmet and getting ready to do a simulation. You have done this hundreds of times. You are now going to beat your best score in the simulator. Now, open your eyes and give me a perfect score."

Miles opened his eyes and headed back onto the field where the offense was already huddled up with unpleasant looks in their eyes. He kneeled down and apologized for the two mistakes he made earlier and said he fixed the problem.

He then looked at Shawn and said, "Are you ready to add to your highlight footage?"

Shawn nodded and said, "Hell, yeah!"

Meanwhile, Andrew was still in the booth fearful of seeing the next disaster on the field.

Down 14-0, the Wildcats lined up to run their third play of the game. The Wildcat fans were still booing Miles for being in the game. They may have also been booing Coach Burdette for allowing him to go back in the game. The ball was hiked and Miles looked to his left. He pump faked an out route to a receiver on his left. That caused the safety to cheat over to Miles' left. Shawn had a 5-yard lead over a solo defender streaking down the right side line. Miles set his feet in the pocket and released a spiraling right-handed 80-yard pass down the sideline that landed softly in Shawn's hands as he crossed the goal line for a touchdown.

As if they had been celebrating the entire time, the Wildcat sideline and fans were bursting with enthusiasm and renewed spirit. Coach Burdette threw his hands up in the air signifying a touchdown. Miles ran down field to celebrate with Shawn. Not much of a dancer, Andrew did some unusual celebratory dance in the video booth.

After Shawn and Miles were done congratulating each other, they both joined the rest of the team on the sideline. Coach Burdette gave Miles a slap on the butt with his playbook when he walked by.

Coach Burdette tried to be as mild with his excitement as possible, so he could continue.

For the rest of the game, Miles lit up the sky with perfect pass after perfect pass. He connected with Shawn for three more touchdowns before the game was over. Miles finished the game with six touchdown passes and two interceptions with over 450 yards passing for the night, leading Oakridge to a 35-14 victory.

The victorious Wildcats hustled back to the visitor's locker room after a brief celebration on the field. Coach Burdette ended up giving the game ball to Miles for his "spectacular debut performance under such heavy pressure." Several media members were outside the locker room requesting comments from Coach Burdette, Shawn, and Miles. The coach allowed them into the locker room for a few short questions. Shawn was used to postgame interviews normally done with Matt, but he enthusiastically reached out his left arm and extended it toward Miles to signal attention to his "new partner."

The media members shouted some expected questions at the two players and their coach, who answered for Miles.

"Coach, where have you been hiding this secret weapon?"

"Shawn, how do you feel about Matt's replacement?"

"Miles, what other football programs have you played for?"

"Miles, how did it feel having to step in and save the day?"

"Coach, do you think the technology Virtual Tech has provided your program is working?"

Coach Burdette had to finally force the media to leave after Miles and Shawn made a few comments, which were posted online on the Phoenix and Scottsdale newspaper Web sites less than one hour later.

Andrew joined Miles and his teammates as they were leaving the locker room. "Miles, you are the man, dude. Talk about a coming out party. You are going to be famous, and I'm going to make sure of it."

Miles didn't have a clue what Andrew meant. At that moment, he didn't care to find out.

Chapter 7
A NEW BEGINNING AT OAKRIDGE

September 2021

The following Monday, Miles was the hottest topic at Oakridge. He was instantly teleported to rock star status after pulling off the big win. The banner of Matt Barkley on the side of the athletic complex was replaced with a banner of Miles next to Shawn. Several guys Miles had never spoken to before high fived him in the hallway, and random girls were supplying him with hugs to congratulate him. The compliments seemingly had no end.

"Awesome game, Miles," said an Asian student who had never spoken to him or anyone, in fact, in his math class.

"You looked great on Friday, Miles," said a woman who Miles didn't recognize but who looked like she was probably one of the new teachers.

"I can't wait to see you play this Friday. Take us all the way, Miles," echoed almost every other girl he passed in the hallway.

Miles even found notes from nearly 10 female students who apparently slid them into his locker, propositioning him for some two-hand touching behind closed doors, in some cases four-hands touching him. One girl took a picture of her boobs and slid it into his locker although the photograph could not identify her by face. Her phone number was written on her boobs so Miles could contact her. He never called, though. He was intrigued and flattered, to say the least, but his inexperience restrained his instincts. At the age of 17, he had never engaged in sexual activity with anyone. Miles had never even made it to first base. However, based on the new attention he was receiving in school, it would appear that a home run was in sight.

Christine was not happy when Miles started getting all the attention. She was threatened by fears of losing him before she ever even had him. Meanwhile, Andrew would not be denied the enormous opportunity to benefit from his friend's fame. When Miles pulled into the student parking lot that Monday morning after his first game, Andrew had a small portable table set up, selling "Starr Power" t-shirts. Lord only knows how he had them made so fast over the weekend. Christine grudgingly helped Andrew. She only agreed because she thought Miles would be impressed with her loyalty.

"Be the first to get an originally designed shirt of Oakridge's new star quarterback. I only have a few left. Don't be left out," yelled Andrew even as students, mostly females, were purchasing the shirts from Christine for $20 each.

The white t-shirts had nothing more than a large blue star on the front with a red M in the middle of it. It was obvious the emblem stood for Miles Starr, as if he was some kind of superhero. Some students began wearing the shirts that day over their yellow polos. The school administrators didn't object to the temporary adjustment in the dress code, due to the fact that they too were overly excited about Oakridge's newfound talent. Andrew was wearing his own version. The only difference was that Andrew's shirt had a Web address on the front and back for ordering more shirts. Andrew's t-shirt strategy turned out to be a good idea. He sold out of his initial supply of 100 before the first bell rang. If he sold enough t-shirts and proved his idea was a profitable venture, he was sure he would be elected president of the Future Business Leaders of America at Oakridge. Miles didn't know how to handle Andrew's action or the added attention from the student body.

Miles sat in his second period French class thinking of how wonderful life was and how it couldn't possibly get any better. Suddenly, the classroom door swung open and Sage entered the room. Miles immediately dropped his pen on the floor. Her glossy, dark flowing hair bounced off of her shoulders with every step. All the guys in the classroom dropped their bottom lips in simultaneous drools. Sage walked up to Ms. Scott, the French teacher, and handed her a piece of paper. Ms. Scott then hopped into her role of welcoming a new student to the class.

"Class, this is Sage McCormick. She just moved here from Orlando, Florida. I want everyone to pitch in and make her feel warm and welcome here at Oakridge. Sage, there appears to be one empty seat over there beside Miles."

Sage looked up and saw the boy that ran into her almost a week ago at Price-Mart. She raised her left brow for a brief moment with the look of surprise. She didn't make a big deal out of it, and simply walked over and took her seat.

Miles mocked Sage. "I guess it was meant to be, Sage McCormick."

She rolled her eyes at him, not appreciating his sarcasm. As Miles leaned over and took in her berry fragrance once again, it triggered a familiar response in his pants. Based on the stares Sage got from most of the horny male teenagers in the class, Miles knew he wasn't the only one having some type of physical reaction to her presence.

When the bell rang, Sage immediately grabbed her things and quickly moved toward the exit so she wouldn't have to make small talk with Miles. Miles was right on her heels, though, swelling and all.

"Do you need help finding your next class?" asked Miles while following her through the hallway.

"No, I'm fine, thank you." Sage resisted his help avoiding eye contact by any means necessary.

"Are you sure?"

Miles continued to offer his help even as the hallway began to empty. "What room number are you looking for?"

"175."

"Well, you're walking the wrong way. It's on the other end of the hall."

He dashed into his next classroom right before the bell rang, leaving Sage in the middle of the hallway.

During lunch time, Andrew, Christine, and Miles sat at their usual table.

"I saw her. She's actually here," Miles explained in a daze to Andrew. He had the look of a 5-year-old boy who'd seen Santa Claus for the first time.

"Who's here? What the hell are you talking about? You are not making any sense." Andrew continued to question Miles.

"Sage is here. Don't you remember the girl I texted you about a week ago?"

"You mean to tell me that same girl is here," Andrew asked?

By that time, Miles saw Sage walk into the cafeteria. He pointed at her so Andrew would know who she was although he figured he would ultimately find out with all the "hubbub" she would cause in the school.

"Oh, her? She's in my calculus class. She's really nice. The teacher paired us together during an assignment. She transferred here from Florida, but she wouldn't give me many details about why her family moved here. Her father owns several businesses and travels a lot, so mostly it's just her, her mother, and her little brother, who apparently has some condition and needs a lot of medical attention. I think she likes me. She keeps smiling at me and blowing kisses in my direction. Do you think I have a shot at her? I think I'm going to ask her out."

Andrew obviously wanted to torment Miles. Christine, however, found nothing amusing about Miles' unabashed interest in Sage. She said, "What's so special about her? She's just another rich bitch at Oakridge as far as I'm concerned."

It finally occurred to Miles what Andrew said. "I'll beat the hell out of you, if you even think about it," Miles uncharacteristically threatened in a joyful voice. He totally ignored Christine's assertion that Sage was typical in any regard.

That was the first time Andrew ever heard Miles curse, but Andrew had no problems swearing at will. He was surprised and amused that Miles pretended he posed a threat. Andrew would never betray Miles like that, and Miles knew it.

"I gotta talk to her."

Miles motioned to get up and head in Sage's direction.

Andrew stood up in front of him and said, "Sit your $5 ass down before I make change."

Miles and Christine stared at Andrew strangely after his outburst.

"Sorry about that. I watched an old movie called 'New Jack City' last night. You already said she was giving you a hard time, so let's approach this from a different angle. Trust me. You may be the new big jock in town on the football field, but I am far more experienced in the area of romance than you."

Miles looked at Andrew like he was crazy or something. He knew Andrew didn't have a girlfriend. Still, he was great at making friends, so Miles was willing to listen to his strategy.

Andrew suggested that since Sage was already friendly toward him, he should be the one to sway her in Miles' direction. "The best way to get a girl is to be recommended by someone she trusts, and that someone shall be the Honorable Judge Andrew Myers."

Miles thought the idea was brilliant and decided to move forward with it. By the look on Christine's face, she didn't appreciate Andrew hooking Miles up with some other girl. The smile she had on her face five minutes prior left. She writhed in agony while watching how happy this unknown girl made Miles. She never had that effect on him and envied the allure Sage held over Miles.

While Miles gained confidence in Andrew's plan, he had no idea that his worst nightmare was about to happen right before his eyes. Just as Andrew rose to walk toward Sage, he noticed that Shawn had joined Sage at her table and was carrying on a conversation. Christine noticed Shawn's actions as well and smiled instantly. It was as if she willed Shawn to go talk to Sage.

Miles saw Shawn sitting really close to Sage whispering perhaps words of seduction in her ears. He knew once Shawn turned the charm on, it was over. Case closed! Lights out! Shawn had a reputation of tapping the academy's untapped resources. If Shawn wasn't the one getting up close and personal with the fresh meat at Oakridge, it was Sam.

"This is not a problem," Andrew reassured Miles, noticing his disappointment. "Don't panic. I know Shawn is the man around here, but I have a few tricks up my sleeve too."

* * *

The next day, Miles saw Sage in French class once again. He was sure he had no chance with her after he saw her talking to Shawn, but this time, she acted very differently compared to their first two encounters. She was inviting and much friendlier. She looked in his eyes when they spoke, and she actually seemed interested when Miles was speaking. Andrew had come through again, apparently.

Miles intentionally didn't say much to Shawn at practice the day before and avoided everyone in the locker room. He imagined some of the football players would make their usual wagers about how long it would take Shawn to conquer Sage between the sheets. Some probably bet on whether Sam would beat him to the punch. Miles envisioned the eager gamblers circling dates on a calendar and placing their wagers. The rumor around school was Shawn's current personal record was 45 minutes from introduction. The rumor also added that it was a new faculty member less than a year removed from her graduate school graduation.

Sage sat with Miles, Christine, and Andrew at lunch that day. Christine more or less dismissed her, mumbling a dry "hello." She only pretended to be interested in Sage's remarks.

"I live with my parents and my little brother, Austin. My dad is out of town on business most of the time, though."

"Well it's just me, my mother, and aunt at my house," Miles mentioned. He wanted to impress her with news about his new role as the QB, so he found a way to work it into the conversation. Miles was unaware that it would backfire on him.

"Did you hear that I'm the new starting quarterback here now? I led the team to a huge win last Friday."

Sage did not seem amused, and neither did Christine at his attempt.

"So, you're just another jock, huh? I will never date another jock. Some lame character came up to me yesterday during lunchtime telling me he was the star receiver and schools from all over the country were begging him to play for them. He thought that would work on me. Please! He must be used to all these tramps around here standing in line to sniff his balls, but I'm not the one."

Sage had authority in her voice. Miles could tell she was very serious, which made him like her even more. He thought it was refreshing to finally meet a girl who didn't care about being on the arms of someone popular. Christine thought what she said was a load of crock. She hung on to only one word, "tramps." She was confident that she could see right through Sage's fake persona. She actually was pissed that Sage didn't recognize how brilliant Miles was. Christine thought, "How dare Sage accuse him of being a jock? How do we know that she's not a reformed tramp?"

Miles started losing ground with Sage the minute he mentioned playing sports. Andrew jumped in to throw him a lifeline.

"Don't you remember me telling you how smart Miles is? I told you he has a great shot at being valedictorian. He wants to be a doctor, Doctor Miles Starr. He is a smart guy who just happens to play football, not the other way around."

While Andrew was being reassuring with his mouth, with his eyes, he gave Miles the signal to keep talking.

"So, ahhhhhh, can I take you out this weekend? Wanna go to dinner and a movie or something?"

"Ok! I'll go out with you on one condition, if you can tell me what the hell these dumb T-shirts are for that Andrew and all these other people have on over their school uniform?"

Sage had a serious look on her face. Andrew looked dejected for a brief moment, not wanting to take credit. Miles and Christine began laughing hysterically and Sage joined them, looking somewhat confused since she didn't know what the joke was. Miles turned and looked at Andrew with a straight face.

"Yeah, Andrew! Why are people wearing those shirts?"

Andrew remained silent, staring blankly at Miles.

Miles stopped laughing and explained that the t-shirt was designed for him without his knowledge. Andrew still remained silent.

"When I joined the team, no one knew me, and everyone, including coach, probably had some doubts about whether I could fill Matt's shoes. Once we won our first game, my unsigned publicist here decided to market some t-shirts to help encourage the fans after losing Matt."

"Is that right, Andrew?" Miles continued.

Without a word, Andrew simply nodded with a frustrated smile.

After that, Sage gave Miles her phone number. "Just text me the details for Saturday, so I can give my mom and dad a heads up," she said before gracefully exiting the cafeteria.

Miles could not help but stare and admire her apple bottom as she moved away. She might as well have been a goddess as far as Miles was concerned. Christine watched his eyes focus on her body. She knew that her frail body was no match for the more voluptuous, curvy, taller Sage. She finished the last bite of her turkey sandwich without saying a word to either Miles or Andrew. When she left them sitting at the table, they didn't even notice her departure.

* * *

Antsy all week long, Miles was more nervous about his date with Sage than the next football game. When Saturday evening finally came, he could hardly think about anything else – even the team's victory the night before. Miles played another away game that Friday night. He and Shawn performed even more amazingly during that game than they did during Miles' debut. They beat their opponent 49-0. The Wildcats were now 3 and 0. Even though Miles savored those victories, his greatest achievement, he hoped, would be winning Sage's heart.

Miles programmed the address to Sage's home in his satellite phone. The navigation system directed him to a very upscale sub-division with which Miles was unfamiliar. All the homes were at least three stories each with well-manicured lawns and impressive swimming pools. When Miles arrived at Sage's house and rang the doorbell, a little boy wearing superhero pajamas opened the door. He had a shaggy hair cut with small brown freckles on his little face. His hair was dark, but not as dark as Sage's. Miles noticed a slight resemblance to Sage in his eyes. He just stood there fumbling with a computer disc or music disc of some kind. Miles said hello, trying to get the little fella to speak, but no luck. The boy just stood there in complete silence with his disc staring at Miles. Finally, Sage's mother came to the door. The boy ran off once she appeared.

"Hello, you must be Miles. I'm Sage's mother, Victoria, but you can call me Vicky. Please come in. That was Sage's brother, Austin. You will have to forgive him. He doesn't say much," Victoria explained, while she ushered Miles to have a seat on the couch in the living room.

Miles smelled cinnamon in the air. Victoria loved the smell of cinnamon and wanted the aroma in every corner of her home. Miles thought it was a very pleasant and soothing smell. It relaxed him from the tension of meeting Sage's mother and going on his first date. Miles could tell Sage got her looks from her mother. Sage had the same long, flowing dark hair that Victoria had. Miles noticed her delicate, tanned skin and toned body. She did not look like a woman with two kids. She looked much too young for that. Although it was 5 p.m., Victoria wore a grey silk house robe that draped down to her knees accompanied by grey slippers. She was enjoying her happy hour at home with a martini glass filled to the rim with several olives. She walked over and sat on the couch next to Miles. Miles felt somewhat uncomfortable due to her close proximity to him, especially considering that it was an oversized couch. He felt she was violating his personal space a little.

"Sage tells me you play football at the academy."

"Yes, ma'am."

Victoria was examining Miles up and down as if undressing him with her eyes. She continued to sip from her glass and occasionally stabbed an olive with a toothpick while slowly migrating them to her mouth. Victoria crossed her legs in front of Miles to reveal how smooth and soft they looked. She was obviously turned on by the tall, handsome, virile teen sitting less than a foot from her. She saw his veins pulsating from the muscles in his arms since he wore a short-sleeve shirt. Victoria experienced a mild form of arousal in Miles' presence. Though she didn't say anything inappropriate, she continued to scan Miles from head to toe while sipping her drink. Miles didn't know how to respond to Victoria. He had never been in a situation like that before. Miles began to feel even more uncomfortable after noticing her gazing at his crotch but thought he might be making much ado about nothing.

"You don't have to 'yes, ma'am' me," she demanded. "I'm not that old."

Victoria didn't know that Miles would have said yes ma'am if she was merely 5 years old. His mom and aunt raised him to always respect women, even the ones that didn't respect themselves.

Sage pranced into the living room wearing one of her famous sundresses. No one could wear them better than she could. This one was black accompanied with black wedge heels which brought her stature closer to Miles'. She really knew how to show off her fabulous legs and accentuate her curves. Her long black hair was pinned up, revealing her soft neck decorated with a shiny gold necklace and matching earrings. With her hair up, he also noticed three small stars tattooed behind her left ear. Miles thought for a second that they could be a sign. After all, his last name was Starr.

Feeling a sudden relief, Miles immediately hopped to his feet.

"You look so beautiful. You ready to go?" He said it without pause. Although not many words were exchanged, he couldn't wait to end the conversation with Victoria.

The two teens said goodbye and closed the door behind them on their way to Miles' car. Victoria eyed them through the front window. She was mainly checking out Miles from a different angle, his rear. Before she could touch the door handle, Miles stepped in front of Sage and opened her door. This was an unexpected sign of chivalry to which Sage was unaccustomed. Mr. Somers gave Miles this little bit of advice, which apparently impressed Sage because she said, "Why thank you."

Miles eagerly jogged to the driver's side and quickly settled under the wheel. They were off, headed up North Scottsdale Road. Miles pulled into a shopping center parking lot. Sage knew they were having dinner and a movie but was not sure where dinner would be. She was familiar with the shopping center, but not sure which restaurant Miles had planned for them, considering there were several to choose from.

Miles parked and then jumped out to open Sage's door. Her right foot was already on the ground by the time Miles grabbed the door handle and extended his hand to help her from his vehicle. When Sage turned her body in the passenger seat to exit the vehicle, Miles couldn't help but see her red thong escaping from under her thigh-high black dress. The dress was already short, so it didn't take much effort for it to slide a little further up during the car ride. Nevertheless, Miles pulled her up from the car and headed toward a Japanese restaurant with his newly-formed woody intact.

Miles had never been to the restaurant before, but he chose it based on Mr. Somers' advice. While the hostess distributed menus to them, Miles couldn't help but notice photographs of celebrities that had dined at the restaurant. Miles was excited to be in the same establishment that so many big name people had patronized. Although the restaurant was rather full and had lots of people waiting for seats, Miles and Sage were escorted past them within five minutes to a table that had two remaining seats on the edge. Eight other patrons already sat at the rectangular table in a sea of 10 other similar tables. Diners held conversations while watching chefs prepare food. Miles pulled Sage's chair out for her, another gesture that Mr. Somers suggested.

The restaurant was set up with Japanese hibachi grills all over the dining area, so the meal was prepared at the table. Miles watched the chefs working at other tables and became even more excited at the unique dining experience. As Miles and Sage began to review their menus, they discovered that neither one of them ate red meat. They both shared a laugh over their newly found common interest. They decided to go with the shrimp and chicken combination along with glasses of water. The chef rolled out a cart full of raw vegetables, beef, poultry, and seafood from the kitchen. Before they knew it, he was throwing knives up in the air, slicing, and dicing food with speed and craftsmanship to the sound of applause from the seated patrons.

While Miles and Sage enjoyed the live cooking show, they began to learn a bit more about each other. Miles told her that before he started playing football a couple of weeks ago, he had a job cleaning up after school.

"I had a job after school and during summers for the last three years, but since I start playing football two weeks ago I had to stop."

"Wait, you just started playing football two weeks ago. How is that possible? Don't you have to practice for years and years to play?"

"It's a long story. I'll tell you about it someday. You should really come see me play sometime."

"Maybe, if you're lucky," Sage replied, with a playful smile.

"She has the perfect smile," Miles thought.

"Are you any good?" she questioned.

Sounding more like Shawn, he responded, "Good? I'm the best you've ever seen." Miles borrowed Mr. Somers' description of the game of football. "Commanding 10 players down a 100-yard field into the end zone is like a conductor instructing an orchestra."

"When you said it like that, you make it sound more exciting."

Sage went on to explain that she lived with her father, Harold, mother and little brother. Sage told Miles that her father traveled a lot on business, forgetting that she told Miles that information on Tuesday.

"We moved to Scottsdale at the last minute when my parents suddenly decided to sell our home in Orlando. I asked them why they were selling our Florida home, but they didn't really give me a straight answer. My father got upset when I pressed the issue. My last boyfriend and I had just broken up around that time, so the timing was perfect for me. I was ready for a change. We have another house in L.A., but my parents said they liked the schools here better. The school Austin attends is expensive, but they work wonders with him."

"Does he have some type of discipline problem or something?"

"No nothing like that."

Miles paused and waited for Sage to elaborate, but she changed the subject to something about school. He figured she didn't want to talk about it, so he didn't pursue questioning her about Austin any further.

Mile couldn't really understand why he was so intrigued with Sage. There were plenty of rich and enchanting girls at Oakridge, but he never felt the way he felt with Sage about any of them. Other than Christine, Sage was the first girl to actually show any kind of interest in him prior to knowing he played football. Furthermore, Sage didn't appear to be the type to want to be with him because of his recent success on the football field. Maybe it was her voice or her smile. Maybe it was the color of her eyes. Maybe it was how passionately she spoke about her family, especially her younger brother that made Miles want to be with her even more. Maybe it was the combination of everything about her.

Sage became curious about Miles when Andrew told her how smart he was and how he wanted to become a doctor. The fact that he played football was just a plus that she both loved and hated. Sage had told herself and others that she didn't want to be with another jock because of negative past experiences, but she subconsciously loved being the girl that every girl wanted to be. That kind of status can become addictive.

Once she began to feel more comfortable with him, Sage shared more details about her brother. "Austin is autistic and requires special medical attention and a special school that's near our home, which is another reason why my parents chose to move here."

Since Miles planned on being a doctor, he was well-versed with characteristics of a disease as common as autism. He knew that one out of every 110 children was born with autism. Sage's revelation explained Austin's peculiar behavior and preoccupation with the disc when he answered the door.

Miles noticed Sage was not very comfortable talking about her brother's ailment. Luckily, Mr. Somers gave him some pointers on how to keep a lady entertained as well. He said, "Just get her laughing. If you can make a woman laugh, she will melt in your hands like butter on a warm knife. Also, ask her to tell you something about herself that no one else knows."

Miles looked at Sage, "So, tell me something about yourself that no one else knows."

"When I was younger, I was a gymnast. I'm very flexible," said Sage seductively. "No one here knows that now but you."

The statement was true, but she said it to mess with him. Miles took a deep swallow. Sage just smiled, knowing the physical effect she had already had on him at their first encounter probably would trigger again after her statement.

"Now it's your turn to tell me something about yourself that no one else knows."

Miles paused for a second. Sage's reversal of the question caught him off guard. There was only one thing that popped into his mind, but he couldn't tell her that. Miles had held on to that secret for many years. His mother didn't even know that secret. He couldn't reveal it now, not even to someone as alluring and trusting as Sage appeared to be.

Miles fumbled for a moment, but then he finally answered.

"When I was a baby, my mother said I hated wearing diapers. She said every time she put on a fresh diaper and turned her head for a split second, it was on the floor without me in it. She said I must have done that for almost a year. Luckily, I was potty-trained very quickly. She got tired of cleaning up my little or, should I say, big messes."

Sage started laughing hysterically at the thought of Miles' baby bottom running around the house and his mother dashing after him before he messed up the floor. Her outburst caused others to pause. The other guests at the table looked anxiously in her direction, as if wanting to be let in on the funny moment. She thought that it was the most adorable story she'd ever heard. Miles was extremely pleased with her reaction, and he was grateful to Mr. Somers for providing him such great advice.

The chef served their meals in parts. First, he gave them steamed white rice then stir-fried vegetables and finally shrimp and chicken. The entire table let out applause for the delectable meal the chef prepared when he rolled his cart back into the kitchen.

Once they left the restaurant, Miles drove a few miles south on North Scottsdale Road and made a left on East Shea Boulevard.

They arrived safely at Harkins Shea 14 movie theatre. Some teens preferred to make their own movies with their satellite phone cameras in the back seats of their parents' automobiles. None of that would be going on with Miles and Sage. He wanted to impress her, not undress her – at least not yet. Miles parked his car in the shopping center near the movie theatre entrance.

"What are we going to see," Sage asked?

"I thought we could check out that new romantic comedy starring Dominique Vickers and Katherine Hearst called Loving Lonely Again." It was a bona fide chick flick, but Miles figured Sage would like it.

"I love Dominique Vickers. He's pretty cute for an old guy," Sage joyfully acknowledged about the 40-year-old actor.

Miles purchased two tickets for the 8:15 p.m. showing. With only a few minutes before the film would begin, the teens bypassed the concession counter. Miles, almost certain she would refuse, still felt compelled to ask, "Would you like a snack or something to drink? We can go back and grab something real quick."

"No sugary soda, greasy popcorn or artificial colors and fillers for me, thank you," said Sage.

"Same here," said Miles almost instantaneously.

Sage moved in closer to him and briefly rested her head on his arm as a show of approval. Miles didn't know whether to hold her hand or hug her in response to her display of affection, so he did nothing but keeping walking. "Let's blitz these folks, so we can get decent seats," he added, using football jargon he would never have used three weeks prior.

They found an empty set of seats on the far right side of the theatre around the middle section. The seats were perfect because they were next to the wall so no one would have to disturb them by crossing over their feet.

Once the movie started, Miles reached out for Sage's hand. He used a technique from the HSC chamber by visualizing it happening before it actually did. In this way, he felt less afraid and intimidated when reaching for her hand. Still, the inexperienced Miles could not believe he was actually on his first date with such a stunning, sensual girl. Her hands were soft. He couldn't help inhaling that wonderful berry fragrance that always got a reaction from his mid-section. Miles kept looking over at Sage to watch her lips adjust whenever she laughed and smiled at a scene in the movie. She was more exciting to him than the movie was. He loved looking at her sexy lips and perfect smile. Meanwhile, she just sat there in that black dress with her legs crossed. Miles could vaguely see her toned thighs when the light from the screen glared occasionally.

Once credits finally started to roll, Miles reluctantly released her hand so he could brace himself to stand up in the narrow aisles. To his surprise and delight, Sage grabbed his hand again once they were outside the theater, headed to the car.

When Miles pulled into her driveway and cut the engine off, he exited his side to run around and open Sage's door. She had gotten used to this by now, so she didn't move until her door was opened. Miles left his door cracked so the interior light in his car would stay on. He wanted to get one last peep at that red thong before the night ended. Sage knew he had been peeping it all night long, but she liked knowing he wanted to see her undergarments. It made her feel like she retained a position of power. That was another lesson about men her mother told her. "Just give them enough to keep them wanting more and more," her mother would say.

Miles walked her up to the front door, where the porch light was lit, so he could get a final gaze into her big brown eyes. His heart was racing at this point. He had never been on a date before, so he didn't know the protocol. Mr. Somers didn't tell him about that part of the date – the end of the night. He only knew what happened in the television or movie version. Miles didn't know whether to shake her hand, hug her, kiss her, or what. Awkwardly, he just stood there in silence, shuffling his feet.

"Well, are you going to kiss me or not?" asked Sage, sensing his inability to make a decision.

He closed his eyes and leaned into Sage, stopping about 2 inches from her face. Sage finished the deal by completing the transaction he started. She gave him a soft, wet kiss while gently stroking her tongue in his mouth. Miles figured he better follow her lead and do the same. He thought, "Her lips taste better than I imagined."

The kiss lasted for about 10 seconds although it seemed like 10 minutes to Miles. Sage slowly withdrew her tongue, abruptly turned to open the door, and vanished into her home without saying another word. Miles was spent. His knees went weak as he stumbled back to his car. He updated his Facebook status on his satellite phone before even starting the car. He typed, "I just kissed the most beautiful girl in the world."

Christine cried herself to sleep that night after reading the update.

Miles drove home with the radio off.

With her shoes in hand, Sage made her way toward her room pass the barely lit living room area. Suddenly her mother turned on a lamp. She was sitting in a dining room chair holding an empty martini glass. She startled Sage by saying, "How was the date?"

"It was fine. Miles was a perfect gentleman. Were you waiting up for me?"

"That brother of yours nearly drove me crazy while you were gone. He won't listen to me. And your father said he's not coming back until tomorrow."

Austin never responded to his mother the way he responded to Sage. She knew how to get him to do just about anything without raising her voice, which her mother couldn't seem to do.

"Where is Austin?"

"I made him go to bed. Miles is really cute. Are you planning on seeing him again?"

"Yes!"

"As long as you're just having fun and not getting too serious with him. I know he's nice and all, but he's not right for someone like you."

"You're right. I should be looking for someone just like dad, someone who's never around. That would be a perfect fit for me. Right, Mom?"

Sage marched to her room and closed the door.

* * *

Miles was walking on clouds when he walked through his front door.

"Miles, can you come in here for a second," his mother uttered from the living room.

He was shocked that she was still up, but he figured she wanted to make sure he came home safely after his first date. He expected her to want details of his evening.

"What's up, Mom?"

"You tell me. How is work going with Mr. Somers?"

"It's going really good mom. You know Mr. Somers and I are really close."

Miles thought it was odd that his mother would ask him about work and not his date.

"Well, let me tell you about my day at work. I was helping this lady in my store today. She was telling me how wonderful my son performed last night during the away game. She said he was a regular Tom Brady on the field. She said all of Scottsdale was raving about the new star quarterback at Oakridge. I just thanked her and pretended to know what the hell she was talking about, thinking there must be some mistake. I knew it couldn't be possible for my son to join a football team and not tell his own mother."

"But, Mom you don't understand the circumstances that led up to this..."

Interrupting, she said, "I just want yes or no answers from here on. Do you understand me?"

"Yes."

"Do you enjoy playing football?"

"Yes."

"Will playing football have a negative effect on your grades?"

"No."

"Will you get hurt playing football?

"No."

"Do you promise me that?"

"Yes."

"Will you ever lie or keep something from me again?"

"I promise I won't, and I didn't tell you because I didn't think you would allow me to even try. Heck, I didn't know this experiment with me playing quarterback would last this long or turn out this well. I thought I'd only play one or maybe two games before getting cut, so I would never have to tell you."

"I love you more than anyone else in the world. You can tell me anything."

"You also worry about me more than anyone else in the world, so I was afraid to tell you."

Melissa bowed her head and began to cry. Sensing her pain and disappointment but not yet noticing the tears saturating her blue gown, Miles immediately knelt, hugged his mother around her waist, and began rubbing her back gently.

Lifting her head courageously, she said, "It's okay, son. My fears forced you to live in a world that doesn't exist, a world with just you, your aunt, school, and me. I can't wait to see you play."

Once his mother started smiling, he gave her the biggest kiss on the cheek he had ever given her. He lifted her in midair, carrying her like a prize trophy. He then plunked her tenderly on the sofa across from his chair and told her all about how he came to join the team only after the coach visited their home once he learned about his HSC chamber scores.

* * *

After his discussion with his mother, Miles retreated to his room. He felt a sense of relief and glee. He looked at his phone and noticed Sage had sent him several messages.

"Are you still up? Are you thinking about me right now? Do you wish I was there lying in bed with you?"

Miles responded, "Yes, yes, and hell yes!"

The two teens carried on their virtual discussion for at least an hour before finally agreeing to end the conversation at once, after a long debate over who would end it first.

CHAPTER 8
ACCEPTING YOUR DESTINY

October 2021

When Miles came to school during the following weeks, he could not imagine his life being any better. His mother supported his new athletic endeavor. Sage seemed to be really interested in him. The Wildcats were 4 and 0, and a strong favorite to win the state championship, with Miles' help. His grades had not suffered, and people were treating him like a celebrity.

Amid all the attention Miles received, Sage enjoyed being the one girl who had him. The other female students envied her for being so lucky. Many of them regretted the fact that he was right under their noses the whole time and none of them displayed an interest. Christine could sense Sage's pride, and she found it interesting for someone who claimed to not want to date athletes anymore. As his closest friend, Andrew, meanwhile, was also a direct beneficiary of Miles' popularity. He was turning a hefty profit from Starr Power t-shirt sales, especially the autographed ones.

Miles still got his normal paycheck deposited into his bank account with an increase even though he hadn't worked for Mr. Somers since he started playing football. Miles didn't complain, though, and appreciated Mr. Somers for looking out for him. Miles assumed it was Mr. Somers making that call.

Shawn treated him like his new best friend mostly because Shawn's stats were higher at that point than they were for all of last season. As a result, his interest from potential colleges doubled. Shawn got flooded with recruiting calls and college visit requests. Miles gained recruitment interest also. Two or three scouts representing top schools were rumored to be in attendance for the upcoming game.

* * *

It was game five of the Wildcat football season. Miles had been spectacular during games two, three, and four. While Miles looked very impressive at the QB position, the Wildcats were facing their strongest division rival, the Broncos. The winner of that game would have a clear lead in the division. Coach Burdette warned the players all week in practice that the Broncos had the number-one-ranked defense in the state. He said their offense was average, but the defense was extremely stubborn and loved to go after the quarterback.

Miles convinced his mother and Sage to join Christine, Mr. Somers and Squirt in the stands during this home debut game. Since his mother didn't want him playing such a dangerous sport in the first place, it was a huge accomplishment. During the pregame warm up drills, Miles spotted them in the stands. He became even more hyped but perhaps less focused because of Sage's presence.

After the game started, Miles would wave in Sage's direction and smile every time the Wildcats completed a first down. Christine was literally becoming sick from his boyish antics. Miles was turning into a typical teenage boy trying to show off for a girl, and Christine had always liked him because he was anything but typical prior to this point in their friendship. Coach Burdette noticed the careless behavior and warned Miles to stay focused. "Don't take this defense lightly," he said.

The Wildcats were leading 7-0 in the first quarter after Miles threw a stellar 67-yard touchdown pass to Shawn during the opening offensive drive. Miles was easily leading the Wildcats down the field on their second offensive drive of the game. With 5:23 left in the quarter, the Broncos called a timeout to delay the Wildcats from further marching down the field for their second touchdown.

Miles began to wonder what Coach Burdette meant by top-ranked defense. In the huddle, he even went as far as to joke about the Broncos lack of defensive presence, "Burdette must have been drinking while he was watching the Broncos' game film. They may have a top-ranked defense, but they left it at home tonight." His teammates laughed at his amateur attempt at humor.

Meanwhile, the Broncos' defensive coordinator stood on the sideline whispering in All-American defensive end Todd Lopez's ear during the timeout.

"That Starr kid is making all of you look like jackasses out there. I need that quarterback out of the game. You do what you have to do to put him down."

Todd hustled back on the field and settled into his stance for the next play. Miles broke the huddle with the play call and walked up behind the center. He made sure he waved at Sage again before making his call. "Ready...Set...Hut...Hut," Miles barked.

Shawn ran a 10-yard post pattern across the middle and threw his right hand up calling for the ball as he glided past his defender. Miles took a three-step drop, set his feet, and pumped to the left before ripping a flawless right-handed spiral pass over the middle. It landed softly into Shawn's hands for a 47-yard touchdown pass.

The home crowd erupted into cheers and celebration. Shawn's fan club engaged in their usual celebratory dance. Mr. Somers, his daughter, Sage, Christine, and Melissa all threw their arms in the air, yelling and hugging each other in honor of Miles' success. Christine didn't hug Sage, partly because she had no plans of doing so but mainly because she remained fixated on the field where their hero lay.

Almost no one else at the time noticed Miles rolling around in the back field holding his right arm near a yellow flag thrown by the head official. Meanwhile, several Oakridge offensive linemen were pushing the Broncos defensive players and trying to get at one in particular, Todd. The cheers in the stands soon turned to silence and immense concern. Several Wildcat players gathered around Miles while he lay on the field. They pleaded with him to stand up, hoping he would comply. The Wildcat trainer then raced onto the field to assist Miles.

The head official made his penalty calls for a late hit and roughing the quarterback on the All-American defensive end. Apparently, Todd made a move toward Miles after the ball was hiked. His advances were met with complete resistance, as the Wildcat offensive tackle didn't move an inch. Once Miles released the ball, the offensive linemen relaxed their protective shield. The All-American saw the opportunity he was waiting for and rushed toward Miles on his blind side. Todd ran into Miles at full speed and pummeled him, forcing his entire body weight onto the unmanned QB. With that, Miles collapsed onto his right arm.

The trainer finally got Miles to his feet and assisted him to the sideline. The fans gave him a standing ovation in a show of support. The trainer took Miles into the locker room to assess the injury. Melissa grabbed her purse and attempted to rush to Miles' aid before Mr. Somers stopped her.

"I'll go check on him. You won't be allowed in the medical room, but I will," claimed Mr. Somers.

With worry in her eyes, Melissa reluctantly agreed with him but decided to follow him anyway. Even if she couldn't go in the locker room, she wanted to get as close to her son as she could. When she saw Christine crying, Melissa abruptly stopped to console her. Sage, however, didn't want to acknowledge the extent of the grief she was feeling for Miles. She had only known Miles for a short while, but she was developing stronger feelings for him with every passing day they were together. She merely bowed her head and pulled Squirt, who Mr. Somers had asked her to watch, close to her. Also concerned for his dear friend, Andrew sat motionless in shock up in the video booth, where the school had taped the entire episode. No doubt, this would make the late news.

Pain radiated from Miles' right shoulder to his hands. The trainer determined that Miles had a stinger, an injury to the nerve supply of the upper arm, and he would not be throwing any more passes for the night. With Miles done for the night, the team had to find a way to win without its new star QB. The trainer gave Miles some aspirin to help with the pain and asked him if he felt like going back out to the sidelines.

"I'd rather be alone for a while."

The trainer then retreated to the sideline to give Coach Burdette and the officials the verdict on Miles. Coach Burdette never came back to the locker room, but Miles could only imagine how he felt after losing a second starting quarterback in one season. Miles lay on his back listening, as the cheers from the visiting side grew louder while the home side energy began to disappear.

By halftime, the Broncos led the Wildcats 28-14. Miles' teammates filed into the locker room one by one. They found him sitting silently in front of his locker with his shoulder pads removed.

Miles donned a sleeveless, blue compression shirt that fit his body snuggly.

Coach Burdette walked in as his players circled around him for his halftime rallying speech about never giving up and nothing being impossible. He had not given that halftime speech thus far all season because that was the first time the Wildcats were behind at the half. Miles sat quietly listening to every word but saying nothing. When Coach Burdette finished, he told the team to get back out there and start warming up for the second half. "We have a game to win," he said with doubt in his eyes as well as his tone.

Each player and coach slowly walked toward the exit to head back up the tunnel. Before they left, one by one they each looked back at Miles searching for evidence of the possibility of a return to the field. Coach Burdette and his players hoped for a sign to give them a reason to continue fighting for a win. Shawn paused longer than any other players or coaches, just hoping Miles would look up to give him some reassurance that he would be back in the huddle. Still, Miles never looked toward anyone. Finally, all the players and coaches left, and Miles was alone in the locker room once again.

About five minutes after everyone left the locker room, Miles heard the crowd respond to the second half kick-off. Miles heard the locker room door open thinking the trainer was coming back to check on him. He heard footsteps coming toward him and raised his head to greet the trainer, but there stood Mr. Somers.

"What are you doing sitting in here listening to your team's season go down the drain?

"You saw me take that hit," Miles explained.

"Don't pull that crap with me, Miles. I spoke with the trainer right before halftime, and I know the extent of your injury. You knew exactly what I meant when I asked you that question," shouted Mr. Somers.

"You think I didn't know that you started using the HSC chamber shortly after I hired you? You know, you can't see others watching you when you have the simulation helmet on. I've watched every skill you've developed over the last three years. EVERY SKILL! Just accept you destiny and use the talents you were given. I would have given anything to be special like you."

Miles didn't want to disappoint his mentor and friend. He didn't want to let his teammates down, but he couldn't let everyone know what he had kept hidden his whole life. Miles had always thought his secret made him weird or, to some extent, freakish. He knew it was anything but normal. Miles just sat there staring at Mr. Somers, realizing that his lifelong secret was no longer a secret. Mr. Somers left to rejoin the others in the stands. He knew they were waiting for a report from him.

Miles stood up and put on his shoulder pads. He grabbed his helmet and headed back up the tunnel to rejoin his team. The home crowd started cheering and clapping when they saw the player wearing the number 1 jersey jogging toward the Wildcat sideline. The Wildcat crowd's former look of desperation and despair turned hopeful when they saw Miles.

Melissa wondered why her son was returning to a game that betrayed his promise to never get hurt. "I thought he was hurt and not returning," she snapped at Mr. Somers. He assured her he was fine, and the injury was not that serious. Even Andrew emitted a sigh of relief when he saw Miles return. Coach Burdette was more surprised than the players to see Miles, however.

"How do you feel, son?"

"I feel like winning this game, Coach."

Miles ran back on the field to retake control of the offense. The relieved look on the players' faces said it all. Shawn just started smiling and said, "It's about time you got your ass back out here."

"You knew I wouldn't let you down."

Miles called the play and the offense moved into formation. Mr. Somers sat on the edge of his seat like he knew something special was about to happen, something that could no longer wait to be unleashed. Miles set up in shotgun formation ready to receive the ball. The ball was hiked and Miles took a step back before throwing a dart to Shawn for a 20-yard gain. Mr. Somers jumped up and shouted, "Yes!"

Most of the fans didn't notice any difference in Miles' play, but the coaches and the players sure did. Coach Burdette stood in amazement on the sideline and asked his assistant coach, "Did you see that?"

It had become clear what Mr. Somers was so eager to witness. Miles had thrown a pass to Shawn with his left hand. The issue in most onlookers' mind was that Miles was right-handed, or so everyone thought up until that point. Again, the Wildcats lined up, and again, Miles bulleted a left-handed completion. After two more plays, the Wildcats were in the end zone, down 28-21. Miles completed a 68-yard scoring drive in less than two minutes.

Soon chatter began circulating amongst the fans, home and away. Everyone was beginning to realize that Miles began that game and every game prior to that throwing the football with his right arm, and now he was throwing it with his left. You could hear the word "ambidextrous" clearly circulating amongst the crowd of spectators.

People on both sides of the stadium started pulling out their mobile devices to begin recording, texting, updating their social media accounts, and everything else to document what was happening before their eyes. Andrew could not believe what he was seeing his best friend do. Mr. Somers' daughter even realized the significance of what was taking place on that October night. Sage, Christine, and Melissa had not caught on yet. They were not big sports fans, so Mr. Somers had to explain. Melissa, however, didn't seem surprised. She always knew he was ambidextrous, but she was still reeling from the fact that he could even throw a football, period, and so well.

On the next Wildcat possession, even the visiting team's fans cheered for Miles as he continued to connect with Shawn from his left arm. The Broncos defensive coordinator decided to double team Shawn since Miles was beginning to go to him on every play. Shawn was the only receiver skilled enough to get open on every play against the stingy defenders. The ball was hiked and for the first time all night, Miles had no one open. Todd was again charging toward Miles, so he had to make a decision. Miles took off running down the field. The crowd on both sides of the field rose to their feet. They all witnessed Miles juke, spin and knife his way for a 51-yard touchdown scramble. Miles also had blazing fast speed. No one knew that, not even the coach, his mother, or Mr. Somers.

The game was now tied 28-28. Coach Burdette was beside himself with disbelief. He peered curiously at Miles in the end zone, now flanked by the entire offensive line. He was witnessing the revelation of the perfect quarterback, like none the world had ever seen before. The defense was mortified, and Coach Burdette, not known for PDE (public displays of emotion), threw his playbook in the air screaming with joy. He had no idea Miles could both throw and run with so much skill. Coach Burdette had never timed Miles in the 40 or anything else when he initially showed up for practice several weeks earlier.

Miles' second-half heroics must have inspired the Wildcat defense as well. They went on to shut down the Broncos' offense for the remainder of the game. Miles threw two more touchdown passes and rushed for two more touchdowns. The final score was Wildcats 56 and Broncos 28.

The fans rushed the field when the final buzzer sounded. Pure pandemonium broke out at Oakridge Stadium. The players hoisted Miles up on their shoulders and paraded him around the field. Reporters scrambled to push microphones in Miles' face to get a comment. Mr. Somers was in the stands clapping like a proud father would after a great achievement by a son. Christine, Melissa, Sage, and his daughter were overwhelmed. Andrew jumped up and down in the video booth. He was already counting the dollar signs from t-shirt sales. He started thinking about pins, caps, and even toothbrushes to sell. Andrew would try to market anything he could with Miles' logo on it.

Eventually, the players let Miles down, and Coach Burdette ordered the team back into the locker room before the fans carried Miles off. After Coach Burdette gave a postgame speech, he awarded Miles the game ball. It was time for interviews with the local media. Reporters only requested Miles. This slight bothered Shawn more than he would ever admit. It was the first instance in his four years at Oakridge that no one questioned him about his performance on the field. They all wanted a piece of Miles that night.

During the postgame media interview, Miles was bombarded with questions. "Are you right handed or left handed? How did you develop the other arm? How old were you when you realized you were ambidextrous? Why did you decide to return to the game after the injury? Why did you hold this back for so long? Are either of your parents ambidextrous?"

Coach Burdette had to finally end the interview after about 20 minutes. The questions usually took about 5 to 10 minutes, but the reporters didn't appear to be letting up any.

Miles showered, dressed, and headed to his car. Awaiting him were his mother, Christine, Sage, Andrew, Mr. Somers, and Squirt.

They all hugged him and congratulated him on his success. Shawn joined the group on the way to his red, two-seat, convertible. He formally introduced himself to Melissa and Mr. Somers. Someone took a photo of the eight of them standing together in the parking lot, which Mr. Somers later acquired a copy of and put in a frame on an end table at his home. Christine made sure she was standing next to Miles in the photo. Sage didn't seem to mind because as she reminded Christine, "I'm leaving with him."

"You are going to be so famous, man," said Andrew. Come Monday morning the world will know who Miles Starr is."

"Well done, son. Well done," complimented Mr. Somers. Miles' performance especially intrigued Mr. Somers' daughter. At 10 years old, she only knew enough about sports to figure that what Miles had done was a big deal. Mr. Somers spent their entire ride home explaining the impact of what Miles did and who he would likely become.

Chapter 9
NATIONAL RECOGNITION

October 2021

Andrew was right. By Monday morning, the entire country was talking about the ambidextrous high school prodigy quarterback in Arizona. Over the weekend, the local media sent footage of the game to national media outlets. Miles was viewed around the world on MSNBC, CNN, Fox News, and USPN (Ultimate Sports Performance Network) as well as on most other major media networks in other countries. Game highlights broadcast in over 200 languages. Nationally syndicated radio networks discussed Miles while most of the country was having coffee that Monday morning. Miles had gone viral. Every sports fan in America knew his name by the end of day on Monday. There had been athletes that could write with one hand and throw with the other, but the world had never seen an athlete, let alone a person, that could use either hand to do everything evenly.

Andrew even posted highlights of the game on YouTube and Facebook with links to his t-Shirt Web site. In fact, Andrew's online store was one of the top-ranked sites to appear in most search engines for the words "Miles Starr." He had so many orders that he eventually had to contract a company to handle them.

USPN contacted the athletic director at Oakridge and worked out a deal to air the remainder of the regular season games live on one of their networks. The contract amount was undisclosed, but it was rumored to be very lucrative. USPN, the largest sports media network in the world, had decided to make young Miles the new face of the network. It was obvious to the network that "Miles Starr Fever" was about to become very contagious.

The phones were ringing off the hooks. Oakridge received several calls from people trying to get group tickets to see who everyone was calling "The Prodigy." The Academy added extra temporary seating to accommodate the hundreds of new ticket requests.

When Miles pulled into the student parking lot that Monday several news vans, reporters, and students were waiting for interviews, autographs, and just plain footage of him breathing. As he stepped out his vehicle, he received applause from students and faculty. They treated him as if he was some sort of military hero coming home after winning a war. Oakridge was forced to hire a private security firm to handle all the additional traffic and for the safety of the student body, namely Miles. After three days of chaos, the school administration had to order the media off of the property.

Christine and Andrew greeted Miles just beyond the parking lot once he made it past the crowds. Andrew wore new sunglasses, new clothes, and a huge smile. They walked with Miles to the school entrance while the private security team ushered a path through the excited mob.

"I told you that you were going to be famous," Andrew said.

"Do you think all these people are here just for me?" Miles asked.

"No. They're here for some other superstar quarterback. What the hell do you think? Of course, they're here for you. When I'm right, I'm right. By the way, you're looking at the new president of FBLA. I received a confirmation text this morning once the members saw my sales numbers on my Web site."

While everyone else was smiling and celebrating, Christine felt dejected. She knew the world had Miles and any hope of him loving her faded way with every Google search of his name.

Andrew continued to fill Miles' head with all the comments that were on all the social media sites and television over the weekend. Miles didn't watch much TV over the weekend because he spent every free moment he could with Sage and the rest of the time doing homework. Miles didn't want to believe Andrew, but it was true. The sports world was talking about this new kid with a talent never known to exist before. Miles had become a phenomenon.

Miles, Christine, and Andrew were walking down the hall when, all of a sudden, Eugene Reynolds III came running into Andrew. Due to the force of the impact, Andrew's new sunglasses fell on the floor along with his tablet.

"Hey, watch where you're going asshole," Eugene insulted Andrew.

"You ran into me," Andrew responded.

"I don't care if your little friend is getting his 15 minutes or not. You three have never been and will never be shit to me, numb nuts."

Eugene just walked away not even waiting to hear a rebuttal from Andrew, Christine, or Miles. They were not worthy of a response in his eyes.

Eugene Reynolds III was a white, 5-foot-2-inch senior who came from a wealthy family. His great grandfather invented a type of aluminum foil that people used for cooking and storing food. The business eventually added plastic storage bags and many other products over the years. His family was so wealthy they purchased a new vehicle for Eugene at the beginning of every school year since he could drive. Before that, they simply had someone drive for him. The new vehicle for this year was a white Cadillac truck. Eugene was known for trying to impress the girls at Oakridge with his new vehicles. He was always offering some freshman a ride in his new wheels.

Eugene had been giving Andrew a hard time ever since freshman year. He was the only person that gave Andrew a hard time, but Eugene treated most people that way. He would stick gum on Andrew's locker or call him names in the hallway. On one occasion, Andrew was in the restroom sitting on the toilet in a stall. Eugene followed him in there, waited until he sat down on the toilet, and then began urinating on the floor in front of the stall. The urine splashed on Andrew's shoes and pants. Andrew didn't see Eugene do it, but he knew it had to be him. Andrew never understood why Eugene tormented him because he never recalled doing anything unjust to Eugene. Some people said he had a "Napoleon complex." He acted out to compensate for his insecurity with his own height, and Andrew was a good target because he was a scholarship student who didn't have the financial resources, physical stature, or clout to defend himself. After three years of dealing with Eugene's crap, Andrew was fed up.

"The next time that little, short bastard messes with me, he is going to regret it," Andrew threatened while checking for damage to his glasses, which he picked up immediately. Miles, meanwhile, picked up the tablet and handed the damaged device back to Andrew. The tablet's screen was cracked, and it never worked again.

Mr. Somers met the group in the hallway and asked to speak with Miles privately. Andrew and Christine continued on to class. Mr. Somers walked Miles outside to deliver a little fatherly advice.

"Miles, I know I encouraged you to let the world know who you really are, but I didn't take into account everything that would happen once you did. People can be very selfish, and I am not excluded from that statement. Now that the world knows what you a capable of, everyone, and I do mean everyone, is going to want a piece of you. The media, college recruits, girls, everyone. There is nothing I can say to prepare you for how your life has changed forever from last Friday night moving forward."

"I understand. You're worried about all of this going to my head. My mother gave me the same speech last night. Just like I told her Mr. Somers, I can handle it."

"Son, I'm not worried about you handling the spotlight. I'm more worried about the wolves in sheep's clothing trying to be your friends. Just be careful is all I'm saying."

Miles understood Mr. Somers' concern. He promised to heed the warning. However, that promise did not make Mr. Somers feel any better about coercing Miles to continue playing the game that night.

The Wildcats did not have a football game scheduled on the coming Friday. It was their bye week. During the week, Miles received dozens of letters offering him full scholarships to come play football at all sorts of schools. The letters were from just about every state that had a major college football program.

Miles' satellite phone was ringing off the hook, so he finally had to get a new number. Less than three hours after changing his number, he received a call from Head Coach Mickey Bradford of the USC Archers located in southern California. Coach Bradford offered him two first-class tickets to come visit the school on the upcoming Saturday. That weekend just happened to be USC's bye week also. After talking it over with Mr. Somers and his mother, Miles agreed to visit the campus. Because it was just an overnight trip, his mother consented for him to go with Mr. Somers.

* * *

Their flight landed in Los Angeles around 3 p.m. that Saturday afternoon. A 22-year-old, sexy, blond hostess with a handwritten sign reading, "Starr" greeted them at the airport. She was wearing a white satin blouse and a black professional skirt. Standing at about 6 feet tall in her black heels, she had long, lean legs built for walking down a runway.

Miles and Mr. Somers walked up to make their presence known. She introduced herself as Nicole Anderson and then led them to a limousine on the curb outside the terminal. The driver took their bags and loaded them in the trunk.

Nicole sat next to Miles while the limo headed toward the interstate. She immediately began talking about the school and how successful the football program was. Nicole said the head coach just received a contract extension and would not be going anywhere next year. The young lady was not aware that Miles and especially Mr. Somers knew more about the program than she could imagine, but they listened attentively anyway.

Making very little eye contact with Mr. Somers, who sat across from her, Nicole gushed at Miles during the entire ride. Miles barely listened to her words and instead, focused on her inviting smile punctuated with sheer, fragrant lip gloss. He also couldn't help but notice her smooth, sexy crossed legs only a few feet from his eyes. For some strange reason, Nicole kept crossing and uncrossing her legs. Miles enjoyed watching them reposition each time.

It was a 25-minute commute before they arrived at USC's stadium, where Coach Bradford was waiting for Miles and Mr. Somers when the limo stopped. He stood outside the athletics office building with two provocatively dressed female hostesses. Coach Bradford formally introduced himself, giving them firm handshakes and welcoming them to the campus. Afterward he cut straight to the chase, giving Miles and Mr. Somers the spiel about the football program and its tradition and success. Nicole sometimes echoed and reemphasized what Coach Bradford told them.

"Being an Archer here at the USC is not just about playing football. It's about becoming a part of a rich tradition and joining a host of professional athletes that had to pass through these walls first." Coach Bradford laid it on thick.

After the meeting, Coach Bradford showed Miles and Mr. Somers the game field, locker rooms, and practice field. Almost on cue, Nicole then drove up on a golf cart to show them the main campus. At 6 p.m., they joined Coach Bradford again along with two other men on the recruiting team to have dinner at a cozy, family-owned Italian restaurant that was walking distance from campus.

Nicole whispered to Miles during dinner, "Coach usually doesn't join us during recruit dinners, so you must be real special, Mr. Starr."

"Mr. Starr," Miles thought, that was the first occasion when someone referred to him with that title. He smiled uneasily, as her lips brushed his ear as she spoke. Mr. Somers noticed his flushed complexion and said, "Are you okay, son?"

"Son," Miles thought. He had never heard Mr. Somers use that expression. He didn't notice that Mr. Somers had acknowledged him as son when he initially warned him about the "vultures" that would begin circling. Miles was too busy soaking in the presidential treatment he was receiving that day.

"I'm fine," answered Miles. "I think I'm just a little warm."

With that, Nicole summoned a nearby waiter and asked that he turn down the thermostat. "We can't have our number one recruit all hot and bothered."

Amazed at her attentiveness, Miles started blinking nervously at his healthy plate of vegetable lasagna.

"So this is your dad?" said Tim Vincent, one of the recruiters.

"No," said Mr. Somers before Miles could answer. "I'm his mentor and friend. I gave him his first job."

"Oh, yeah," said Nicole. "Doing what?"

This time Miles answered for Mr. Somers. "He's like a father to me. He comes to all my practices and games." He never made mention of the job, and no one else did either.

Mr. Somers smiled broadly at Miles' comment and stuck his chest out like a proud father. For the rest of the meal, Mr. Somers bragged on Miles' talent. He alluded to the fact that Miles had more athletic surprises to reveal. Miles was unsure what he meant and thought that Mr. Somers might have simply been trying to sell him to the coach.

* * *

When the tour officially ended after dinner, Nicole accompanied them in the limo to an exclusive five-star hotel where they would be spending the night. She told them to charge all meals and anything else they needed to the room. Before leaving them in the lobby of the hotel, Nicole told Miles that she and some of her friends were going out to celebrate her 22nd birthday that night and she wanted him to come. Miles hesitated, but Mr. Somers told him, "You only live once."

With Mr. Somers' blessing, Miles agreed to go. "I guess it's fine," he said.

"Great. I'll pick you up at 10."

Nicole walked away and winked at Miles. Although he felt guilty, he couldn't help watching her curvy figure move gently through the hotel lobby before disappearing in the back of the limo. The driver closed the door behind her, and she was gone.

Miles and Mr. Somers went to their separate suites. The rooms had hot tubs, steam rooms, a kitchen stocked with snacks and drinks. Miles and Mr. Somers were very impressed. They each recognized that USC really knew how to treat their recruits with style.

The two of them began to video call their loved ones to tell them about the trip. Mr. Somers called his wife and daughter. Miles contacted his mother at work and then Sage. Sage joked with Miles about not hooking up with any whores while he was in Los Angeles. All Miles could do was laugh it off and reassure her, "You're the only girl for me, Ms. Star with one R. You're gonna have to convince me to give you the other R to make this official."

"What do I have to do, Mr. Starr, with two Rs?"

"Come up with something. I know I'll like it." No longer shy about his feelings or desire, Miles spoke with new confidence. However, Miles didn't mention a word to Sage about his plans for the evening with Nicole and her friends.

At 8:59 p.m., while Miles watched television, he heard a knock at the door. He was already dressed for the party, wearing a long-sleeve, baby blue dress shirt, black slacks, black dress shoes, and a black sports coat. Miles opened the door to find Nicole dressed in the most amazingly tight bandage dress. The royal blue dress complemented her 4-inch, blue stilettos with a bejeweled strap around the ankle. The dress accented her sea blue eyes in a way that made them seem magical, and it lifted her firm breasts to command immediate attention. Her blond hair was lying across her shoulders and shifted smoothly whenever she turned her head. Miles wasn't sure if it was her complexion or the makeup, but her skin looked flawless. She wore a sweet, erotic fragrance that emanated from her entire body. It wasn't the fragrance Sage wore, but it had the same effect on Miles.

"You ready to go?" Nicole asked enthusiastically.

"I thought we were leaving at 10."

"That was the plan, but since you're already dressed, we might as well leave now before we get into trouble," said Nicole with an alluring grin. She then turned to walk back toward the elevator.

Miles didn't notice the outfit revealed her entire back until she walked away. Just like her face, her back was smooth and flawless with no moles, freckles, or any other type of blemish. The back of the dress was open down to the beginning crease of her backside. There, Nicole had a 6-inch tattoo. Miles didn't know what the tattoo was, but he knew it looked sexy. As she strode gracefully down the hallway Miles thought, "She has one hell of a walk." He stayed focused on her rear while it moved seductively in his presence. He was convinced that she was not wearing any underwear after failing to notice a panty line.

Nicole escorted him outside of the hotel where the same limo they rode in earlier sat parked. The same driver from before waited to open the door. Miles entered the limo with Nicole. Two women from the tour were sitting patiently and dressed in a similar fashion as Nicole. All the striking young ladies greeted Miles with smiles and admiration. They could not have made him feel more welcome and accepted. Miles grinned like he had been welcomed into the pearly gates of heaven.

They arrived at Nitro, a trendy L.A. nightclub, at 9:40. The entrance line wrapped around the building. Miles noticed the doorman checking IDs for admittance. The club was obviously for the

21-and-older crowd. Miles was only 17 and began to worry about getting admitted. "Hey, I'm not old enough to get in here, am I?"

Nicole grabbed Miles by the hand and walked right up to the doorman, an intimidating 6-foot-5-inch man with a shiny, brown head and goatee who looked like he once played nose tackle. He took one look at Nicole and opened the red velvet rope that barred everyone in line from entering. Miles and the three ladies bypassed the aggravated patrons standing in line. He heard one woman ask her boyfriend, "Who is he?"

"Probably some pro athlete," the man answered.

Nicole's display of power and influence impressed Miles.

A man, who appeared to be some sort of manager, greeted the group at the door. He was in his 40s and dressed in a nicely-tailored, tan suit. Nicole kissed him on his cheek right before he led the foursome up stairs to a private table overlooking the dance floor. One of the girls, Brooke, slid in the circular booth first followed by Miles then Nicole and then the last girl, Erica. The ladies all ordered drinks for themselves and tried to encourage Miles to do the same. Instead, Miles ordered bottled water. He was not about to put something as toxic as alcohol in his system.

Nicole sat really close to Miles as if trying to co-occupy his seat. She started asking him questions about how he was handling all the media attention and being pretty much an international, Internet sports star. Miles answered her questions with a huge grin on his face the entire night. He felt like some kind of kingpin with all those overly attractive women surrounding him.

Without even asking, the three women grabbed Miles and rushed him to the dance floor when the DJ played their "song." The lovely ladies surrounded Miles and grinded their backsides up and down the much taller Miles while dancing. Nicole was directly in front of him and literally felt how excited Miles was getting from their interaction. Occasionally, she faced Miles and extended her arms around his towering neck. Miles had to bend his knees some just so she could interlock her fingers. Nicole looked deep in his eyes while she seduced the inexperienced teen with her slithering moves. Nicole and her friends put on a show and got Miles worked up in the process. Miles was out of his blazer before long as the temperature in the club seemed to rise after dancing for more than 30 minutes straight.

Nicole turned her rear to Miles' front. She took both his hands and rubbed them on her breasts. She guided his hands down the side of her body until he felt how firm her bottom was. Meanwhile, Brooke and Erica rubbed Miles' broad muscular shoulders and chest, getting him more and more excited. This went on for another 20 minutes until Nicole figured that she had him primed and ready.

At that point, Nicole led the foursome outside and back into the limo so the driver could take them back to the hotel. Miles stepped out the car with Nicole trailing him, leaving Brooke and Erica in the limo. They stuck their heads out the window to tell Miles goodbye and rewarded him with a kiss on the cheek for helping them celebrate their friend's birthday. The limo pulled away from the hotel entrance and vanished down the street when Miles and Nicole entered the hotel.

Miles looked confused, wondering what Nicole was still doing there. Still, he didn't ask any questions or make any assumptions. Once they got to Miles' room Nicole led Miles toward the bed, threw her purse on it, and removed his coat. She sat Miles down on the foot of the bed and began undoing his belt. As Nicole lowered herself to her knees, Miles' satellite phone rang. Sage was calling. Miles didn't answer. He looked Nicole in her eyes and lifted her to her feet. He grabbed her purse from the bed and said, "You have to leave."

"Why? I thought we were both having fun," Nicole asked.

"I have a girlfriend. I don't know if it will lead to anything really serious, but I don't want to do anything stupid before I find out."

Nicole looked perplexed. She had never experienced rejection from a man before. It was an embarrassing and uncomfortable feeling. She began crying softly. Miles responded with a gentle hug while escorting her to the door. "It's okay, Nicole. You're a great girl and maybe I'll see you again."

With Nicole gone, he called Sage back. They talked until about 4 a.m. Miles didn't mention a word about what happened or didn't happen with Nicole. He only got three hours of sleep before having to wake up for a 10 a.m. flight back to Phoenix with Mr. Somers.

CHAPTER 10
ANDREW AND SAGE STRIKE BACK

October 2021

M iles received several offers and visited several schools before the season ended. However, none of his recruiting trips came close to matching his experience on the USC trip. Even as the season was about to end, he was still nowhere near making a choice. While Mr. Somers did provide lots of insight into the history and potential benefits of the various football programs, Miles still remained unsure. He figured he would get an academic scholarship for college. He never dreamed he would be actually playing football in high school, let alone college. All the attention he was getting, along with the numerous students bombarding him with questions about which college he was going to, made the decision that much harder. It seemed like everyone had a favorite college team and wanted it to be Miles' choice. Even faculty members were promoting their alma maters. Miles was totally confused now that football had been thrown into the equation. He was sure of one thing, however. He didn't want to fly half way around the country and be far away from his mom or Sage.

Both Andrew and Sage talked about going to USC if Miles decided to go there. Sage's family had a house in L.A., and plus, she truly loved the California atmosphere because it reminded her of Florida. Andrew, however, outright declared that he wanted to trail Miles to wherever he decided to play collegiate football. At that point, seemingly everyone in Miles' life wanted to relish in or benefit from his fame. No one individual at Oakridge capitalized on Miles' new international acclaim quite like Andrew did, though. Andrew made so much money from selling Miles paraphernalia he was able to purchase a new car. He tried to give Miles some of the money, but Miles refused it. Unlike most, Miles wasn't playing football for the fame or glory. He truly loved the game almost as much as he loved helping people, almost.

Even though Andrew set up a small-scale process to handle online orders, he still sold items in the student parking lot. The principal, Dr. Cecil Edwards, had been hounding Andrew for two weeks about using school property for his private business venture. Andrew delayed Dr. Edwards' harassment when he lied about donating half of his proceeds to a charity on behalf of the Oakridge. Andrew had one additional week to provide proof of his assertion before Dr. Edwards shut his little operation down.

All of Andrew's Starr Power merchandise was scattered across a portable table, which he stored in the trunk of his new car. He looked and acted like a real entrepreneur. Andrew began taking on the demeanor and appearance of a man who could possibly be a judge or anything else he wanted to be one day. He spoke with a cool confidence, most times leading the conversation. His hair was now always freshly cut. He began wearing shiny patent leather dress shoes with his freshly dry-cleaned Oakridge uniforms. Andrew even kept his hands and toes manicured and pedicured. He was starting to blend in with the trust fund babies at Oakridge.

On one particular Wednesday, Andrew was set up in the student parking lot like he always did. Eugene drove by in his new Cadillac truck and bumped Andrew's table with the fender, sending half his items tumbling to the asphalt. His face bright red, Andrew was visibly furious. Eugene pulled into the empty parking space right next to Andrew. When Eugene walked by heading to the building, he laughed at Andrew, who was struggling to gather his items back to the table. Several other students witnessed what Eugene did, but no one said anything. A few students helped Andrew put things back in order. Normally, Andrew would dispense a few choice words to Eugene. That morning he remained silent and resolute, simply watching Eugene disappear into the building.

As soon as Eugene was completely gone, Andrew noticed the rear window was open on Eugene's vehicle. Andrew reached into his trunk and pulled out a pair of latex gloves. He put on the gloves right before reaching for a one-gallon freezer bag filled with some strange looking dark colored pellets. The pellets were, in fact, two week's collection of dog shit from Andrew's toy poodle, Sydney.

He scanned the parking lot for any onlookers. None were present at the moment. Andrew then climbed onto the back of Eugene's truck and emptied the contents of the bag into the driver's seat through the window opening. He quickly hopped off of the truck and parked himself back in the chair behind his car. It was a clean get away, or so he thought.

Later that day, right after lunch, Sage was parked in a stall in the lady's restroom. No one else happened to be in there at that time. Suddenly, she heard the restroom door open and two voices entered giggling while in conversation.

"I don't care what you say. He is too cute and sexy to pass up. Sexy and cute equals two points for Miles in my bedroom category. He is definitely on my 'to do' list," said Voice 1.

"So what are you saying? Are you going to approach him or what?" Voice 2 commented.

"I'm still deciding if I want to give him some of my goodies. I can't go wrong if I do. He is definitely going to be big time. My brother is a college scout, and he said every sports writer in the country is writing or having a conversation about Miles and his potential at the next level and even as a pro."

Sage raised an eyebrow when she heard Miles' name, but she kept listening to see where the conversation was going. She had heard this type of conversation many times before among girls in Orlando.

"Yeah, my boyfriend said the same thing."

"Every chick he comes across is going to be trying to get at him. Why not offer myself as an option?"

"Does he have a girlfriend?"

"Meagan said she thought he was talking to that new girl," said Voice 1. "What's her name?"

"Sage!" proclaimed Voice 2.

"Yeah, her name is Sage, but I don't give a damn if he was married. If I want to get with him, I'll get with him, and there's not a damn thing that Sage or any other woman can do about it."

Sage swung open her stall door and stared intensely at the girls before she walked up to the shorter blonde who she felt referred to her during the conversation. "So what were you saying about Miles?"

The young lady took a big swallow and headed toward the exit with her friend at her heels.

Sage shook her head while looking into the restroom mirror and thought, "That's why I don't like dating athletes." She remembered the many encounters, a few of which almost got violent, with girls throwing themselves at her superstar athlete boyfriend. Sage was unwilling to experience that again, not even for Miles.

Miles had biology as one of his late classes. It was his favorite subject, and he outperformed all his classmates. When the bell rang ending class for the day, Miles gathered his things. Jessica Simon caught Miles before he left the classroom heading to practice.

"Hello, Miles!" Jessica said.

"Hey, Jess. What's up?"

"I'm really struggling with the stuff we're going over right now. I don't think I'm going to do well on the test next week."

"Sure you will. You've been doing fine so far this year."

"I know, but this stuff is a little more difficult."

"Well, if there's maybe something I can do to help, just ask."

"OK. Well, I'm asking now. Do you think you could come over and help me tonight?"

"I have practice this afternoon and then I..."

"Just for a little while. Please," Jessica begged. "If I don't get an A on this test, my dad is going to take my phone away."

"Email me the address, and I'll stop by for a minute right after practice. It shouldn't take long."

When the final bell rang for the day, many of the students poured out of the building heading toward their vehicles. Eugene was walking out with another unwitting freshman, Rosa Galindo, whom he snagged with his chatter about his money, his house, his truck and whatever else he could muster to impress her.

Offering her a ride home, Eugene walked the girl to his truck. He unlocked the doors with his satellite phone as they approached the vehicle. Rosa walked around to the passenger side with her backpack in hand. She climbed into the truck at the same time as Eugene. He thought his rear felt a little off balance in the seat, which was pulled forward as much as possible to accommodate his small stature. He began sniffing to identify an unusual smell. Noticing an odor as well, Rosa soon identified the source oozing from under Eugene's pants. She screamed before jumping out of the vehicle.

It took a moment, but Eugene finally came to grips with what he was sitting in. He then started to swear out loud and bang his truck horn.

Whispers of the phrase "dog crap" began circulating among a large group of students heading to their vehicles.

Eugene lifted his head up enough to see Andrew standing in front of his truck laughing hysterically. A few other students noticed the show and added their jokes and laughter.

"Hey Gene, you sure have a stinky booster seat," one male student said and brought himself to tears laughing so hard. That statement really prolonged Eugene's embarrassing moment with additional students joining in.

Because of his attitude, Eugene was not very well liked, so the other students just stood around laughing without offering any assistance. Humiliated and embarrassed, Eugene burned the rubber on his rear tires as he sped out the parking lot. He never bothered Andrew again that year. In fact, he avoided him.

* * *

Miles kept his word and went straight to Jessica's house right after practice. He pulled up in the circular driveway and was amazed by the size of her home. It was twice the size of Sage's home. Miles rang the doorbell while waiting in front of two 10-foot custom wood doors. A woman wearing a housekeeping outfit answered the door and invited Miles in.

"Miss Jessica will be joining you in the study," the housekeeper informed Miles.

Miles followed the woman through a maze of rooms before finally arriving at the study.

A ton of books towered up each wall, neatly aligned on dark cherry wood bookshelves. A few animal heads decorated the few bare spots on the walls. Jessica's father was obviously a wild gamer. Miles also noticed several University of Dallas-Texas flags, rugs, golf bags, and other such items with the same markings placed around the room.

When Miles heard a door open, he turned expecting Jessica to walk in with her books. To his surprise, a man walked in smoking a cigar. He was a round man standing about 6 feet tall wearing a business suit with a University of Dallas-Texas tie.

"Hello, Miles. I'm Jessica's father, John Simon."

"Hello, Mr. Simon." Miles shook his hand to greet him.

"Call me John."

"OK, John. You have a beautiful home, sir."

"Oh, it's nothing. I have several more around the world. I have been very fortunate and successful in my business ventures. You see, I'm a developer. I develop property around the world for commercial or industrial use. Let me show you a project I'm working on right now. You may want to back up about 10 paces, son."

Miles backed up till his back met the bookshelf. John flipped a switch on the wall, and the floor opened on two sides. A table rose from the floor. It had a miniature model of a shopping mall completely covering its top. Miles' eyes stretched with surprise, impressed that he had just seen something rise out of the floor.

"We're building a new shopping mall in the town of my alma matter, the University of Dallas-Texas. We're nearing the completion and should be opening early fall next year. We have to catch those Christmas shoppers, you know. We're beginning to staff the place, and we're in the process of looking for some people with experience in retail to manage the place. I understand your mother works in retail?"

"Yes, sir. She works at Fashion Square Mall."

"I may need to talk to her and see if she interested in moving to Dallas. Our mall managers are furnished a house and a car, and we pay them very well. Man, it would be something if you and your mother moved to Dallas. They have a wonderful football program there, too. The facilities are the best in the country. I should know. I paid for and built most of them."

Miles finally realized he was not there to help with any schoolwork. Jessica lured him to her home so her father could pitch his school to Miles. "Here we go again," Miles thought, recalling the many times that even strangers on the streets suggested that he attend a particular school. This was the most extreme solicitation because no one had ever tried to entice him using his mother as a beneficiary.

"Are you ready to get started?" Jessica asked as she walked in the room with her books in hand.

Miles looked at his satellite phone, pretended to have an emergency text from his mother, and explained that he had to leave. Miles apologized to Jessica and made haste toward the front door.

During the drive home, he thought a lot about what Mr. Somers had said to him about the "vultures." Because everyone was coming at Miles trying to get something, he eventually changed his social media profile to private. He drew tired of the questions, requests, and suggestions regarding the university he would attend. Miles eventually had to stop watching USPN and reading anything related to sports to avoid the predictions and speculation. One thing made him feel better, though. He felt that the people he loved would never try to exploit him. His mother, aunt, Sage, Andrew, Christine, and Mr. Somers were the only people in his life he thought he could truly trust.

The next day, Dr. Edwards called Andrew into his office to discuss the incident with the dog poop. The incident would later be named "Poopgate." While Andrew sat down, Dr. Edwards remained standing and focused his attention to a flat screen monitor on the wall. He picked up a remote and pressed play. They both watched a recording of Andrew making a poop deposit in Eugene's truck. When a clear shot of Andrew's face turned toward the camera, Dr. Edwards froze the frame and zoomed in. He turned to Andrew, saying, "Do you have anything to say for yourself?"

Andrew remained unusually calm during the entire viewing. As a matter of fact, he seemed more interested in playing with his satellite phone.

Andrew was good at making friends and finding out things that most people didn't know. For instance, over a year ago, Andrew found out about a certain married principal and a certain unmarried French teacher named Ms. Scott. They had a weekly love session in the head counselor's office when school ended for the day. Wednesday was normally the day of choice. Andrew knew the information would come in handy one day, so he hid a tiny camera in the office to catch all the action. During his meeting with Dr. Edwards about Eugene's vehicle, Andrew accessed the recorded rendezvous from his electronic device.

While Dr. Edwards stood in front of him waiting for an answer to his question, Andrew seemed unfazed and finished dabbling with his phone. Finally, he stood up and held the device up to Dr.

Edwards' face. The video showed Dr. Edwards hitting Ms. Scott on her bare rear with a paddle, as she moaned in delight. Andrew even turned the volume up so Dr. Edwards could hear himself squealing like a pig.

"If I press this button right here," Andrew said smugly, "this video will be all over the web. Now, do you have anything to say for yourself?"

Dr. Edwards didn't say a word but turned as red as a fire truck.

Andrew gathered his backpack and then headed for the door, but before he left Andrew brought up one last matter.

"I consider the issue about me providing proof of my charitable donations settled."

"I agree," Dr. Edwards replied.

Chapter 11
MARK WELLS

November 2021

The USPN television ratings on Oakridge's football games were better than anyone expected. They ranked among the top-five most-watched events on television and the Web during its time slot. Miles was becoming a household name, and kids all over the country wore the number 1 jersey and pretended to be Miles. Stories hit the news about fathers around the country forcing their sons to use their off hand when they played sports. Mr. Somers told Miles one about a father who was arrested for duck taping his son's right arm to his body and forcing him to throw a football with his left.

Shawn's receiving stats were among the best in the nation. He got more scholarship offers than he could have ever imagined. With all those positive things going on in Shawn's life, he was unhappy. The spotlight that he had solely retained his entire athletic career had been taken from him. To make matters worse, he kept hearing several of the girls he was involved with making suggestive remarks about Miles. Even their teammates bragged about how amazing Miles performed during the games in the same manner they used to brag about Shawn. Still, the one thing that infuriated him more than anything was the fact that his father wanted to meet Miles. Shawn's father had never wanted to personally meet any of his other friends or teammates in the past.

When Shawn was 12, his father sent him to a receiver's camp instructed by professional wide receivers. Some of them were his father's clients including Shawn's favorite receiver, Troy Mitchell. Troy taught him that the key to being the perfect receiver was conditioning.

"Any fool with two hands can catch a football. But when you're in the fourth quarter of a game, and you look across the line of scrimmage at your defender and his chest is going up and down, up and down, up and down, his ass is exhausted and you're just warming up it's because you put in the hard work, the conditioning, and he didn't. He might as well not even be on the field because you have beaten him before the ball is even snapped."

Troy was the one who told Shawn about Echo Canyon Park in Scottsdale. Echo Canyon sat at an elevation of 2,704 feet. It took the average hiker approximately one hour to travel to the top of the 1.3 mile trail of rock and rugged terrain.

"When you get to the point where you can run to the top without stopping, then and only then will you be ready."

Shawn never forgot those words and was at that park every weekend from that day on. His mother took him to the park before he started driving. Anyone who ever attempted to conquer the behemoth of a mountain would understand how Shawn obtained his superior athletic abilities. He was never really serious about anything else in his life, including the women, but when it came to his training, no one was more focused and dedicated to his craft. So what if it was all motivated from the thought of not disappointing his father, the results were outstanding.

* * *

One weekend, Shawn asked Miles to join him for his routine workout on Sunday morning at Echo Canyon. Miles agreed. The two young stars began stretching in the parking lot before heading toward the top of the mountain. The sky was very cloudy that day. The weatherman predicted rain, which would explain why only a few adventurers were on the trail. On any given weekend, the parking lot was normally at capacity, and people would have to park a mile away and walk to the park entrance. That was not the case that day.

Shawn led and Miles followed. Miles was in great shape, but the rugged terrain and steep inclines were enough to challenge anyone not used to such a workout. Even though it was difficult, Miles stayed on Shawn's heals. Each was smart enough to strap a water bottle pouch around his waist. They each took a few sips every few minutes but never broke pace.

After about 20 minutes the rain started pouring, but they had practiced in weather much worse than that so it didn't bother them at all. Rocks, which were slippery when wet, caused the main issue. Meanwhile, others on the trail headed in the opposite direction to escape the rain. They made it to the top in about 45 minutes. Miles stood near the edge of the cliff taking in the view and catching his breath for the journey back down. Shawn got some amusement from watching his obviously worn-out teammate.

The rain eased to a light downpour but still more than a sprinkle. While no thunder erupted during the rain shower to indicate a threat of lightning, out of nowhere, a bolt of lightning struck the mountain about 30 feet from where Miles and Shawn stood. Startled, Miles slipped and fell over a cliff. He reached out and grabbed the edge before barreling down the side of the mountain to his death. Miles dangled, trying to get a good enough grip to pull himself back up. He was losing his grip on the slippery rock.

Shawn saw his teammate in need of help, but he hesitated for a couple of seconds. For a brief moment Shawn saw an opportunity to be number one again, a chance to reclaim the spotlight he once commanded. However, Shawn was not cold hearted enough to allow his friend and teammate to meet such a tragic end. After all, who would throw him the ball if not Miles? Shawn extended his hand and pulled Miles to safety.

Miles' heart raced as he realized what almost happened. The two young men found refuge from the storm in a small covering embedded in the side of the mountain.

"Thanks, Shawn. I owe you big time. That could have been it for me."

"If something happens to you, who's going to throw me the ball so I can continue making highlights?"

"I see your point."

Shawn stood there with his hands resting on his waist and stared at Miles, who was in a seated position resting on a rock to calm his nerves. He was still jittery from his unsettling ordeal. Shawn gave Miles a reassuring, comforting grin, but in his mind, he was wrestling with the thought of what he was almost capable of – not helping his friend in order to help himself.

"By the way, my dad wants to meet the person that guaranteed I could play at any school in the country."

"Oh...really? It would be an honor to meet your dad. I've heard a lot about him. He's very well known in the community."

"I'll come by and pick you up around 8 tonight."

"I'll be ready."

Once, the storm faded within the next 15 minutes, they both maneuvered back down the treacherous wet terrain and left the park.

Miles' mother and aunt were both at work when Shawn arrived to pick Miles up at 8:27 p.m. He pulled up in a 2020 model Ferrari with the top dropped. Miles rushed out of the front door and hopped in the passenger side. He was very excited, considering he'd never ridden in a Ferrari before. Shawn backed into the street and smoked the rear tires when he pulled off. Luckily for Miles, his mother and aunt did not witness Shawn's wild driving. Miles would have undoubtedly been given grief about putting himself in such a potentially harmful situation. The fastest Miles' mother ever drove was 55 on the highway. She valued safety on the road and taught Miles to do the same, which he did, for the most part.

Shawn headed toward the interstate to get back home. Because of his jeopardous driving, he needed the additional lanes. Miles figured Shawn was an Indy driver in his former life by the way he zoomed in and out of traffic reaching speeds over 100 mph. Miles wanted to ask Shawn what the rush was, but decided to make sure his seatbelt was securely locked instead while listening to Shawn ramble on about the fine girl he was with the night before. Shawn described her soft breasts and buttocks in great detail. Miles would have never been able to recall any of those details because his eyes alternated from the white lines streaking up the paved interstate to the speedometer in Shawn's Ferrari.

Shawn drove too fast to notice a sofa lying on the roadway covering two lanes. It had fallen off of a beat-up, old pickup truck that had no business hauling furniture on such a busy roadway. Shawn had a split second to make a decision. If he made the wrong decision, the outcome would end very badly. Shawn pumped the breaks and swerved to the right only missing the sofa by two feet. He turned the wheel slightly back to the left, and the high performance tires quickly re-obtained their grip on the roadway. The two teens avoided their second life-threatening encounter of the day.

Their next encounter would not be life-threatening, but still troublesome. A police officer saw Shawn swerving after his near upfront and personal encounter with a sofa. The blue lights were in Shawn's rearview mirror within seconds. Shawn cursed under his breath and pulled the speeding vehicle over on to the right shoulder. Miles thought for sure they were going to jail. He closed his eyes, clinched his lips, and rested his head back, waiting for the worst.

The blue flashing lights were almost blinding in the dark Arizona night. The overweight uniformed officer of the law walked up to the passenger side door to avoid exposure to oncoming traffic.

"Do you know how fast you were going? May I see your license and registration?"

Reaching over Miles, Shawn handed the officer the information he requested.

"You're Shawn," the officer said with excitement in his voice. "You're Mark Wells' boy. Your dad sure has been good to the Scottsdale Police Department."

"Yes, sir, he does do a lot of charity work," Shawn added.

"Shawn, because I know your daddy, I'm going to let you off with a warning on two conditions."

The officer handed Shawn back his information.

"What's that, officer?"

"You promise to slow down out here and tell your daddy old Wendell said hi."

"Sure thing, I'm on my way to see him right now."

The officer walked back to his patrol car. Shawn started the engine and continued to his home. Miles was relieved and grateful for the generosity the officer had shown them. He finally exhaled when the officer moved out of sight.

"I thought we were going to jail for sure. The only thing I expected that officer to say was 'You have the right to remain silent.'"

"I wasn't worried at all. If these Mayberry-ass cops arrested me, my dad would've been all over them and they all know it. You have to learn to relax when you're rolling with me."

Even though the worst had passed, Miles almost became tearful at the continued thought of having to explain to his mother why he was in jail. He already knew he would probably get a question or two about the black tire marks on the street in front of his house.

For the remaining stretch of drive, Shawn only drove 15 miles over the speed limit.

Shawn turned off the main street and stopped in front of a gated entrance. He pushed a button in the Ferrari and the large brass gate swung open. Shawn drove up the cobblestone driveway and parked the Ferrari in an eight-car garage containing several expensive cars. Miles had never seen so many cars in one garage.

Miles followed Shawn through a door leading them from the garage into the kitchen, where Shawn's mother, Kim, was finishing washing dinner dishes. She didn't have to do manual chores, but she loved the idea of taking care of her family. Even wearing an apron, she was a very attractive 38-year-old woman. His mother's face lit up when she saw Shawn walk through the door.

"There's my baby."

Shawn gave his mother a kiss on the cheek and hugged her so tight he picked her up off the floor.

"Mom, this is my friend Miles."

"So this is Miles. I heard your father talking about how talented this young man is. He said how this young man was helping show the world what a superstar my baby really is."

"Thanks, Mrs. Wells." Miles blushed.

Shawn loved getting praise from his teammates, coaches, and groupies. None of them compared to hearing them from his mother. She was his biggest fan. Shawn always dreamed of being with his mother at a professional football draft and giving her a big hug on camera when they announced his name after a team selected him.

The story of Mark and Kim Wells was an interesting one. Shortly after finishing law school, Mark accidentally impregnated the 20-year-old college sophomore, so he married her. He was the type of man that took care of his responsibilities, but that's where his good intentions toward her and Shawn ended. Mark lived the bachelor life throughout the marriage. Because his work kept him on the road several days at a time, nights of infidelity were routine.

Kim knew about the other women Mark was involved with, but she didn't say anything as long as he didn't parade his infidelity in her face. Shawn also knew of his father's appetite for the many flavors of female fruit. His father's actions explained why Shawn was such a womanizer. Shawn didn't care much about the feelings of the many girls with whom he had been involved. His mother would always say, "You're just like your father." Shawn only loved one woman, his mother, and he treated her better than all the others combined.

Shawn never felt a connection with his father, however. He always felt more like a client than a son. This bothered Shawn, but Mark seemed unfazed by their impersonal relationship. Mark cared about his son, but he cared about winning more, so he spared no expense on Shawn when it came to sports. Shawn never remembered a summer that he didn't attend several football, basketball, and baseball camps throughout the country. Through his work, Mark had access to the best in the business, many of them clients. It was like Mark was trying to create a more valuable asset for him to manage one day. No matter what anyone thought about Mark's abilities as a husband and father, there was no better person at negotiating contracts.

Mark was one of the most successful, well known, and highly respected professional sports agents in the country. His clients worked in all three major sports: football, basketball, and baseball. Mark always got what he wanted, no matter what the cost. All professional sports managers revered him. The saying went, "If you ever met Mark Wells, you would never forget him because he wouldn't let you."

Shawn hugged his mother one last time and took Miles into his father's office, which Mark occupied 80% of the time when he was actually home. Shawn knocked on the door before entering.

"Come in."

Mark was heavily involved in a heated phone conversation with a Fulton County district attorney in Atlanta, Georgia. Apparently, one of Mark's clients assaulted his girlfriend, and the police got involved. Mark worked out a deal with the DA and convinced the girlfriend to drop all charges.

He said, "You let me know what three games you want to use my suite for, and I'll have my assistant send you the credentials... Sounds good. Bye."

Mark instantly redirected his attention to Miles. "You must be Miles. Shawn has been raving about you for weeks now."

That was a complete lie. Mark Wells knew about anything worth knowing in Scottsdale, especially high profile athletes. Exposing a mouth full of capped white teeth after every sentence, Mark went on to extol Miles, which Shawn didn't like at all. Jealousy framed Shawn's face.

Mark suggested they go somewhere a little more formal for having male conversation. They all piled in his Bentley and went to a popular "shoe modeling" establishment in Phoenix, better known as a strip club.

The three of them walked up to the main entrance, where a tall, muscular doorman awaited to check their identification. Miles and Shawn were both under the age of 21, so surely they would not be getting in.

"May I see your IDs please?" The doorman's tone was firm.

"IDs, you want to see our IDs. Who the hell are you? Don't you know who I am? You must be new. I'll tell you what, here are our IDs right here." Mark pulled three crisp $ 100 bills from his jacket pocket and stuffed them in the collar of the doorman's black t-shirt. They each walked past the doorman, who didn't utter another word.

The music pounded. The place was not busy on the Sunday night, nevertheless, nude women were dancing at various locations on a stage that curved from one side of the club to the other for little to no tips. Mark took some of his clients to this strip club when he wanted to show them a good time.

"Your usual table, Mr. Wells?" asked a toned, voluptuous, barely-dressed, young hostess. She escorted them to a private table. Shortly thereafter, a different attractive, high-heel wearing, scantily dressed woman came to their table. She asked if they needed anything. Mark ordered two club sodas for the teens and vodka mixed with cranberry juice for himself. Meanwhile, two petite women came over to the table wearing only G-strings and bikini tops. Within seconds, they pulled the strings on their tops, which then fell to the floor. They began dancing directly in front of Shawn and Miles. Shawn had seen more naked women than most men would see in a lifetime, but Miles, on the other hand, was trying to maintain his composure. He was still a virgin and a horny teenager. It wasn't long before a woody made an unseen appearance in his pants.

With the mood properly set for male conversation, Mark began sharing some of his knowledge with the youngsters. "Money trumps everything in life. It trumps love, looks, and age. Hell, it don't even matter if you have a little "wiener" if you got plenty of money. Of course, I'm not speaking from personal experience. Take these two naked young girls dancing in front of you guys. If I gave them both a thousand dollars, they would have sex with all three of us right here right now in front of everybody. Do you know why? Because you can't do a damn thing in life without money."

"Tell me the difference between signing a letter of intent and signing a professional football contract. The answer is about $60 million, 32 teams, and seven rounds. Both put you in a position to make someone else a lot of money. Both put restrictions on your life that normal people don't have to worry about. College football and professional football are both ran by a bunch of pimps. The professional whores get money from their pimps through revenue sharing known as a salary while the college whores don't. Prostitution is indeed legal throughout this country in sports. Instead of everyone making money from you spreading your legs, they make money from you playing a game. Most players make the school about 10 times what it costs the school to have them on their campuses. College football has become a farming system for professional football. They will love you guys as long as you don't get injured. Yeah, the relationship will go south pretty quick once you can no longer earn your keep."

Miles seemed distracted by the nude dancer waving her right nipple just inches from his forehead, but he heard every word Mark said. When he got home later that night, Miles lay in his bed trying to find some major differences in how both systems were set up. He could not find any other than the one main point that both Mark and Mr. Somers emphasized.

While Miles listened, he almost thought he was listening to Mr. Somers. Mark basically echoed what Mr. Somers had said to him a thousand times in his living room in front of the big screen on game day. It never failed. Whenever Miles watched a game with Mr. Somers, he always reflected on how "horrible" the system was set up for college athletes and how that same system had started corrupting high school programs. He said, "Coaches at every major college program want to lock down the next great corner or

300-pound lineman before their rival, so scouts are using every trick possible to entice the best high school players. Millions of dollars a year are being spent scouting high school talent, just like college talent. High school recruiting is being televised and on the Web more and more each year, just like the professional draft.

"It's all set up like a business at both levels," Mr. Somers would say, "but the only athletes that are compensated for the amount of money they help bring in are the pro players. The revenue in college football is enormous, with very little operating expenses considering you don't have to compensate the most valuable employees in the process."

Three years ago, when Mr. Somers started those lectures, Miles tuned him out. Now, Miles was paying close attention to the news reports and articles outlining the one-sided benefits of the current college football structure. What he once thought to be jibber jabber was now his impending reality.

Chapter 12
A PERFECT SEASON

January 2022

Before the two-week winter break for Christmas and New Year's, more than half the teachers at Oakridge had Miles sign items to give away as Christmas gifts. However, some of those items ended up for sale online.

Miles surprised Sage with a thin platinum necklace with a custom-made black stone star pendant. Andrew suggested using the star rather than a heart pendant. Miles thought it may have been cheesy, but Sage loved it. "This is so special," she said.

"And it may be worth quite a bit some day," Miles added with a wink, relieved that she liked it. He had never given a "real" gift to any woman besides his mother and aunt, and their gifts never cost more than $50 combined.

Sage, however, gave him an even bigger surprise. She collected every newspaper article ever written about him in every major United States sports market, including New York, Los Angeles, and Boston, just to name a few. She compiled the articles along with a few original pictures that she had, and she created a scrapbook. Miles appreciated it because he knew it took her several weeks to put it all together. Not as if he had questioned her loyalty before, but with her gift he knew she was undoubtedly devoted to him. "This means more to me than you'll ever know, Sage," said Miles before kissing her tenderly on the forehead and stroking her long dark hair as he held her closely.

"And it may be worth quite a bit some day because those pictures came from my own personal stash." They both chuckled and continued to embrace each other.

Miles met Sage at her locker that Monday morning immediately following the holiday break. They snuck a kiss when they thought no one was looking, but everyone at school knew they were an item by then. In fact, Miles and Sage were a celebrity couple. If anyone searched "Miles Starr girlfriend," pictures of Sage, shots of them together on dates, or photos of them holding hands on the field after a game would instantly appear in the search results online. At the time, every guy wanted to be Miles and every girl wanted to be Sage. She loved being by his side. At first, Sage didn't like the invasion of privacy created by her boyfriend's superstardom. She tried to seem unimpressed when people stopped them on their dates to get an autograph from Miles or asked to take a picture with him. Often, Miles couldn't keep himself from showing off. Several photographs and videos surfaced of him signing his autograph on two different items simultaneously with both hands. The younger kids got a real kick out of watching him. Some fans would even ask Sage for an autograph and to join the photo.

* * *

During the break, Miles had a lot to celebrate. He and Shawn took Oakridge all the way to the state championship. Miles finished the undefeated season with 3,826 passing yards, 88.3% completions, 40 TD passes, 3 interceptions, 15.5 average yards per completion, 46 rushes, 642 rushing yards, and 10 rushing TDs. Both Miles and Shawn broke every quarterback and receiver record in the state of Arizona. Rumors circulated about retiring their jerseys before the season was even over.

The state championship game wasn't even close with a score of 56-7. USPN did a national broadcast and live web stream of the entire game. The two young stars took care of business early and didn't even play most of the second half. In official, public commemoration of the perfect season and the decisive championship win, the school had a trophy presentation ceremony in the gymnasium during the last class period.

Oakridge's athletic director, Mike Parker, welcomed the state championship football trophy and dedicated it to Miles and Shawn during the ceremony. The players had a presentation of their own. Some of them captured footage of him doing some sort of victory dance in the locker room following the championship game. Most sane people wouldn't have called that a dance at all. Even after viewing the evidence, Mr. Parker never admitted it was him.

The mayor and other local politicians attended the ceremony. All the local news stations provided coverage, and even some radio stations. Rather than a reporter, USPN sent one of its prime-time anchors to interview Miles, Shawn or anyone directly connected to them.

The students, faculty, administrators, and just about everyone at Oakridge loved the fact that they were getting national recognition for the school's dominance on the gridiron. The fan base for the Oakridge football program grew to an unthinkable magnitude, including local, national and even international fans. The local community and new fans from the surrounding areas filled the stadiums to maximum capacity at home and on road games throughout the regular season and playoffs. Everyone was a little sad knowing the cameras would be leaving and the notoriety would be going away, or so they thought.

Immediately following the ceremony, Coach Williams, the Oakridge boys' basketball coach, approached Miles. Coach Williams had apparently found out about Miles' HSC scores in basketball. After discussing the proposition with his mother, Miles agreed to join the team. Like football, he was shocked to learn he was being considered for a starting position, moreover, as point guard.

USPN returned to Oakridge to air Miles' latest athletic undertaking. The network wanted to capture every basketball game with Miles, the point guard who made jump shots with both hands and sometimes switched shooting hands in mid-shot. Shawn wasn't about to miss out on any of the fanfare. He didn't attend all those basketball camps for nothing, and so he volunteered himself as the team's small forward. Whether by parental coercion or sound judgment, Coach Williams added Shawn to the rooster. He became Miles' go-to guy on the basketball court. During the games, fans lost count of the number of alley-oops Miles threw Shawn so he could finish with a massive dunk. Some of the other players took bets on who Shawn would "posterize" first from the opposing teams. Unfortunately, they fell two wins short of winning the state championship trophy in basketball that year. Still, it was an unforgettable season for the players and fans.

Miles' sporting career and the USPN coverage didn't end there. Shawn typically played football and baseball each year. This season, he wanted to add Starr power. Shawn and the baseball coach, Brad Johnson, convinced Miles to, once again, show the world his athletic prowess. Shawn was ranked one of the best shortstops in that part of the country. He had never seen Miles play baseball, but he just knew Miles "had it in him."

Melissa Starr had some objections because she said, "This may be too much."

Petitioning on Miles' behalf Shawn explained to her, "We won't ever be 17 again, and we may never have this opportunity again. If me and Miles don't do this... Nah, we gotta do this. We can tell our children, your grandchildren, that we were some bad mothersuckers back in the day."

She chuckled at Shawn's rather blunt and somewhat sincere petition. She agreed as long as Miles kept his 3.9 GPA intact. Like he did with his own mother, Shawn hugged her so tight, he lifted her off the ground.

"What do baseball moms wear to the game?" Melissa asked half serious and half joking. Until Miles started playing football, she had never donned sporting apparel.

"I got you," promised Shawn.

The day before the season-opening baseball game, Shawn personally delivered, as promised, a custom-made jersey with Miles' name and number for Melissa. He also gave her a matching cap, tennis shoes, socks, and fitted sweat pants in various sizes. "Miles, man, you have to get your girl Sage up some gear," said Shawn.

"I guess I wasn't thinking," said Miles. "You think I can get her a jersey before the game tomorrow?"

Shawn reached down into another shopping bag and handed Miles a second custom jersey for Sage. He didn't, however, provide any of the other wares that he gave Melissa.

"Aw, man, how can I repay you?"

"You can't. Ya'll don't have that kinda money, at least not yet. Just get out there and do what you do tomorrow."

* * *

The same precision Miles showed in the quarterback pocket revealed itself on the pitcher's mound. Miles threw left-handed and right-handed strikeouts. His pitches were, in fact, a thing of beauty. They were the only part of his game on the field that looked better than his switch-handed batting techniques. Miles thoroughly enjoyed messing with the opposing pitcher by batting with opposite hands for each pitch. For many years afterward, sports writers continued to tell stories about what Miles was able to accomplish on the pitcher's mound and batter's box.

Shawn and Miles both received numerous offers from professional baseball teams, but they declined. They had a pure passion and love for the game of football. Their decision bothered Mark Wells, for he knew the earnings potential for professional baseball players was greater than that of football. Moreover, baseball players had longer careers and guaranteed money in their contracts.

* * *

During the same time Oakridge's gymnasium was filled with screaming teens, a boardroom in Phoenix had a very different but related set of events taking place.

James Garrett, Virtual Tech CEO, had just ended a meeting with his direct reports at the company headquarters. He thought everyone had left the room, but William Finigan, the Chief Financial Officer at Virtual Tech, was still lingering in the room to get a word with his boss.

"James, I need to speak with you about an email I received during the meeting."

"What is it regarding?" he asked.

"Do you remember the HSC training simulation program we implemented at your son's old high school four years ago?" asked William.

"Of course. How could I forget? We had high hopes that the HSC chambers could turn-around their program."

You asked me to let you know if any substantial results were generated from the technology. Well, the results are better than expected. Have you ever heard of Miles Starr?"

"He is that ambidextrous kid that throws the football with both arms. Didn't he win the state football title at my son's school?"

"Yes, and it gets better. Apparently, he has had three years of quarterback preparation training using only our chambers. He had never played one down of organized sports prior to the beginning of last season. Mr. Starr learned to play and dominated the quarterback position solely from using our technology."

"Can we prove that our technology developed the use of both arms?"

"No one can prove that it didn't contribute to developing such an amazing skill set. Miles has become an international sensation. USPN took care of that for us. When we make our sales pitches to college and professional teams, we'll be sure they know that this kid was created solely from using equipment developed by Virtual Tech. Just think, every athletic organization on the planet will be placing orders for our chambers when they discover Miles used our technology. He has become our ultimate marketing tool."

"How soon can we get him on video endorsing the chamber?"

"That's the only issue. Technically, high school and college athletes aren't allowed to make money from their accomplishments while still being affiliated with those organizations. We would have to wait until he turned pro to get an official endorsement. Until then, we'll just mention it to prospective buyers."

"Who made that rule? That's the dumbest thing I ever heard of. If these kids can sell themselves, they should be allowed to."

"I agree," acknowledged William.

"Do you think we can give him and his mother a little something to keep them happy until we launch a full public ad campaign? I hear he has a single working class mother. I'm sure she'd appreciate any kind of help."

"I'll have to talk to legal to see what we can do without getting the kid or us in any kind of trouble."

CHAPTER 13
THE DECISION

January 2022

During basketball season, Miles' only free day was on Sundays. He always visited Sage then. Miles enjoyed spending time with Sage more than any audience of screaming fans. His only discomfort came from Sage's mother, who undressed Miles with her eyes when her husband wasn't around. Some Sundays Miles and Sage kept Austin entertained, which kept him out of his parents' way. They seemed extremely grateful for those small breaks and would make plans for outings without Austin.

Miles had come to enjoy his talks with Sage's father, Harold, who was at home almost every day now. This was a change from when Miles and Sage started dating. His businesses seemed to keep him traveling very often early on. Harold was extremely nice to Miles and let it be known that Miles was welcomed in his home anytime. Sometimes Miles didn't leave Sage's house until after midnight even considering that he had often been there since 9 a. m. Sage didn't understand her father's reaction to Miles because he never made any attempts to get to know Sage's previous male acquaintances.

Nevertheless, Miles realized he was completely in love with Sage. Something about the level of love and concern she had for Austin showed him a side of her that no one else at Oakridge knew existed. He loved the way he felt when he was with her. Another plus was that Sage always planted a long wet one on him before he departed.

Miles and Sage had been together for almost four months and Miles hadn't pushed beyond second base. His woodies had been lasting long past removing himself from her presence. He often endured them well into his rides home. As a 17-year-old virgin, Miles had raging hormones. Andrew was surprised he lasted that long. It wasn't like he didn't have numerous options available.

Andrew volunteered to record the boys' basketball games just like he did with football. He edited the footage and uploaded Miles' basketball highlights to YouTube. Andrew noticed when Miles sat on the bench at away games that provocatively dressed female students would always sit behind him. They would make catcalls and try to pass their numbers to him with no success. He loved Sage. Only love must have prevented him from sealing the deal with Nicole in Los Angeles last year. Shawn continued telling him he was a fool for letting that "piece of ass" walk away "untapped."

On the last Sunday in January, Miles received his eagerly anticipated tongue wrestle with Sage before departing for home at 6 p. m. This was fairly earlier than his normal routine, but his mother called nearly two hours before saying he needed to come home because they were going to have important guests. Miles noticed an unfamiliar black SUV in the driveway when he pulled up at his home. The tag read "AAM WIN 1." Miles entered his home to find none other than Arizona A&M Coach Nigel Banks and three of his assistant coaches sitting in the living room talking to his mother. Miles had received several letters and missed phone calls from Coach Banks. He wasn't really interested in speaking with Coach Banks because he was nowhere close to selecting a college even with the decision deadline within sight. All four coaches stood up when Miles walked in the room. They had on khaki pants and short-sleeve, red polo shirts with the team logo stitched on the top left side. The Rock Warrior logo was a rock with a spear and bow on it. The scene was very reminiscent of the day Coach Burdette sat in the same room talking to his Aunt Evelyn.

"You finally were able to pull yourself away from Sage. It's a miracle," said Melissa, shaking her head. "These men are from Arizona A&M University in Phoenix. We were just discussing their curriculum for pre-med majors. It sounds really interesting."

Coach Banks shook Miles' hand first and the other three immediately followed before retaking their seats. Still standing, Coach Banks chewed a stick of gum like it was the last day for gum to be legal. He led into his sales pitch like many others before him. The coach was a smooth talker. After all, he was nationally known for successful recruiting. Miles witnessed a master at work. The one thing that Coach Banks mentioned that no other school could offer him was the ability for his mother and Mr. Somers to watch him play live at every home game with two complimentary tickets.

Miles listened attentively for over 30 minutes while the words flowed from Coach Banks' lips. He laid it on thick. Fortunately for Miles, due to recruiting restrictions, the coach could not speak with Miles longer than 30 minutes. He eventually wrapped up his monologue, thanked Miles and his mother, and left with his staff.

"So, what do you think, Miles?" Melissa asked. "It would be nice if you were close to home."

"I still don't know yet, Mom. There are so many choices. I'm just not sure yet."

"You'll make the right decision by February 2. I have no doubt in my mind. Whatever you decide, I'll support you, and I'm sure your aunt will too. She has really taken an interest in where you're going to school. She asks me all the time, 'Has he decided yet?' She must be as concerned about your future as I am."

Miles knew the February 2 national signing day would be there soon. Miles hadn't worked for Mr. Somers since he started playing football the previous fall, so he didn't see him as much to get regular fatherly advice. Still, he would sometimes call Mr. Somers to discuss his many, ever-expanding college options. While Mr. Somers would describe the history, benefits, and downsides of each football program, in the end, he would reiterate that it was ultimately Miles' choice to make.

Andrew didn't waste an opportunity to capitalize from Miles popularity. He started a betting pool at Oakridge for students to guess which school Miles would eventually play football for. Miles worried about leaving all the people he cared about. His mother, Sage, Andrew, and Mr. Somers all meant a great deal to him. He anguished over making new friends and new acquaintances at some school far away from the people he loved.

On February 1, Shawn was in his room surfing the Web on his I-Pad when his satellite phone rang. He answered the call, had a brief conversation, and hung up. Shawn grabbed his car keys and left his room heading for the garage. His father opened his office door just as Shawn walked by.

"Did Miles tell you where he was going yet?" Mark asked.

"No, not yet."

"Well, let me know as soon as you hear something, so I can make arrangements for you there."

"Dad, I thought we already agreed that I would play in Florida."

"That was before I ever heard of Miles Starr. Son, you have a once in a life time opportunity to become the greatest receiver to ever play the game. That won't happen unless Miles is throwing you that football. You name me one person on any campus that is as much a triple threat as Miles. With him being such a threat to run, no defensive coordinator can afford to double you during any game. You're going to have a field day and you'll continue to break records. I also need you and Miles to stay real close before he turns pro. I don't want him looking anywhere else when it comes time for him to sign. Miles is an agent's dream. He is a white, tall, attractive male playing the most important position in the most popular sport in the world, and he plays it better than anyone on the planet. The endorsement deals will be the biggest ever. I am going to represent the highest paid quarterback and receiver combination in the history of football."

Shawn had always felt like a commodity to his father, but at that moment he knew that's all he was and would ever be in his father's eyes.

"Speaking of endorsements, I told your mother to stop letting you get all those damn tattoos," Mark shouted.

Shawn's mother heard the elevated tones from the other room and came in to see what her son and husband were arguing about that time. Mark redirected his frustration at Kim.

"Why in the hell do you keep letting him degrade his body like this? Don't you realize how many dollars you are taking off the table from companies who want someone with a clean image to represent their products?"

"Is that all our son is to you? Some marketing tool," Kim asked?

"You know I take good care of both of you around here. Is it too much to ask for him to do something in return for his family?"

"He's not breaking his back on that god-forsaken football field for his family. He's out there for you, and you know it. You have asked him to abuse his body year after year, summer after summer, and he did it all just hoping you would show him that you loved him just for one second. He gets those tattoos to piss you off, and it must be working."

At that point, Shawn had heard enough and stormed out of the house without saying anything to either of his parents.

Miles asked Christine, Sage, Andrew, and Shawn to meet him at a local Mexican restaurant in Scottsdale. Everyone arrived on time and sat down with Miles at a table. A waitress brought over four menus with salsa and warm chips.

"Guys, thanks for meeting me here. I invited you all here because you are the closest friends I have in the world. I've been doing a lot of thinking, and I know who I'm going to play football for next year. Before I tell you, Shawn, have you made a decision yet?"

Miles turned and looked in Shawn's direction.

"Man, you're my ace in the hole. I'm guaranteed to go first round in the draft as long as I have you calling the plays in the huddle. I'm going where ever you decide to go."

Shawn led his friends to believe he came up with this decision on his own, but nothing could have been further from the truth. Miles continued the conversation with his friends. "I was hoping you would say that."

When Miles told the group where he decided to go, Andrew cringed due to the fact he lost the pool he created. He made everyone promise to keep it a secret. Shawn was just relieved it was a top-10 school, so he could compete with the best via nationally-televised games, which he became accustomed to during his last season at Oakridge. Shawn did break his promise to Miles when his father asked him the question again that night. Mark, like Shawn, was only interested in the choice being a top-10 program. He knew that the higher number of people that saw them win, the higher they would be drafted. He thought they both had the potential to go one and two in the draft.

The next morning, Miles woke up a little unprepared for the circus he was about to walk into at Oakridge. Just like the televised games, USPN worked out a deal with the athletic director to air Miles' decision live. A multitude of sports reporters, news vans, and other media members cased the entire campus to try and break the story before USPN had the opportunity to. The scene was similar to the Monday after Miles showed the world his unique ability. USPN pulled out all the stops, scheduling Miles' announcement for a one-hour time slot. The nation wanted to know where Miles Starr would take his world-renowned talents. The frenzy was reminiscent of a certain professional basketball player's announcement back in the summer of 2010. Media estimated that over 40 million homes would tune in for the big surprise, not to mention about half that streamed online. In the end, the numbers were even better.

All 536 students and faculty showed up for the 6 p.m. broadcast. The school set up a podium in the gymnasium with chairs for the media. The student body sat in the stands. The band played school fight songs for entertainment. Along with Miles' closest friends, Mr. Somers, his daughter, Mark, Harold, Aunt Evelyn, Sage, Christine, and Melissa were all in attendance. Shawn's mother showed up, although late, to support her son. Cameras were stationed to capture every angle of the event. Miles and Shawn both dressed professionally, donning dark suits with pastel-colored ties.

The time came for Miles to make his big announcement. When he began his approach to the podium, cameras flashed in succession. For a brief moment, they blinded as well as startled Miles. He finally made it to his spotlight position. He couldn't believe how nervous he was, but no one could tell.

"I want to thank everyone for showing up to show support for my decision. I especially want to thank my football coach, Coach Burdette; my mentor, Mr. Somers; and most importantly, my mother. I'd also like to thank the best receiver in the country, Shawn Wells, for making my success look really easy."

Miles waved to his mother, who was already crying before he began speaking, while standing next to Sage. Miles continued, "This decision has not been an easy one. Whoever knew that a kid could become so popular just from throwing a football? After careful consideration of the people most important to me in my life, I have decided to stay close to home and to attend Arizona A&M University."

The entire student body erupted in screams and cheers from his news. With tears streaming down her face, Melissa went to hug her son while he still stood at the podium. The media launched a question tsunami. The athletic director silenced them so Shawn could make his school choice announcement.

"Looks like *we* plan to attend Arizona A&M," said Shawn with a noticeable flatness in his tone. Shawn didn't really appreciate the fact he had to play second fiddle to what he called "The Miles Starr Show." The crowd cheered and clapped wildly as his parents walked up to accompany Shawn at the podium. Seeing his mother's tender smile triggered an eruption of emotion within Shawn. He stepped back from the microphone to give her a long embrace and kiss on the cheek.

None of the students had ever seen the tender side of Shawn, and the girls reacted in unison, saying, "Awwwww."

The media questioned Miles and Shawn for more than 30 minutes until the one-hour timeframe had expired, and then the athletic director, Mr. Parker, ended the news conference. "That's enough. These two young men have told you every and anything you need to publish good stories about Oakdale's athletic program," said Mr. Parker with a wink. "And unless you want to hear all about my high school and college football days, I think you better escape while you can."

Meanwhile, Coach Banks, after watching the announcement live, was in his office on the campus in Phoenix celebrating with his assistant coaches. The entire phone system in their building began lighting up. Several news vans were scattered across the building parking lot within minutes. Coach Banks had microphones and cameras shoved in his face without warning as media bombarded him with questions. They totally caught him off guard, but he pretended to expect and know the answers to all the questions.

The media asked him to make predictions about the next season. "Will Miles be the starting quarterback? How many wins do you anticipate next season?"

"The media is a joke," thought Coach Banks. He just gave them vague fluff answers like he always did when they asked him questions he didn't care for or thought were ridiculous. The blogs and chat rooms for the Arizona A&M fan clubs were teemed with comments. The entire Web, in fact, crawled with talk of Miles' announcement. USPN analysts had plenty of material to go over during their normal nightly prime-time broadcast, which some claimed had become "The Miles Starr Show."

Miles' number one Arizona A&M jersey went on sale the next day. Even though the jersey didn't have his name on it, it became the number one selling college jersey in the country. College football fans could not wait until kickoff in September. The university later launched a supplementary school football Web site with only Miles' face on it along with a clock ticking down the months, days, hours, and seconds until the Rock Warrior season officially began. It seemed as if the entire nation had begun the countdown to kickoff 2022.

Andrew was upset that he couldn't capitalize on the Miles Starr college paraphernalia due to copyright restrictions and possible trademark infringement. With the money he had already made from his own Starr Power Web site sales, he didn't need any extra. In fact, he made enough to pay for his first two years of tuition at Arizona A&M, where he proudly declared he was attending on the night of Miles' announcement. As much as she adored Miles, Christine, who was slated to graduate the following year, decided to attend Radcliffe College on a full science scholarship as a premed major. Sage was the only one in the group who still hadn't announced her college plans or whether she would even go.

Chapter 14
THE BIG NIGHT

April 2022

Miles was very excited when he woke up the morning of April 2. He had finally turned 18 years old that Saturday. His mother and Aunt Evelyn burst into his bedroom around 8 a. m. with a small cupcake that had only one candle. They sang, "Happy birthday to you."

That routine had become somewhat of a tradition in the Starr household on his birthdays from as far back as Miles could remember. Melissa made the cupcake herself using organic flour and honey along with frosting made with fresh strawberries. Just as always, Miles sat up in bed with a huge smile while listening to the off-key vocals of his housemates. He didn't have the heart to tell his mother and aunt how much they sounded like two squealing pigs on their way to a butcher shop. As a matter of fact, he thought the pigs would sound slightly better. For him, the highlight of the mini-celebration was when the singing ended.

Melissa was overjoyed by the thought of Miles' first prom experience later that night. She almost cried when she accompanied him to her store several weeks earlier to be fitted for his tuxedo. She thought he looked so tall and handsome in front of the mirror.

"Look at my gorgeous son all grown up."

"Mom, please stop it. Can you please stop grinning so hard? People are starting to stare."

"I work with these people. They all have known you for years and are just admiring the man you have become. They are so proud of the success you have had playing sports. That's all they ever seem to want to talk about. And it's not just the people who work here. I get customers all the time who come in the store just to meet me. That reminds me, can you sign some things for me? Some of my coworkers want to give some things away as gifts."

Most of those so-called gifts ended up on some online auction Web site.

* * *

On prom night, Miles had not yet realized how significant that day would eventually become to him. Shawn's father, Mark, supplied a stretch black limousine for the group of friends, consisting of Miles, Sage, Andrew, Christine, Shawn, and his two dates, Dana and Dara, a set of twins who were sophomores at Arizona A&M. Anything involving Shawn and a female rarely involved only one of them. While dating two women at a time was nothing new for Shawn, it literally almost gagged Andrew. He didn't even have one real date for the evening. Christine would be his makeshift date for the prom. If Christine had her way, though, Miles would have been her date. She was pissed knowing she had to watch Miles and Sage smiling and laughing like the perfect couple. Watching them holding hands in the halls at Oakridge was torture enough.

Just three hours before the prom, Sage was at home scrambling to make sure she was ready before the limousine arrived. She still felt as if she had a million tasks to finish. Her day began with an 8 a.m. hair salon appointment. While she was at the salon, her mother agreed to pick up her dress after the final alterations were made. Victoria dreaded having to deal with Austin alone while she ran errands to assist Sage in her preparation, but she had a vested interest in making sure Sage was ready when Miles arrived. Furthermore, Sage's father, Harold, wasn't about to handle Austin alone.

The limo finally arrived at Sage's home around 7:30 p.m. She was the final stop before heading to the Camelback Inn. Miles hopped out from the rear of the dark colored multi-passenger chariot and rang the doorbell. As usual, Austin answered the door with his customary compact disc in hand. He always answered the door, no matter what he was doing at the time, and Miles came to expect no other face than his.

Victoria quickly came to the front door and greeted Miles. She immediately noticed how attractive he looked in his tuxedo.

Victoria had never seen Miles dressed up, and she was impressed – maybe too impressed. "Wow, Miles. You look even better than I imagined. Sage will be here in just a second."

"Thank you. I bet Sage will put me to shame."

Victoria turned her head back into the house to hasten Sage's finishing touches. "Sage, hurry up and get out here," she yelled. "Miles and your friends are waiting."

"I'm coming, mom. Jesus, just calm down," Sage yelled from another room.

Harold sat in the living room watching television. He was normally in Miles' face carrying on conversation. For some strange reason, he was not that thrilled to see Miles that day. Harold didn't acknowledge Miles at all.

In just a few seconds, Sage emerged from behind the door to reveal herself in a magnificent, sparkling hot pink prom dress. Her back was completely visible all the way down to within a few inches of her rear. She was breathtaking. The design fit her curvy frame perfectly, draping all the way down to her hot pink high heels. Her hair was pinned up to reveal her mother's shiny diamond earrings, and Sage's three star tattoos. Miles was completely blown away. Sage looked more striking than he could have ever imagined. She was a modern day princess. For a second, he forgot it was prom. Hell, he even forgot it was his birthday. Miles completely zoned out from the sight of his stunning date. He only came back down to earth when Shawn told the limo driver to blow the horn. His friends were getting restless. They were ready to party.

"You look amazing. Seeing you look like this is worth standing out here all evening," Miles said.

"Thank you. You clean-up really well yourself, Superman." She knew Miles didn't like that name, but she knew she could get away with most anything that night, especially with the dress she was wearing.

* * *

The Camelback Inn was a premiere 5-star resort for the vacationing wealthy. It had everything a person with time and money would need. Staff on hand all over the grounds readily assisted with almost any request. Golf excursions, horseback riding, spa services, and fine dining were available on site. The resort had about 250 private villas that cost about $800 per night. The Oakridge Prom Committee rented the largest ballroom at the resort, the Arizona Ballroom. The committee spared no expense to make that year's prom the most memorable and talked about event for years to come. They went with a Hollywood movie premiere theme. The committee even had four spotlights, which could be seen a few miles away, pointing and rotating toward the sky.

Miles and his friends pulled into the rear of a line of about 10 limousines. The line moved extremely slowly and Shawn grew restless.

"What the hell is taking so long?" Shawn said.

"It's ok, baby. We're here to keep you company all night long," said Dana.

"Yep, you're going to forget time even exists tonight," said Dara.

The other four passengers thought deeply about the comments the twins made. There were definitely plenty of inferences in their statements.

Shawn's patience soon ran out. He opened the limousine's sunroof and popped his head out to take a gander at what was causing the convoy to move so slowly. He could not get an answer from his vantage point. Thus, he impatiently withdrew back into his chariot.

After almost 20 minutes their limo reached the exit point, and they understood why the limos inched along. A gentleman in a tuxedo opened the car door so the group could begin their prom experience and handed the ladies a flower. Each girl was given a choice of a rose or carnation accented with baby's breath and bound with a gold ribbon that said "Class of 2022."

Andrew and Christine exited onto a red carpet while dozens of cameras flashed. The red carpet was about 5 feet wide and lead up to the entrance of the ballroom. Several Oakridge students lined up on each side of the red carpet to get a few camera shots of Miles as memorabilia. Rumors swirled that USPN had a film crew on site to capture footage of Miles' prom experience. USPN pitched a reality show idea to Miles and his mother months before, but they declined. The committee hired several photographers to take pictures of everyone exiting their vehicles and a professional film crew to create the ultimate Hollywood experience. They even hired two guys to record and interview the teens when they emerged from their luxurious transportation. The edited footage of the entire even was later sold to the students. The man holding the microphone shoved it in Andrew and Christine's face for a quick interview.

"Who are you and who are you wearing?" the interviewer questioned. It was just like when a famous actor or actress arrived at a Hollywood movie premier.

Andrew responded, "This was made by Italian designer Leonardo Donelteli. He flew in last week to take my measurements and put together this wonderful ensemble."

Christine gave Andrew a strange look, thinking how much of a difference a year made. The year before, Christine usually had to pay for Andrew's meals when they went out to eat with Miles on the weekends.

Christine responded to the interviewer's question as well saying, "I bought this off the rack for $49.95." She answered as sarcastically as possible because the prom committee's over-the-top antics failed to impress her.

After Andrew and Christine answered his questions a prom committee member quickly waved them on. Shawn and his dates exited the limo next and met the same cameras and same questions except the "who are you" one. Shawn wore his signature wide-toothed grin and gloated due to the fact he had two sexy women, who wore sleeveless, micro-mini sequined dresses. Nearly a foot taller than his dates, Shawn towered over the twins as they strutted down the red carpet. He could not wait to run into Sam and to watch the look on her face when she saw his dates. The trio were making their way up the entrance stairs to join Andrew and Christine when a loud burst of applause and screams made them pause and look back. The crowd was responding to Miles and Sage emerging from the rear of the limo. The scene mimicked actual movie stars making a grand entrance. The interviewer immediately launched into his questions but added a few more for Miles.

"How are you feeling tonight?"

"I'll let my beautiful girlfriend answer that," said Miles.

Shocked by Miles deferring to her, Sage said, "Well, um, we're great."

"How is everyone else feeling?" asked Miles, who was playing up to the crowd. The crowd erupted with cheers and whistles as

Miles waved to people standing behind velvet rope barriers on each side of him.

"The crowd seems to really love their star athlete. I'm sure they are all wondering how much success you feel you will have next year playing quarterback at Arizona A&M?"

Miles answered a few questions. He shied away from the ones about predicting the future. The interviewer didn't give up so easily. He followed Miles up the stairs, continuing to ask various questions until Miles and Sage disappeared into the building, where cameras were placed in various locations to capture all of the night's events.

When Miles and his friends walked into the main ballroom, they were amazed by the elaborate Hollywood-themed decorations. Life-size cutouts of actual movie stars were located at various spots in the room. Many students took pictures with the props. Projections, without sound, of recognizable movie scenes played on the walls throughout the ballroom. A few early arrivals occupied the dance floor as the DJ blasted popular songs from movies past and present.

The group was about to head to a table when Sam walked up alone wearing a tuxedo. Shawn grinned at the sight of a dateless Sam.

"What's up, Shawn? I see you went and hired some poor girls to take pity on you and escort you to the prom?"

"Very funny, Sam. I see you came all alone. Too bad."

"Oh, I wouldn't say that. Ladies, would you please join me."

Sam snapped twice with her right hand, and Shawn's mouth twisted at the emergence of three beautiful girls now accompanying Sam. He stood there speechless, brimming with bitterness and jealousy. It soon subsided because Shawn remembered his player code: "Don't hate the player; hate the game," which means Shawn could be no more upset with Sam than Sam could be with Shawn.

"So what does this mean?" asked Shawn. "I have one, two, three, four, five, and maybe six women to choose from tonight." He pointed to his two dates, Sam's three dates, and then Sam.

"Go to hell, Shawn," responded Sam with a smirk.

"Hell is no place for us. You all do need to join me on the dance floor at some point tonight, though."

After Sam's departure, Miles and his friends eventually found a table near the dance floor. Everyone danced with their dates, and sometimes even switched partners. Sam danced with Shawn's dates, and Shawn danced with Sam's dates. Their rivalry would officially be over in less than two months once they graduated. Though neither would ever admit it, they had an enormous amount of respect for one another.

While Miles did let Andrew steal one or two dances with Sage, he otherwise kept her in his arms all night. Christine and Andrew danced some but not that often. When they were dancing, Christine tried her best to dance seductively on Andrew, hoping that Miles would look her way. However, he never took his eyes off Sage. Andrew and Christine mostly stood off to the side critiquing the many different takes on appropriate prom attire worn by the other students. Still, Christine made random glances in Sage and Miles' direction throughout the night.

Sage couldn't help but notice what Christine was trying to do. She figured out that Christine had a crush on Miles when they met and thought it was cute but harmless. However, she was getting a little tired of Miles being unaware of Christine's feelings and decided to mention it.

"How can you be so smart yet so clueless sometimes?" Sage asked.

"What are you talking about?"

"Christine has had a crush on you for the longest. She keeps doing things hoping you will notice her, but you seem to be totally in the dark."

"Christine is like a sister to me. I could never think of her that way. It actually sounds really gross."

Miles was not playing dumb. He really didn't look at Christine in that way. It drove Christine crazy knowing that Miles would never be hers. She often stared in her bathroom mirror comparing her looks to Sage's. She knew Sage was far better looking, and she believed that if she looked as beautiful as Sage, Miles would love her. For the prom, she dyed her brown hair brunette in an almost subconscious attempt to mimic Sage. Only Andrew really mentioned the change, saying, "So I guess you're channeling Elvira as your Hollywood muse."

Andrew was being his normal witty self, but Christine didn't find his comments amusing at all. "I thought this was a Hollywood-themed dance, not amateur hour at the comedy club."

* * *

About 30 minutes before midnight, when the prom was scheduled to end, Sage slipped something into Miles' front left pocket and walked off the dance floor. Miles retrieved a sheet of folded paper from his pocket and began reading one side of the unfolded paper.

"Happy birthday, baby. I have picked out the perfect gift for you. I hope you like it. X marks the spot."

Miles turned the paper over to reveal a map of the resort. An X was marked on Villa 224, which was a short walk from the ballroom location. Miles told Andrew and Christine he was leaving, and Andrew just smiled and said, "Have fun." Christine, however, looked crushed. She knew very well the types of actions that traditionally took place on prom night. Andrew noticed that her mood had changed and asked her for another dance to distract her from the emotions she was obviously experiencing at the time. Miles didn't bother mentioning anything to Shawn because he was entertaining the crowd with his amazing acrobatic dance moves in the middle of onlookers.

With his tuxedo jacket folded across his right forearm, Miles walked nervously toward the marking on the map. Approximately four minutes later, he arrived at his destination to find a door ajar. Miles walked in slowly, not knowing what to expect but having an idea. He had already allowed himself to consider the possibility that he would finally make love to Sage. He closed the door behind him after entering a room lit only by candles with soft music whispering throughout. He heard Sage's voice from another room tell him to "go sit on the bed." After he complied, she presented herself from the bathroom, and her hot pink prom dress was nowhere to be found. It had been replaced by sexy pink lingerie. Miles didn't really get a good look at her seductive outfit until she came closer to him near the candlelight. Sage wore a see-through, lace bra with a matching see-through, lace thong. He was excited by the clear view of her, but his erection arrived well before she had exited the bathroom.

"You look amazing. Almost too good to believe."

"Who? Me? Happy birthday, baby," said Sage, pretending to act shy and surprised by his comments.

Miles forgot it was his birthday. He forgot everything outside of Sage standing half naked in front of him. Sage walked over to the bed and stood in front of the seated Miles. She rubbed her fingers through his hair, getting him more exited from her touch. Sage kissed his forehead, then his nose and then his lips. She unbuttoned his shirt starting from top to bottom, sliding it off his masculine body revealing his smooth, toned biceps. Miles sat there frozen, not knowing what his role was. Sage loved his body and told him, saying, "Lois Lane should be jealous because I have the real super sexy superman."

Miles finally kicked off his shoes after realizing that he was going to lose his virginity on his 18th birthday. He had no desire to lose it from any other woman. Sage was the one he loved.

Miles didn't know what to do while Sage finished removing his pants. He never told her he was a virgin, but she figured it out months before. Sage took control of the moment, so he didn't have to do too much thinking.

The couple was anxious to perform in front of an audience of slow burning candles. They both stepped to the edge of their desires and leaped into a night filled with passion and warm sweat.

As Miles lay on his back, Sage collapsed on Miles' chest and hugged his body tightly, and Miles caressed her exotic frame. They fell asleep in each other's arms.

The next morning, Miles was awakened by a beam of sunlight torturing his eyes through a small crack in the curtains. Sage was still resting quietly on his chest, and he could feel her heartbeat pounding on his abs. Throughout the night and morning, his satellite phone vibrated on the nightstand. He knew there had to be several voicemails of concern from his mother about his whereabouts. He was in no hurry to hear her angry voice and compromise his mood. He had just had the most amazing night followed by the most peaceful night's sleep he had ever had. Miles tried to reach for his phone without waking his love, but he was unsuccessful.

She moaned when she shifted her nude warm body on top of him under the covers.

"What time is it?" Sage asked.

She didn't want to open her eyes and let the light fully awaken her, but she knew she had to get home to check on Austin. She knew her parents had been alone with him way too long.

"The clock says 7:45. Did you sleep well?"

"Like a baby. What about you?"

"Best night's sleep and everything else of my life. I can't imagine life being anymore perfect than it is at this very moment."

They lay in bed another 20 minutes laughing and whispering the kinds of things that young lovers say when they're in love. They didn't want to leave, but they knew people were expecting them. The front desk arranged transportation to deliver them home before Melissa had the Scottsdale Police Department looking for Miles. Little did she know the police department received many calls about teens not coming home every year after prom night, so officers usually placated parents because the teens always turned up the next morning or afternoon.

The two finished getting dressed just before their shared ride arrived. Sage put on shorts, sandals, and a tank top. She put the rest of her things in a bag she had placed in the room the day before. However, Miles was forced to put back on his tuxedo.

Miles' home was closer, so the driver dropped him off first. After several forged attempts to coax Miles to stop kissing and fondling her, Miles finally closed the car door so the driver could continue with his second delivery. Miles took a deep swallow before heading into the house to hear his mother's lecture. He was sure she had a good one prepared.

The driver pulled into Sage's driveway. She gathered her bag and headed to her front door. Sage saw her father sitting in the living room watching television and heard Austin screaming in his room. Sage dropped her bag and ran into his room to see what was going on. She found Victoria leaning against his room wall with a martini in her hand and just staring at Austin sitting on the side of his bed pounding his fist on the mattress and screaming as loud as he could.

"What's wrong with him, mom?"

"He can't find his damn CD. Hell, I looked everywhere for it, and I don't see it."

Sage walked over to Austin's bed and lifted up his pillow to reveal the CD in question. She handed it to Austin, and it silenced him abruptly.

"Sometimes he puts it under his pillow and forgets he put it there."

"How the hell was I supposed to know that?"

Sage didn't make a fuss but managed to roll her eyes while walking back past her mother when she left Austin's room. Before going to her room, Sage went back downstairs to retrieve her bag. Victoria followed her to the living room, where her father Harold was still watching television as if nothing was going on.

"So, how did last night go? Did you two have a magical night?" Victoria asked.

"The prom was great, mother. We had a fabulous time."

"Did you give Miles a night he would never forget?"

Sage looked at her father expecting some reaction from her mother's comments regarding her and Miles having a sexual encounter. She knew her father had figured out by now that she didn't come home last night. Harold didn't raise an eyebrow. He was a mannequin.

She couldn't believe her mother said that in front of her father. Completely embarrassed, she left the living room and went into her bedroom. Victoria followed, now carrying an empty glass. Sage turned to face her mother and wanted some clarification.

"I don't get it. When I first brought Miles here, you couldn't have cared any less about us getting serious, but for the last few months you have been asking about our relationship an awful lot."

"He makes you happy, and your father and I think you two are good for one another."

"Bullshit, mom."

"Watch your language. You're talking to your mother."

"You are up to something, and I want to know what it is."

Victoria walked out of Sage's room headed toward the kitchen to pour another drink. Her glass had gone dry for far too long. Sage followed her this time. She kept on pestering her mother until she got answers to her questions.

"We're broke," Victoria explained. She figured Sage was old enough to handle it and would find out soon enough anyway.

"Broke, what do you mean we're broke? We can't be broke. What about dad's businesses? We have several homes. That doesn't sound like broke to me."

"Your father made some really bad investments and some deals fell through. He used our other two homes as collateral, and we lost them both. We didn't move here because of Austin's medical condition. We moved here because this was the only house that was not involved in his investments."

"So the houses in Orlando and L. A. are gone?"

"Yes."

"How long have you known this?"

"Six months now."

"So I guess Miles is *our* ticket back to success," said Sage. Before her mother could respond, she added, "That's why you suggested the villa and the special lingerie. You probably even hoped I was stupid enough to get pregnant."

"Darling, things have to work out for you and Miles. Everyone knows he is going pro one day, and that could help you and your family."

"Are you crazy? You're not pimping me because dad made some bad financial decisions. Have you even told dad about this sick idea you have for Miles and me?"

"You have never been asked to do anything for this family. You will not turn your back when your family needs you the most. Do you know how expensive Austin's treatments are? What do you think is going to happen to him when he doesn't get his treatments? Do you want him to end up in some state-run home?"

"Never," responded Sage with tears in her eyes. Victoria finally hit the right nerve with her daughter, for Sage loved her brother more than anything or anyone else – even Miles. Sage didn't want Austin to suffer because of what her father did. She knew Miles was going to college in a couple of months and wanted to attend college herself, but she feared what would happen to Austin if she wasn't around to take care of him. She figured she could do some online courses and maybe catch a few classes here and there. With the news her mother sprung on her, she thought she might even have to get a job. Sage was willing to do whatever it took to keep Austin from being institutionalized.

Even as her thoughts ran rampant, Sage realized that her mother never answered her question. "Does dad know about this?"

"It was his idea."

The bomb her mother dropped completely stunned Sage. She knew that her mother had to be lying. There was no way her father would do that to his own daughter. She marched into the living room and stood in front of the television so her father could disprove the lies her mother told.

"Dad, tell me that mom is lying." At that point, the faint sounds of the actors on a TV commercial were the only audible remarks. Sage continued, "Dad, tell me this was not your idea."

She begged him to say it wasn't true. He never did. He couldn't even look Sage in her eyes when she questioned him.

Chapter 15
WELCOME TO ARIZONA A&M

Summer 2022

It's not like Christine didn't know that Miles would eventually graduate and leave Oakridge. She predicted they would be together enjoying his moment as valedictorian instead of him and Sage. Christine walked up to them after the ceremony and asked to speak with Miles alone. Sage walked over to accompany her parents and Austin, leaving Miles and Christine to have a much needed conversation.

"Congratulations, Miles, my best friend and hero."

"Thanks. You know it will be you up there giving a speech next year."

Christine smiled at his attempt to lighten the mood before becoming really serious.

"Miles, I know you will be leaving for camp this summer, and I won't see much of you after today. I just want you to know that you will always be more than a superstar quarterback to me, and I'll miss you dearly." With her voice cracking, she mouthed a barely audible, "I love you."

Christine gave Miles a loving hug and shed a few tears. Sage looked over at their embrace and smiled because she had become sympathetic to Christine's feelings for Miles. It wasn't until that moment that Miles understood and fully acknowledged how Christine really felt about him. It made him feel good knowing that Christine didn't care if he ever picked up another football again. She loved him unconditionally.

"Don't be like that Christine. You act like we're never going to see each other again. I'll be only a few miles away at A&M. During the season it will be tough to get away, but I'll be around." Miles' attempt to make Christine feel better didn't work although she appreciated it.

After graduation, Andrew enrolled in summer courses so he could get a head start on his grueling pre-law class schedule. He also wanted to network with other pre-law students so he could one day be accepted into Phi Alpha Delta, one of the largest and most well-known law fraternities in the world. Andrew knew that arriving prior to fall and making some contacts would give him an advantage over other prospective inductees. He knew that Phi Alpha Delta would be a major step toward his ultimate goal of becoming "The Honorable Andrew Myers."

Along with the other newbies -- consisting of freshmen, junior college transfers, and walk-ons -- Miles and Shawn reported on campus for football orientation, summer training drills, and practices. The College Athletic Association mandated the orientation for all new student athletes. It took place in an auditorium classroom on campus.

The players were given three-ring binders full of information and participated in detailed discussions about the risks of being a high-profile athlete at a major university. The players were also warned about having communications with agents, and they even received practical advice about avoiding women who would try to have sex without a condom or an altered one. Most of the players, except Miles, who looked shocked, had heard the stories about women willing to get pregnant from potential professional athletes to cash in on huge child support payments. For one particular freshman, the warning came about 17 months too late. He had extended his bloodline during his junior year of high school.

The players were told to avoid any illegal activities, school ethics violations, or CAA rules violations. The list of violations was almost 15 pages long. Shawn thought, "We need a Ph.D. to remember all the things we can't do. It would've been simpler to just give us a short list of the things we can do."

From the time training camp started until the season ended, college football players followed a very structured daily agenda. Certain A&M football staff actually guarded them to keep the players out of trouble.

One facilitator repeated one key statement over and over again to make sure everyone in the room heard it. "Under no circumstances are you ever allowed to take any gifts, loans, money, or anything of value from any person, at any time," he said. "That goes for your family members as well."

A second speaker joined in the conversation. "I don't care if your mother calls and asks you to sign a few jerseys for the church fundraiser. You will be in violation if you do. You are now the property of Arizona A&M University and only approved charitable events will be coordinated through the athletic director's office. Understood?"

It was a CAA violation for any player to take any money from anyone while on an athletic scholarship at a college or university. The players weren't even allowed to have jobs during football season or training. Many players from poor families struggled to survive on the small stipend the university gave them. Miles and Shawn noticed the uneasy reactions and muzzled whispers circulating the auditorium when the facilitators discussed their stipend and inability to earn anything else.

One player sitting next to Miles, Rodney Fuller, a transfer from a Division III school in Florida, mumbled in frustration at the thought of not being able to work. He said, "This ain't going to work for me. My mom has always counted on me to be able to send her a little something every month to help out. My last coach let me put in a few hours here and there. I didn't know that's how ya'll do it at A&M."

Although the information was vital and very thorough, it could not maintain the attention of all 23 young men seated in the auditorium. Some players nodded sleepily and a few eyelids closed completely.

The newbies each had less than two months to prove themselves worthy of playing time before kickoff in September. College rules limited the final roster to 70 players, so all 92 players who showed up for camp would not be there for the opening game. Before any of the newbies were allowed to meet their teammates or perform any drills, Assistant Coach and offensive coordinator, Terrance Copper made them all attend a special introductory meeting with him and him alone.

The meeting was nothing new. It was sort of like his personal orientation to set the record straight. Copper was Head Coach Banks' right-hand man, performing roles as the quarterback's and the receiver's coach, as well as the offensive coordinator. Copper was a professional quarterback for three years before an injury ended his career at the age of 25. Five years later, he joined Banks' coaching staff. Prior to beginning his coaching career with Banks, Copper won a couple of championships as head coach at a junior college in Florida. He was the best at what he did and many football analysts claimed that he was the reason Banks' winning percentage was so high in recent years. Copper's offensive genius improved the team's offensive performance each year for the last five years. The offense, under Copper, averaged 29.7 points per game his first year and kept creeping north. Although the players changed each season, his results stayed the same.

Some football analysts questioned why Copper hadn't been offered a head coaching job at a Division 1 program. No one knew that Coach Banks was the reason. Banks was not going to lose his golden goose. Several schools had called Coach Banks over the past two seasons to get a feel for Copper's potential. Banks would always say that he was "difficult to work with at times" or that he was often "unwilling to take instruction."

None of these remarks were true. Initially, Copper couldn't figure out why he kept getting rejection letters and calls after interviewing for head coach positions at other schools. In fact, the Dear John letters and phone calls began to irritate him after three failed interviews over the last two years. Privately, Copper questioned himself about the successful candidates' abilities over his own. He knew he was more qualified and had a more successful winning percentage than any of the men that got the jobs for which he interviewed. He was a proud, confident man and never once thought being black kept him from receiving a head coaching job at a top-tier program.

* * *

The veteran players were already on the field warming up in shorts, t-shirts, and helmets. The newbies assembled in the Rock Warrior locker room. No shoulder pads had been placed in the players' lockers. It wasn't time yet. Many of the younger newbies crowded around Miles and Shawn, discussing some of the high-lights from their senior season at Oakridge. Every player in the locker room and on the practice field had either seen or heard of the dynamic duo from Oakridge. All of them were amazed by Miles' unique skill set.

One newbie commented to Miles, "Yo, I saw that 87-yard run you had in that game right before half time. That was the most amazing shit I've ever seen in my life."

Another newbie was in Shawn's face, "How in the hell did you make that one-handed diving catch in the back of the end zone during the state championship game? The defender was all over you. How could you even see the ball at that angle?"

Before the young stars were able to respond to any questions, the chatter ended abruptly when Coach Copper joined them and told everyone to pick a locker and to have a seat. Miles and Shawn sat next to each other near where Copper loomed.

None of the potential players in the room had ever met Copper prior to that moment because Coach Banks was in charge of recruiting. At 6 feet 4 inches, Copper stood about eye level to the taller players, but his aura made him seem 10 feet tall. He stood in the middle of the locker room wearing khaki shorts, running shoes, a red visor, and a short-sleeve red polo shirt with the team logo. It was the same outfit Coach Banks and his other three assistants donned when they visited Miles' and Shawn's homes. Copper held a clipboard with a list of everyone who was supposed to be in the locker room. Some of the newbies were nervous, especially the freshmen. They were concerned with getting "red-shirted" their first season and having to sit out a whole year before getting an opportunity to play next season. A red-shirt would have been better than getting cut altogether.

As he surveyed the candidates, Coach Copper cleared his throat and finally spoke to the young men in a strong voice with an intense look on his face. He stuck the clipboard under his left armpit and grabbed his right wrist with his left hand behind his back. At that moment, he looked more like a drill sergeant. He paced back and forth in the locker room, intentionally making eye contact with each and every potential player.

"My name is Coach Copper. I know what some of you are thinking right now," he said. "You're thinking that I was a five-star recruit or that I kicked ass at my junior college and that means something around here. You're thinking that Coach Banks came to my home and begged me to come play football at this fine institution. You're thinking that your past accomplishments will grant you some sort of special consideration in this program. What you're thinking is wrong. I don't give a damn what kind of king of the hill you were in whatever mud hole you crawled out of. As far as I'm concerned, none of you have done shit until you prove it here to me first."

He looked directly at Miles, and Miles raised his eyebrows and swallowed. Miles knew what he meant when he looked at him. Everyone in the room knew who Miles was and how big of a deal he was on the global level. Copper made it known to Miles and all the other newbies that he didn't care how many YouTube videos, Facebook fans, and Twitter followers they had. If Miles was going to be the starting quarterback, he had to earn the position. Copper finished his speech and dismissed the young men so they could change and join the veteran team members on the field, where Coach Banks was waiting to begin drills.

Coach Banks didn't deliver the locker room introduction speech because intimidating newbies wasn't his strong point. More of a politician, he excelled at attending public events with donors and rich alumni. He could charm the checkbook from anyone's purse or wallet after only five minutes. This was the reason he wanted to do all the recruiting. Coach Banks learned his interpersonal skills from his father, who was a successful college and professional football coach. In fact, many speculated that Banks received favorable consideration in his coaching career because of his father's success. Prior to working with Copper, Coach Banks' career winning percentage was under .500. Banks bounced around a couple of college coaching jobs and one professional head coaching job before landing back at Arizona A&M, where he once worked as an assistant coach.

Journalists, cameramen, photographers, and student onlookers surrounded the practice field. Many made up the usual crowd, but this year the numbers tripled from normal summer practice session totals. Everyone wanted to get a firsthand look at the international football prodigy. Upon exiting the locker room with the other newbies, Miles saw people holding up signs with notes for him: "Bring home the trophy Miles" and "Miles, I love you." Others yelled out their own version with the same sentiment.

Some of the bystanders and professional sports writers took notes for books they planned to write about Miles. Students whipped out satellites phones to capture video of Miles throwing passes so they could post it online and share with friends. USPN had camera crews stationed on the practice field as part of an on-going documentary. Normally, the media was not allowed on the field during practice. After USPN made a large financial contribution, the athletic director forced Coach Banks to accommodate the network.

Coach Banks blew his whistle. All the veteran players began forming lines on the practice field. The newbies caught on and formed identical lines behind them in July's scorching Arizona heat. They stretched and exercised for 30 minutes before separating into groups based on skill sets. Quarterbacks and receivers went with Copper. Other offensive and defensive groups went with other coaches to different sections of the practice field to run drills.

Two hours later, the exhausted players dragged their drained bones back to the locker room lounge area for a three-hour break before doing another two-hour practice and then another later that afternoon. Coach Banks always did three-per-days for the first two weeks of summer practices as part of his conditioning regimen. Just like all the other coaches across the country, Coach Banks knew that conditioning played a big role in winning close football games. He prescribed to the same principle on which Shawn based his conditioning.

Coach Banks' teams were known for being in better shape during the fourth quarters of games when other players waited anxiously to catch their breath after ever play. Conditioning in the Arizona heat gave the team an added advantage over teams that weren't used to playing football in such extreme conditions. That was evident from some of the newbies who arrived from milder climates. Some players passed out and vomited during agility drills and sprints. The medical trainers had their work cut out for them.

After the last practice of that day, the tired young men filed into the locker room for showers and downtime. Miles sat near his locker getting ready to head towards the shower when five players approached and stood in front of him, surrounding him in a half circle with their arms folded. They were barefoot, but still wearing their practice shorts and t-shirts. Miles was a tad intimidated. He knew all of them from watching them on television. From across the room, Shawn noticed the group gathering, so he grabbed his helmet in case Miles needed some assistance. Shawn wasn't about to stand by and allow someone to haze his friend. Shawn stood just behind the group and held his position, waiting to see what was going to happen.

Starting from Miles' left to right was starting center Daniel Ryan, a junior better known to his teammates as "R'Kansas" because he hailed from Arkansas. The Irishman was the main person responsible for protecting the quarterback from injury, and he happened to be Miles' roommate. At 300 pounds, he was a large 21-year-old.

Standing next to him was starting tight end and Shawn's roommate Anthony Hernandez. Tony, a proud Mexican American, lived in a tough neighborhood in metro Los Angeles. Growing up in that environment made Tony even tougher on the gridiron.

Team captain and starting middle linebacker Cody Carpenter stood next to Tony. Cody was from Valdosta, Georgia, which was well known for being a football factory. He had long, blond hair that stretched a foot down from his football helmet. The straggly senior needed a shave and a haircut desperately. When Cody took the field during game time, he morphed into a mad man. He led the team in tackles during the previous season.

Next to Cody stood starting running back Mike Jones, a Jamaican who grew up in Rhode Island. Sometimes the dialects of the Caribbean and New England cultures collided and understanding him proved difficult. Also a senior, Mike had been under much scrutiny since the conclusion of the last season due to one critical play that prevented the Warriors from a chance to compete in the national championship game. Still, Mike led the nation in all-purpose yards the previous season and remained a huge reason for the team's overall success.

To Miles' far right was starting safety Paul McKinsey out of Miami, Florida. His teammates called the junior "Big Mac" because of the big hits he put on offensive players over the two previous seasons. Bruises, indicators of his ferocity, dotted the skin on his pale forearms. However, Big Mac was probably one of the nicest guys you'd ever met as long as you weren't on the opposing offense.

As they approached Miles, Shawn tried to read his friend's facial expression through a small clearing between the brutes towering over the seated Miles. Cody finally broke the silence. "So you're Superman? You're the famous Miles Starr who the whole world has been going crazy about? I know Coach Copper told you already, but I'm going to repeat it. I'm the team captain, and until you prove it in the game with the players in this locker room you're just another quarterback. None of us could care less what you did back in high school. Those days are over. You get to test your skills against the best college athletes in the world now. Let's see if you can last."

Cody then turned around and walked toward the showers.

Big Mac spoke next. "Man, I don't give a damn about that mess Cody was talking about. You and my man Shawn over there was on some real hype Batman and Robin straight out a comic book craziness."

Hernandez was next in line to speak. "Yeah, I'm with my man Mac. Those plays were crazy, man. How in the hell can you throw the ball with so much precision with both hands? I still can't believe it, man. You're like an alien or something, man. Yo, what planet you from?"

The other players started laughing at Hernandez' attempt at humor.

Mike said, "Welcome to the team, man. We're glad you're here." He then headed to the showers. Mike wasn't about to give any players a hard time after the criticism he received for one bad play.

R'Kansas said, "Just stay behind me, and your little scrawny behind will survive the season. You start all that running around shit, and you're on your own. Comprendes? Welcome to the team." He then headed in the direction of the showers.

Miles responded, "Thanks, I'll do my best." He didn't really know what to say. He suddenly realized the huge burden that was being put on his shoulders from the most faithful fan to the last man on the team roster.

After all five players left for the showers, Shawn asked Miles what they said to him as if he didn't hear. He really just wanted to demonstrate his loyalty to Miles.

After they showered, Miles and Shawn joined the rest of the team for a bite to eat before heading back to their apartment-style dorms. The football team at Arizona A&M had gorgeous upscale campus housing available to student athletes. Each apartment had new furniture, appliances, carpet, electronics and everything else to make living arrangements as comfortable as possible. Coach Banks made sure his players had nothing but the best. This was only fair since the football program funded approximately 90 percent of the athletic department's budget.

The next day at practice, Miles demonstrated that he picked up where he left off at Oakridge. He completed his passes, and his technique was flawless. Coach Copper was impressed with Miles' development straight out of high school. Although he never revealed it in front of the other players, Copper had seen film on Miles and Shawn. He attributed their success to mediocre competition on the prep school level. He now witnessed why the hype around them, namely Miles, skyrocketed. Even so, he still wanted to know how they would perform on the battlefield with live ammunition.

Coach Banks stood off in the distance watching Miles and Shawn work their magic, anticipating the start of live action in September with his two young studs. He stood alone with clipboard in hand, wearing expensive sunglasses and smiling from what his heart felt was about to happen in the coming season. He knew that if Miles and Shawn did half of what they did on the high school level, his team would win the national championship that season. He could hardly wait to finally make it to the big game after all his years of coaching and to have his name mentioned as one of the elite coaches of all time. For Coach Banks, the days went by slowly and the hours went by even slower. The university countdown to the first kickoff still cycled down the days, hours, and minutes on the school's Web site.

* * *

August finally arrived and Coach Banks had to finalize his roster and decide which players would either be cut or red-shirted. After the decision, one of Banks' assistant coaches put the final team roster up on the locker room board so the players could learn their fates. Shawn didn't even bother to look at the list because he knew he was the best receiver on the team. Miles wiggled his way through the crowded combination of disappointed and cheerful players, and he found his name on the list underneath the letter "S". His eyes scrolled down the list until they rested on "Starr, Miles." The other two quarterbacks were relieved to see their names on the list even though they knew they would see little to no action with the starting offense during the season. Neither the freshman nor the sophomore had a skill level even close to Miles.

Despite many attempts by the media to get him on the record, Coach Banks didn't announce his starting quarterback until a week before the premier game of the season. Anyone who watched the Warriors practice would have noticed Miles taking 80 percent of the snaps. The mock defenses were drained at the end of every scrimmage drill from chasing Miles and Shawn all over the practice field. Coach Copper loved making defensive coordinators look bad – even if one was his colleague.

Two weeks prior to the opening game that season, Miles went to visit Mr. Somers. He hadn't seen much of Mr. Somers or Andrew since he arrived for football practice in July. Miles wanted to surprise him before he visited Sage.

"Come in and have a seat."

Miles entered the Somers' home and felt comforted by his warm and friendly smile. He could tell Mr. Somers was glad to see him. Wearing her faded old football jersey, Squirt ran up to Miles and gave him a hug. He had to squat so she could complete her action. Just as always, she followed Miles over to the sofa and sat beside him.

"Are you hungry?" asked Mr. Somers. "Do you want something to drink?"

"No, I'm fine. We can pretty much eat all we want on campus, and some of the players actually do," said Miles with a chuckle.

"Well, you don't look like you're overindulging. You look great."

"I pretty much stick to my same dietary regimen and drink mainly health shakes between meals."

"Tell me all about how practice is going and how the team looks this year. I see they have you boys ranked number five right now. They would have you guys ranked higher if the defense hadn't lost so many starters from last year."

"Everything has been fine. The team looks real strong. Shawn hasn't missed a beat, but..."

"But! What is it, son?"

"I just feel an enormous amount of pressure to perform now. In high school, it was just fun, but now everything is so structured and serious. Every moment outside of the class is football related.

Every night there's a story about me on USPN. A blogger online has been ripping me to shreds, saying I'm a phony and someone created me in a lab and all kinds of stuff. Some of the people who believe in aliens are starting rumors that I'm from another planet. They say no person in history has ever been documented as being able to do what I can do."

"Miles, I'm sorry you have to go through this. Just stop watching TV and reading blogs. For every one person who says something negative about you, there will be 10,000 who say something good about how you inspire them or give them hope somehow."

Mr. Somers paused and hesitated before he made his next comment. "You don't have to play football, you know? I told you that everyone would come after you once they discovered what you were capable of."

"I love seeing the faces of the fans when we score a touchdown. It's kind of cool having everyone know who you are everywhere you go. I want to play, but I just wish it could be fun again. Everything feels more like a business now. We spend more time on football-related activities than we spend on class-related activities. Most of the courses we take are online now, so some players don't ever go to a classroom."

"I know, son. The system has changed over the years. Sometimes I feel sorry for you guys, but just remember what I said."

"I will."

"Remember that I'm here for you if you need anything."

"Thank you, sir."

Miles headed toward the door then stopped. "I almost forgot. Here are your season tickets. They only give us two per game. I kept one for the first game for my mom. I don't want her to miss my college debut. You and Squirt can go to the rest of the games. My mom will more than likely be working, and you know she's not much of a football fan."

"This is quite a gift. Thanks, Miles," said Mr. Somers.

"I get to see you play in real life?" Squirt asked.

"You saw me play in real life when I was in high school, but this is a little bigger, more people, more players, more everything."

The youngster went running through the house in celebration.

Once Miles left Mr. Somers' home, he went to visit Sage and then his mother before heading back to campus to his apartment.

CHAPTER 16
RANKED #5

September 2022

On opening game day, Saturday, September 8, the temperature spiked close to 95 degrees. As fans piled into Rock Warrior Stadium anxiously waiting to see their fifth ranked team, the heat visibly bothered them. Still, not even 120-degree temperatures would have prevented them from seeing freshman starting quarterback Miles Starr play his first college game. Former and current Oakridge students also came out to see Miles and Shawn, a starting receiver, together again. Kickoff was scheduled for 1 p.m., but fans arrived as early as 9 a. m. to ensure that they would be seated on time to catch every glimpse of the superstars.

Some of the fans had never seen or heard of the opposing team, but that didn't matter to them. Apparently, Arizona A&M paid $2 million to a small private university in Nevada to play against the Rock Warriors on opening game day. Arizona, like most schools with major football programs, always wanted to make sure they never lost a season-opener.

The game ended before it started. The smaller team from Nevada presented no match for the bigger, stronger, faster, more skilled Warriors. The score reached 42 to 0 at halftime. The starting offense and defense never took the field again during the game after the offense, led by Miles, put 35 on the board. Cody led the team in tackles, picking up from where he left off the previous year. Miles had zero rushing yards that game, mainly because he felt no pressure from the opposing defense. When he actually did throw, he seemingly had all day to make the pass. Mike Jones rushed for over 200 yards, which left Shawn very few opportunities to see many balls thrown his way. It was a less impressive victory, but a victory nonetheless.

Mr. Somers and Melissa left shortly after halftime. Melissa normally worked an early shift at her store on Saturdays, but she didn't want to miss her son's debut college game. Besides, Miles made her promise to be there. Mr. Somers didn't mind leaving early. He actually wanted to get home to watch some of the day's remaining match-ups on TV. Sage wasn't able to attend. Her mother, Victoria, was out of town with her father, so she had to watch Austin for the weekend. Nevertheless, she and Austin watched the game on TV. Austin kept yelling, "Go, Miles, go," for the entire game – even after half-time when Miles was no longer in the game.

Shortly after Miles removed his helmet, the media began post-game interviews. Coach Banks and Miles took seats at a table with two microphones. Shawn was not requested. Behind them was a red USPN banner serving as the backdrop. Reporters bombarded Miles with questions. Whenever he thought the final question was being asked, five more followed. After about 20 minutes, Coach Banks rescued his star quarterback.

"That's enough questions for now. My player needs to clean up and rest for next week's game."

Miles thanked him privately when it was over.

After every early home game Cody, Paul, Mike, R'Kansas, and Tony always visited a sports bar near their apartments called Harry's Place. Paul called Shawn and Miles because he wanted his two new freshman teammates to join them in celebrating an outstanding season-opening victory. Normally, a place like that was off limits to the players. The owner was a personal friend of Coach Banks. Thus, he permitted the veteran players to patronize the establishment.

When Miles and Shawn arrived at Harry's Place, their teammates were enjoying nachos with cheese and sodas, while laughing over highlights from their game on a projection screen broadcast on the USPN channel. All the players except Cody seemed excited by the rookies' presence. Unlike the other veteran players, Cody wasn't convinced of Miles' abilities. Cody played with his share of superstar athletes dating back to his high school days, yet had never won a title. His starting quarterback from the previous season was the first quarterback taken in the professional draft, and he didn't deliver the hardware at the end of the season. Cody was not about to get his hopes up about Miles just because he completed a few passes against the unranked, non-divisional opponent they drug through the turf a few hours earlier.

"Grab a chair from over there and come join us," Paul said to his young invitees. They both found chairs at a neighboring table and slid them over to where their teammates were stationed. A waitress came over shortly after and asked the newbies what they wanted to order. Miles was distracted from her request by the extremely short, red hip-huggers she had covering her mid-section and the revealing tank top from which her big breasts tried to escape. Shawn also admired her assets. He remained well restrained under the circumstances. He only said, "She's nice."

Shawn had not had sex since arriving on campus for practice that past July. It was the longest drought he had ever experienced, probably since freshman year at Oakridge. Coach Banks had the entire team on such a time restrictive and physically exhausting summer schedule that most players only wanted to rest when they got a spare moment. The coach knew that the less free time his players had, the less he had to worry about them doing something stupid to embarrass the program or the university. Miles used most of his spare moments to spend time with Sage, who he was seeing less and less of since classes had finally started. Normally, their conversations took place via video calls on their satellite phones.

After Miles and Shawn only ordered bottled spring water the waitress asked, "Are you sure that's all you want because we have new items on the menu like onion and garlic fries, and beer burgers?"

"I'm not that hungry, plus I don't really eat fast food," said Miles

"We make everything fresh," she said, looking somewhat offended.

"Nah, he's good. Trust me," said Shawn.

Everyone knew Miles wasn't going to consume any of the fried, cardiac arrest-inducing items on the menu at Harry's Place. Shawn wasn't as big a health nut as Miles, but he did watch what he consumed as well. If it wasn't full of lean protein and complex carbs, he usually wouldn't partake.

Several fans and students stopped by the table to congratulate the players on their victory and to speak to Miles personally. Based on the comments, the players knew the fans considered anything other than a national championship trophy a failed season. The owner of the bar, Harry, came over and said a few words praising them all for an outstanding performance.

"You boys looked good out there today."

Knowing Harry was trying to compliment Miles as much as he was the entire team, Paul said, "Miles did his thing."

* * *

The group was joking with each other and speculating about their next game when they noticed Candler Levingston Wyatt walk in with five of his rich friends. The starting punter for the Rock Warriors, Candler was a senior who really wanted to play tennis instead. His father and grandfather were both punters at Arizona A&M. Therefore, his spot on the team was a tradition that Candler was not afforded the luxury of breaking.

Candler's family was extremely wealthy and well-respected mainly because his mother was a U.S. senator representing the state of California. He had the best of everything, which included a 2023 Mercedes Benz. Maybe it was because of his mother's political position, his family's football legacy or his own narcissism, but Candler was an "asshole," according to most accounts. In fact, he was not just any asshole. He was the ultimate asshole. He treated everyone who didn't come from money, including his teammates, as if they were beneath him.

Everyone in his social network had a so-called noble last name. That criterion excluded every other member of the football team. Therefore, Candler didn't fraternize with many of his teammates. He came on the field to punt, and then he would leave the field immediately. He stood on the sideline away from where the majority of his teammates gathered. He wasn't even the best punter on the team. But because he had connections, he wasn't about to sit on the bench. Financial contributions from his family to the university made sure of that.

Candler walked in talking with his friends and didn't even acknowledge his teammates. His group settled down at a table located near the restroom, which was directly across the room from his teammates.

Unaware of Candler's traditional antics, Miles asked Paul, "Hey, isn't he on the team?"

"Yeah, maybe he doesn't see us," said Shawn.

Before Shawn could lift his hand to wave at Candler, Tony gently grabbed Shawn's forearm and explained, "He's not really one of us. He doesn't know the meaning of the word team. He thinks he's better than all of us. Just look at his snobbish ass."

With that, Shawn settled back in his seat and shook his head.

After Miles guzzled a third bottle of water, his bladder begged for relief. He excused himself and headed toward the restroom. When he walked past Candler and his crew, the chatter at the table grew silent. Although 12 eyes focused in his direction, Miles kept moving toward the restroom and ignored their stares.

As soon as Miles exited the restroom, he heard one of Candler's friends make a comment about him. He said it loud enough to get the attention of all the patrons on that side of the sports bar. "Look up in the sky. It's a bird. No, it's a plane. No, it's super freak."

Miles froze and looked directly at his detractor before walking over to the table. "Is there something wrong, guys?"

Murray, the young man who mocked the much taller Miles, engaged him in a conversation. "Nope, my friends and I were over here wondering what your story is. We want to know what type of lab experiment you were a part of? I looked it up, and I could not find one single person in history that could use both hands evenly the way you can. Everybody else has had one dominant arm. Now logic tells me that something is not right about you, and we're just waiting for the other shoe to drop. You must have signed up to try one of those experimental drugs."

"Guys," said Miles calmly, "I was born this way. I don't know what else to tell you."

"Maybe you are a product of some type of gene splicing. Maybe I should pay your mother a visit and ask her about your father. Maybe someone did experiments on him like in the movies."

Miles' friendly demeanor turned to aggression when the guy mentioned his mother and his father. Miles balled up his fists and put a frown on his face. Candler and his friends instincts told them Miles was about to do some damage. They rose to their feet to anticipate an altercation.

Suddenly the rest of his teammates, led by Shawn, ran over to the table and stepped in between Miles and Murray. Shawn was the first to speak, beckoning Candler's group with his hands to invite a confrontation. "Is there a problem here? If so, we can settle this real easy."

"There's no need for violence," said Candler. "I know that's how they settle things in the hood, but you're just going to have to realize that you're not in the hood anymore, unfortunately for us."

Shawn responded, "What did you say to me? Boy, I will..."

Harry appeared from the back and tried to reason with them, saying, "Why risk the entire season over a minor disagreement? I don't want to have to call Coach Banks, but I will." He reminded them that they were representing the university and any fight would eventually end up in the news or, worse, the Internet. Proof of his words was evident from the surrounding patrons who held up satellite phones, eagerly waiting to record something newsworthy.

Members of both groups realized that Harry was right, especially R'Kansas. He said, "Why give the university or the CAA a reason to suspend us and jeopardize a shot at a national championship?"

"Let's go," added Paul, who couldn't resist trading one last insult. "What would the team's chances be without our punter?"

Afraid to say anything further, Candler and his friends sat down and remained at the sports bar, pretended nothing happened so onlookers would stop staring.

Once Miles and his teammates went back to their apartments, they told some of the other players what happened. Most were not surprised, and one player even went on to explain to Miles saying, "Candler is who he is, and don't expect anything other than his arrogance." Still, Miles felt something he had never felt since he started playing football – rejection.

Neither Candler nor his friends lingered on anyone's mind the next day because three polls ranked the Rock Warriors number two in the nation.

CHAPTER 17
MELISSA STARR'S INTERVIEW

October 2022

Miles never talked about his father to anyone and no one had ever asked him about it. His best friend Andrew never even questioned Miles about his father. Mr. Somers was as close to a father figure as anyone was to Miles, but he never asked Miles or Melissa about Miles' father. As far as Miles was concerned, there really wasn't much to talk about since Miles never knew the man responsible for the number 1 jersey he wore on game days.

USPN had been begging Miles' mother, Melissa, for months to do an interview for a human interest piece they were putting together on Miles. She always declined. They even asked Miles to influence his mom. He told them the decision was up to her. The reason Melissa didn't want to do the interview was because she knew the question would come up about Miles' father, and she didn't want to speak about him at all.

One day the VP of USPN's programming department called her again about doing the interview. Melissa paused for a few seconds and then agreed. The VP expected a negative response, but told her a crew would be at her doorsteps within the next three hours. The senior executive called everyone on her team to make sure they stopped what they were doing and had every resource available headed toward the Starr residence. The VP was not about to give Melissa time to change her mind. The world needed to know more about Miles, and she was going to give it to them.

Over the next three hours, vehicle after vehicle and person after person arrived at Melissa's home to set something up for the interview. The makeup and hair people arrived. Next, the lighting and camera crews arrived. Then, the setting and wardrobe people arrived. Finally, just a little over three hours after Melissa's phone call, Doug Stewart arrived to do the interview.

Doug was a 45-year-old black male who worked at USPN for over 20 years. He was well-known for his in-depth and revealing interviews. The interview was not on his schedule when the day began. He just happened to be in Phoenix when he got the phone call. Nevertheless, Doug was extremely happy to nab such a high-profile and highly sought after interview.

The USPN staff rearranged Melissa's entire living room, installing props and a fake background. When they were finished, the room looked nothing like her original arrangement. Melissa's worries were put to rest when Doug reassured her that everything would be put back exactly as they found it.

After the hair and make-up people did their thing, Melissa and Doug took their seats on the newly created set. One of the UPSN staff members attached a wireless microphone to Melissa's shirt. She sat in her cushioned chair and tried to relax, but had little success. Doug sat about five feet across from her with most of the cameras to his back. Someone yelled, "We're ready to roll Mr. Stewart," and before Melissa knew it, she was being asked her first question. Her nerves were rattled by the thought of answering questions about Miles' father, which were sure to come up during the interview.

"When did you realize that Miles had a special gift?"

"I first noticed something different when he was just a baby. Sometimes he would suck his right thumb and then other times he would suck his left thumb. I thought that was kind of odd. Then when he was about to eat on his own, sometimes he would eat with his right and then sometimes his left. The thing that really confirmed everything was when I played catch with him when he was 10 years old. Sometimes he threw with his left hand and sometimes with his right. That's when I knew he had a unique quality about him."

"Did you ever get worried and take him to see a doctor or anything?"

"No, Miles is completely healthy. I made sure of that with nutritious meals every day. I did go look up some information on left-handed people. I learned that they make up between 5 and 15 percent of the population. They are better in sports like tennis, baseball, swimming, and fencing. Lefties are more likely to become creative geniuses. They are generally better at three-dimensional perception and thinking."

"But Miles is totally ambidextrous. Only 3 to 5 percent of the population is that way. Truthfully, those numbers are a little high because most of those people can maybe write with their off hand, but not perform physical tasks with ease like Miles can. How do you explain that?"

"I really don't know. As long as he's healthy, I just don't worry about it that much."

"You mentioned a moment ago about lefties being better at three dimensional perception and thinking. Do you think that played a factor into Miles excelling in the simulation chamber at a much faster rate than most other athletes? The fact that he was able to master multiple sports in three years is astonishing."

"I guess. Some scientists believe lefties process information using a visual simultaneous method in which several threads can be processed simultaneously, plus they have an excellent ability to multi-task. There have been plenty of brilliant left handed people such as Michelangelo, Albert Einstein, Benjamin Franklin, Bill Gates, Oprah Winfrey, and former President Barack Obama."

"That's quite an interesting list, but Miles has both skills. Doesn't that make him more exceptional than all those you have just named?"

"Of course not, I just think the sky is the limit for him even though I'm scared to death of him playing a dangerous sport like football. I hope he will continue with his plans of being a doctor when he's done with college."

"Well, most sports fans hope he plays until he's 50 years old." Repositioning himself in his seat and dropping the tone in his voice, Doug said, "Now, you know that I would probably get fired if I didn't ask you this next question. Where is Miles' father?"

Melissa took a deep swallow and lowered her chin to her chest. Doug didn't know what to make of Melissa's reaction. He remained silently anxious to hear her response. Melissa raised her head and started telling Doug the story of David Hunter.

* * *

On February 12, 2002, Melissa and her sister, Evelyn, were out at a local bar celebrating Melissa's 24th birthday. They both sat at the bar flirting with the bartender while Evelyn kept whispering to Melissa about how cute he was every time he turned away to assist another customer.

"Just look at that cute little tight butt of his. I just wanna eat him up."

They each continued to sip on their drinks as the night unfolded. Melissa was so engaged in small talk with her sister that she paid no attention to an attractive man staring at her from across the room. Finally, the stranger built up enough courage to walk over to the woman whom he had admired from afar for well over an hour.

The young, tall dark and handsome man walked up behind her and said, "I know you must be a twin."

Melissa playfully spun around on her bar stool and responded, "Oh, yeah, why is that?"

He continued, "Because God wouldn't have been foolish enough to create only one of you."

Melissa and Evelyn both turned and looked at each other before breaking out into an uncontrollable laugh at the corny comments from the attractive stranger. He could only stand there and smile as he found his own amusement from their reaction. He was going for the funny approach and succeeded. When he asked Melissa to dance, she figured, "What the hell. Why not."

He grabbed Melissa's hand and led her onto the dance floor. Soft and subtle music played in the background, and it created a romantic overtone. The man grabbed Melissa gently by her waist and she put her hands around his neck as they faced one another. The couple swayed back and forth and side to side to the gentle, pleasant sound echoing in the background from the speakers throughout the building.

He asked for her name and she responded, "Melissa Starr, and yours?"

He responded, "My name is David."

"Does David have a last name?"

"Hunter. It'll be yours one day, so you might as well start practicing it now."

Somewhat tipsy, Melissa giggled and kept dancing. As the night advanced, the two continued to dance and to ask each other personal questions. Melissa learned that David was 26 and in the military. He lived in an area not far from where Melissa and her sister lived. Melissa told him that she worked at a clothing store and was out celebrating her birthday with her sister.

Before they knew it, they'd danced for over half an hour. The only way they realized how much time passed was due to Evelyn walking onto the dance floor to interrupt them. She grew bored from watching them flirt on the dance floor in each other's arms. She was more jealous than bored, however. She was not amused that no one had asked her to dance much less eyed her all night.

David followed the two women back to their seats at the bar and bought them both drinks. He said that was the least he could do for keeping Melissa away from her sister for such an extended time. The three of them joked and laughed while sipping beers and wine until the bartender made the last call for serving alcohol.

"It's getting late. We should get going," said Evelyn, interrupting Melissa while she was smiling in David's face.

"So soon? It's my birthday, Evelyn. Can't we stay a little longer? He's just so darn cute."

"Yeah, yeah, he's cute. He's cute. I get all that, but I have to get up early in the morning and I'm not leaving you here alone with a total stranger. I don't care how cute he is. This place is about to close anyway."

David stood there amused by the sibling rivalry unfolding in front of him.

Once outside the bar, Evelyn walked toward the curb to wave for a cab. Melissa and David stood a few feet away, continuing their conversation.

"How can I contact you?" David asked Melissa.

She said, "I work at Fashion Square Mall."

"Which store?"

Melissa simply began backing away and turned to enter the backseat of the cab Evelyn flagged and was already seated in. David continued to beg Melissa for more clues while she closed the door.

"You have to tell me more than that. We were practically on a date tonight."

All Melissa did was blow David a kiss through the back window of the cab as it drove off into the night. She felt as if keeping in contact with him would be a waste of time since he was traveling in the military. Still, she relished their short time together. She had a huge grin on her face while she watched David through the back window of the cab getting smaller and smaller as they sped away.

The following Saturday morning, Melissa diligently helped customers and kept items in her department neat and organized. She was helping an older woman try on something in the dressing room. Apparently, the older woman didn't have the right size garment and asked Melissa to bring her the appropriate size. After she gave the garment to her customer in the dressing room and started heading back out to the shopping floor, she was startled by David standing there smiling with a bouquet of flowers for her.

Melissa asked, "How many stores did you have to check before you found me?"

"None, I just asked that nerdy looking guy who works at the cookie counter where you worked. After I gave him your description, he told me exactly where to find you. If you want to know how to find a woman in a mall, just ask the guy at the cookie counter. They notice everything."

Melissa tried not to seem impressed by David's clever actions, but she couldn't help it.

* * *

By September 2003, Melissa had been living with David for three months. She was sad because four weeks earlier, the military issued orders for David's deployment to Iraq. Melissa experienced episodes of crying ever since David told her one morning less than a week prior to his departure. He grappled with how to tell her he was going to be gone for 18 months, which just so happened to be about the same number of months they had been dating.

Melissa drove David to the base in his car, which he asked her to take good care of while he was gone. When they finally arrived, they both exited the vehicle so David could retrieve all his belongings from the trunk. Melissa stood toe to toe while gazing up into his eyes. Tears suddenly began flowing from both of their eyes. David dropped his bags. They gave each other the most passionate kiss they had ever given or received in their entire lives. It must have lasted two minutes.

David picked up his bags, backed away from Melissa, and said, "I love you, and I will see you soon."

"I love you too. Please come back to me safe and sound." Melissa whispered under her breath, "We need you."

Once David disappeared into a building, Melissa finally pulled herself together, got back in the car, and drove away. She must have been driving for about five minutes before she picked up her cell phone and dialed David's phone. He answered but said he couldn't talk long because he was about to walk into a meeting. "Well, this won't take long." She paused before continuing, "You're going to be a father. I'm pregnant."

After a moment of complete silence he said, "Really, are you being serious?"

"I have never been more serious in my entire life."

David yelled with joy, causing so much commotion that his peers and superiors started staring. Once David regained his composure he asked, "Will you marry me?"

"Please don't just say that just because of what I just told you."

"I swear I've been thinking about asking for a while, but I was waiting for the right moment."

"Well, yes, I'll marry you."

"We can get married as soon as I get back. Start making plans."

"The only plans I'll be making for now is figuring out how to ease my nausea."

"So my leaving has made you sick?"

"If pregnancy is an illness, then yes," said Melissa, trying to force a chuckle.

David's superiors urged him to get off the phone immediately so the meeting could begin. "I love you both. I have to go now."

"I love you, too," said Melissa,

Four months later, on January 26, 2004, Melissa was at work when her cell phone rang. Before she looked at the phone, she immediately thought the call was from David since he said he would call her on that specific day every week whenever possible. When she answered the phone, she heard a male voice on the other end. "David?" she asked.

The voice responded, "This is David's father, William Hunter. He gave me your information before he deployed and said to contact you if anything ever happened to him. I'm sorry to be the one to tell you this, but David was killed in active duty two days ago while fighting in Iraq."

Melissa dropped the phone and started screaming in a loud panic. Customers turned to look and co-workers rushed to her aid.

* * *

Doug was almost speechless after hearing Melissa's story, which she had never shared with anyone other than Evelyn up until that point. Melissa had tears running down her face when she finished telling the world how Miles came to be.

"That was an amazing story. Are you okay to continue?"

"I'll be fine," sobbed Melissa. A USPN employee handed her a Kleenex to dry her eyes.

"I just have one more question, if that's okay?

"That's fine."

"There is a former Arizona A&M football player who claims that Arizona A&M is among several schools that offered him and his family money to play football. Are you aware of any such activity? Were you or Miles offered any financial compensation?"

"My son would never engage in anything like that, and neither would I. This interview is over."

Melissa ordered Doug and the entire USPN staff to leave her home immediately. Evelyn was just arriving home from her job at the hospital when the last van pulled away. Melissa remained at the door, making sure they all left.

Evelyn questioned her sister. "Who was that who just left?"

"Just some people looking for dirt on my son. They tried to accuse him or me of taking money for Miles to play football. I made sure he knew that no one in this house ever took a dime from anyone."

The hair on the back of Evelyn's neck stood up.

CHAPTER 18
EVERYTHING BEGINS TO CHANGE

November 2022

By the fourth week of November the Rock Warriors were ranked #1 in the country, mainly because Miles and Shawn lit it up on Saturday afternoons. With a stunning record of 11-0, Miles and his band of juggernauts seemed unstoppable. Their next opponent was a conference rival and ranked #2 and, without a doubt, the toughest competitor they would face all season. The Southern California Archers' defense was anchored by Senior Safety Demetrius Term a.k.a. "The Terminator." Coach Copper drilled into Miles' head that no plays would be called to send receivers in Demetrius' direction. Demetrius was responsible for three players during the previous season and one player during the current season being rolled off the field on a medical cart. Copper wasn't about to give "The Terminator" a shot at his prized receiver, Shawn. "No throws over the middle" were his non-negotiable instructions for the game.

Just like the terminators who existed on the field, female versions prowled off the field or even on the sideline in the case of Candice Kane, better known as "Candy Kane." Considered an All-American girl, her resume was full of superficial accomplishments that included gymnastic trophies, homecoming queen, Miss Teen Arizona, president of her sorority, and current Rock Warrior football cheerleading captain. She was also known for donating her time and raising money for various charities, which was part of her Miss Teen Arizona civic responsibility. She aspired to gain the Miss Arizona crown eventually.

She had perfect everything: lips, legs, teeth, long blond hair, breasts, you just name it. Candy wasn't known for being loose, but she was known for getting what she wanted once she put her mind to it. She wasn't about to share her body with just any old trust fund baby who could buy her anything she wanted. She wanted to be married to someone famous one day. Candy wanted to guarantee that she would always be a person with a recognizable name when her looks started to fade. Everyone knew that Miles would be a star professional quarterback one day. In fact, most people who were knowledgeable about football said he would probably go down in history as the best quarterback and athlete to ever play the game. Miles was just the type of guy Candy had been waiting for but 10 times better.

Candy and her attractive group of female friends would sometimes hang out at Harry's Place after a home game and chat with Miles and his teammates. That is also where Candy met Sage. Sage's sixth sense told her that Candy had her eyes set on Miles, but she downplayed it when Miles asked her about it.

"Are you okay, Sage? You seem a little ruffled by Candy. She's just chatty and high energy."

"Do you think I feel threatened by a girl with a name like Candy Kane?"

"Her name is Candice. Candy is just a nickname."

"She's not even your type."

"You're right. You're my only type." Miles kissed her forehead.

Sage thought that was the end of anything relevant involving Candy Kane. She knew Miles loved her and had never given her a reason to distrust him.

Candy found out that Sage's brother, Austin, suffered from autism. She figured that getting Miles to help her raise money for autism research would be a way to spend time with Miles while making her seem strictly professional. She was right.

Candy also had another card up her sleeve, but she had to wait for the right time to play it. Her father was a businessman who just so happened to be one of the people to whom Sage's father owed money. She stumbled onto that information while looking for some fundraiser flyers in her father's office one day. The document listed Harold McCormick as the defendant in a $300,000 lawsuit for unpaid compensation. She knew that information would become useful to her at some point. Given that Sage's family was in debt, Candy figured that Sage was merely cleaving to Miles so that she could cash in on his success at the next level.

For now, Candy wanted to do a 12-month calendar of Miles with a different theme for every month. She knew Miles had favorable ratings with the 13 to 35 female demographic, so the project would be successful.

Cornering him one day after football practice as he was leaving the locker room she said, "Miles, I'm thinking about doing a fundraiser for autism. My plan is to create a calendar featuring one of the cheerleaders each month. We would do pretty well with sales alone, but I was thinking that you could be featured in each shoot."

"Doing this for autism research is an awesome idea. It's a condition that's close to my heart."

"Well, could you lend us your face...and possibly your bare chest."

"So you want me to pose topless with the cheerleaders?"

"Yes, please, please, please. You know how much the female fans love you."

Taking a deep breath, expressing anxiety more than hesitation, Miles said, "I'm not much of a voyeur. I kinda leave that to Shawn. But if you think it will really help, I'll do it."

With that, Candy swung her arms around his neck and said, "Thank you so much. You don't know how much this means."

Miles told Sage about it, but she could not oppose such a noble effort that hit so close to home. Regardless of how she felt about the coordinator, she encouraged Miles to help with the fundraiser. When Candy told the other cheerleaders that Miles had agreed, they were all excited about being near him with his shirt off. Candy used the opportunity to set special planning meetings with Miles on some days after practice. She asked him about his wardrobe and what he possibly had that would match their themes. Even though their meetings would always begin about the calendar, Candy would always divert the conversation to learn more about his personal life and feelings about Sage.

"How did you and Sage meet? How long have you been together? Can you ever see yourself with anyone else?"

Miles wasn't even aware what Candy, as seasoned manipulator, was doing when she came dressed in skintight jeans, a plunging neckline, alluring perfume, and camera-ready makeup.

On the Friday before that year's rematch against the Southern California Archers, Candy and the rest of the cheerleaders were getting ready to shoot the picture for the calendar's month of July. The photo shoot was a car wash scene in the Rock Warrior Stadium parking lot. Candy thought that the stadium created the perfect backdrop to promote the football program while raising awareness of a worthy cause. She and the rest of the cheerleaders were all wearing two-piece bikinis. They pretended to wash Candy's car, a red 2022 convertible BMW coupe. The idea was a soapy, sudsy, sexy car wash where all the cheerleaders were wet and Miles would hold a slippery, wet Candy in his arms in front of the car. Normally, the university would prohibit any commercial or even non-profit activities on campus that promoted sexual content. Since the money was going towards a good cause, no resistance was met from the school administration.

Prior to the beginning of the photo shoot, Sage decided to surprise her man at his apartment on campus. She put on light brown shorts and a white blouse and headed to Miles' apartment. When she knocked on his apartment door his roommate, R'Kansas, answered with a game controller in his hand.

"Oh, hello, Sage. Don't take the game off pause, man, damn," R'Kansas yelled back into the living room at Anthony and Paul, who were trying to gain an advantage on the game while their teammate was distracted at the door.

"Miles isn't here."

"Do you know where he is?"

"He said something about a photo shoot at the stadium today," explained R'Kansas, who was turned only partially facing Sage at the door. "Man, we are going to start this shit over again, because ya'll don't want to lose." He kept turning away from Sage to keep his eyes on his cheating teammates. R'Kansas was obviously too distracted to provide her any information, so Sage hopped back in her car and headed to the stadium. When R'Kansas turned back around to finish his conversation with Sage, he saw her car heading toward the complex exit. He just closed the door and went back to playing the game.

When Sage turned into the stadium parking lot, she didn't see anyone other than a few cars parked near the main gate entrance. Upon closer inspection, she noticed women in bikinis walking around with sponges. Sage parked her car next to one of the others near the entrance. When she exited her vehicle, she saw a bikini-clad photographer shooting a scene with Miles carrying Candy. They both had suds all over their bodies. He was bare-chested and wearing his red Arizona A&M practice shorts. Candy wore a red two-piece bikini that matched his shorts and her car. While Candy hoped this scene would provide some titillation for consumers, she herself was getting a little warm while pressing against Miles' abs and biceps.

Miles didn't see Sage from the angle he was facing because she was off to his left. However, Candy's eyes met Sage's anger and jealous face. Meanwhile, the camera was snapping multiple shots every few seconds. Candy's friend and cheerleading teammate, Valencia, held the camera and directed their actions.

"Candy put some suds on his nose and head," said Valencia. "Keep that beautiful smile going Miles. Candy, act like you are going to kiss him on his chin."

Candy did better than that; she actually kissed Miles on his chin. She ended up very close to his lips. From Sage's view, however, she saw Candy kiss Miles and him allowing her to do it. Sage decided that she had seen enough. She left and sped off in a furious rage.

Talking to herself in the car she said, "Who was I kidding? I can't live with this constant worrying about some tramp tempting Miles at every turn."

While driving down the street exceeding the speed limit, Sage pulled out her phone and called her mother to tell her she had made a decision. She said, "Mom, I can't see Miles anymore. It's over."

"What happened? What do you mean? Calm down. You're not making any sense"

"You're not going to talk me out of it. I've made up my mind."

Sage hung up. Victoria made several attempts to call her back but kept getting voice mail. She began to panic. Victoria had to speak to someone else about this matter but not to Sage's father, Harold, who wasn't home at the time. She dreaded the thought of speaking to the person she had to call next. She pulled up her list of contacts on her satellite phone and selected a very familiar name. It rang a couple of times before a male voice answered.

"Hello."

"It's over. They broke up."

"What the hell do you mean it's over? Nothing is over."

"What am I supposed do? I can't force her to be with him."

"The hell you can't. Where the hell are you?"

"I'm at home."

"Don't you move one muscle until I get there."

Thirty minutes later, there was a harsh knock at Victoria's door immediately followed by the door bell ringing multiple times. Victoria moved hastily toward the door because she was scared and also because Austin was still napping. Another loud bang on the door occurred just before she was able to unlock and open it.

When she opened the door, an angry Mark Wells was standing on her door mat. He barged into Victoria's home and slammed the door behind him. The noise didn't wake up Austin, but it should have. With her husband away, she alone would face Mark's wrath. Victoria backed into the living room with fear in her eyes. The back of her legs met the couch where she immediately collapsed into a seated position.

Mark stood in front of her and set the record straight. "Now, let's go over our arrangement one more time, since you seem to be a little shaky on the details. You called me over a year ago and told me about this kid your daughter was dating and how he was the next Michael Jordan of football. You also told me that you and your piss ant husband were in some real financial trouble and needed to borrow some money. Now because you and I go back a long time and obviously I'm not low on cash, I said we could work something out. All you had to do was make sure your daughter kept Miles happy and focused on football. When it came time for Miles to sign with an agent, you and Sage were going to make sure he looked in my direction. If all that happens, everybody wins. Miles is the permanent solution to all your financial problems and I go down in sports history as the sports agent who signed the greatest quarterback to ever play the game. Now, did I leave anything out?"

"What do you want me to do?"

"You get her ass back on the phone and tell her that you, her, her piss ant daddy, and her crazy ass little brother are about to be homeless unless she makes things right with Miles. I can promise you this. If you don't fix this, I won't make another payment. The beautiful drapes, cars, fine dining, country club memberships, your life of glamour and living with the Jones', you can just kiss all of it good-bye. I guess your husband won't be able to afford his legal fees anymore either."

Victoria knew Mark was right. He was the reason they were able to sustain their comfortable lifestyle over the past year. Victoria reluctantly called Sage back, but still she didn't answer. Sage had nothing left to say to her mother. She needed to hear a friendly voice, so she dialed Andrew's number. When Andrew didn't answer, the only other person she could think of calling was Shawn.

Sage called him and he answered after recognizing her number. "Hey, Starr child. What's up?"

"Shawn, I need to talk to you."

"What's wrong?"

"I just need to talk to someone right now. Are you home?"

"Yes, I'm at my apartment."

"Well, I'll be there in four minutes." Sage said nothing else and hung up the phone.

CHAPTER 19
ACCUSATIONS OF WRONG DOING

November 2022

On that same Friday afternoon, Andrew attended an open house for the law fraternity he wanted to join. The event was at the Phi Alpha Delta fraternity house. The email Andrew received informing him of the event stated that no phones would be allowed, so he left his in the glove compartment of his car. That's why he missed Sage's call.

Andrew and Miles had not seen much of each other since their arrival on campus over the summer. With the tight schedule Coach Banks had his players on and the class load that Andrew had, it was next to impossible for them to hang out like they did at Oakridge. They exchanged an occasional text message. However, Sage did keep in regular contact with Andrew. Since Miles was hardly ever available, she would meet her friend for a quick lunch to catch up on the details of their lives.

Andrew stood next to a punch bowl admiring an 80-inch flat screen monitor mounted on the living room wall of the frat house. He was about to pour a cup for himself when a curly-haired young man with light brown freckles introduced himself to Andrew. The young man wore a dark suit and a yellow tie with the law fraternity pin on his jacket. Staring at the pin, Andrew began adjusting his collar. The event invitation said candidates had to wear professional attire, so Andrew had on a dark blue suit with a red tie.

"Excuse me, are you Andrew Myers?"

"Yes, and you are?"

"Pardon my rudeness, I'm Teddy Fitzpatrick." They shook hands.

"Fitzpatrick, are you any relation to Chase Fitzpatrick?"

"Chase is my cousin."

"How do you know my name?"

"Chase received a letter of recommendation from Professor Ferguson about you. So, he asked me to get to know you a little better and find out if you're a good fit for our fraternity."

Chase Fitzpatrick was the president of the fraternity, so Andrew's eyes lit up with excitement. Teddy stood next to Andrew and pointed out several members of the fraternity and gave their names. Andrew tried to record them in his memory so he could speak to them before he left. Teddy looked around the room and noticed there weren't enough folding chairs for all the guests they were expecting. He asked Andrew if he would help him bring more chairs down from upstairs. Andrew happily agreed.

Meanwhile, Miles finished the photo shoot with Candy and headed back to his apartment. R'Kansas, Anthony, and Paul weren't there when he arrived. Somewhat tired from getting up at 7 a.m. for the shoot, Miles plunked on the sofa and decided to watch some TV, which usually put him to sleep when there was nothing exciting on to watch. The TV was already on USPN. He decided to leave it there because no game highlights or games were scheduled for that Friday, only dry interviews and so forth. To his surprise, USPN's Doug Stewart was interviewing Kaymon Jordan, a former dominant Arizona A&M linebacker who was dismissed from the team for receiving gifts and money from boosters. Kaymon had threatened to expose the university and others if they didn't reinstate him. The university lacked options once the charges were made public and the CAA began investigating.

Doug had been working on a story about players receiving money to play college sports for years, but he was unable to get anyone to speak on the record. He finally got the break he needed with the Jordan interview. Knowing Doug asked his mother was about similar allegations, Miles listened intently.

"Tell me what happened to you and your family," said Doug.

"When I was in high school, I came home from football practice one day and my dad said a man came by and offered them $200,000 for me to play football at Arizona A&M."

"Did they say what the man's name was?"

"No, they said he didn't give a name and they didn't ask."

"What else did they say this man told them?"

"He told my parents that the money would be put in a Swiss bank account overseas until I completed two seasons."

"Why a Swiss bank account?"

"He said that the money couldn't be traced back to the university that way, and my parents could start making small withdrawals at the end of my second season. He said that it was more than likely that I would turn pro after my second season and everyone would think the money came from my professional contract."

"Kaymon, everyone knows you were dismissed from the team before the conclusion of your second season. Based on what you just told me, no money ever changed hands. So, there is no proof to what you are saying. Still, I wanted to ask you something else. Are you aware of any other players on the team who took money?"

"I don't have any evidence of any players getting the same offer I did, but I do know of players that took money during the season last year."

"Can you give me a name at this time?"

"Sure. Mike Jones."

At that moment, Miles started receiving several text messages from players who were watching the same show. They were trying to find out if he was watching the interview. Miles didn't respond to any of them, though. Instead, he left his apartment and headed straight for Mike's apartment.

Miles started banging on the door really hard and calling Mike's name to get his attention. He could hear the hip-hop music blasting loudly from Mike's apartment. Miles heard the volume of the music go down shortly before Mike opened the door. Apparently, Mike was online playing a college football game against someone who lived on the East Coast. An angry Miles walked in and stood squarely planted in front of the television on which Mike was playing the game.

"Is it true?" asked Miles.

"Is what true?"

"There is a USPN story airing right now about you taking money from someone to play football here, so is it true?" Miles continued to question Mike hysterically.

Mike threw the game controller he had in his hand across the room and started yelling. "Don't come in here Miles with that holier than thou shit. You know what time it is. My mom got robbed on her way to pay her rent. She said they took the money she was going to use to pay the light bill too. She called me crying, asking me if the school or coaches could do anything since I was such a good player and all. It can get really cold in Atlanta sometimes in the winter. Imagine no electricity and no heat, and I got a younger brother and sister living with her. You know they won't even let us work and play football. Why do the players have to do all the work and watch everybody else line their pockets? I'm not as dumb as you might think. I did a little research. Do you know that the football program generates over 90% of the revenues that fund the entire athletic department, and that's not just at this university? It's at most universities. Each player on this team generates over 800 grand for this school. They give us a little measly $2,500 a year and expect us to have any kind of a life with that. Do you think the swim team paid for all these nice new facilities on campus? Hell no! You, me and the players before us did. You think Coach Banks got that huge contract extension because of his hard work or does he just capitalize off the sweat from our backs? He sure does live in a nice big house and his kids go to a really nice private school.

"Take a look at that college football video game over there. The players on that game are us. They have the same height, weight, skin tone, and jersey numbers. That game made $22 million within six hours of being released. The school, the conference, the CAA, the retailers, everybody made money off of that game, that is, everybody but us. The list doesn't stop there, the bookies in Vegas, the airlines, the hotels, the food vendors and the list goes on and on. We are the ones out here risking our lives every single game. We are one hit away from ending our football careers. You know what happens when we get hurt? We lose our scholarship and get shown the door. They recruit our replacements every year just like they recruited us to replace the players before us.

"Candler's mother is a U.S. senator, and his family has old money. You know where he took his girlfriend after the bowl game last year? Skiing in Sweden. Don't I look like I would like to take a girl to Sweden? Why don't the poor players have the right to provide for ourselves if we have the means to?

"I had over 1,300 yards rushing last year. I missed one pass that kept us out of the national championship game last year, and I got seven death threats. I only missed that pass because I was playing with a stress fracture in my right arm during the last three games of the year, but they didn't report that in the news. I had to change my phone number five times. I had to cancel my Facebook and Twitter accounts because I got tired of reading the hateful comments about me dropping that one pass. Keith Piper, Jr. has me ranked the third best running back in the draft next year. I played hurt, bleeding, or whatever. I got two concussions in the four years I've been here. I still play every game to the max no matter. I made one mistake, and I got to hear all this shit from everybody. Everybody loves you until they don't need you anymore, when you can't make them anymore money. When we stop giving them something to cheer for, they stop cheering for us. Five years from now, half of our fans won't even remember my name. They will be cheering for the ignorant fool that will be running the ball then just like I am now.

"If a guy on the soccer team beats the hell out of his girlfriend, it might make the local evening news. But let me jaywalk or get a speeding ticket and I get an alert from USPN on my phone before I make it back to my apartment. All these wannabe super cops want their 15 seconds of fame for being the guy to catch the big name athlete doing something wrong. The other student athletes get the same scholarship, the same education we get, but we have to live under the microscope because nobody cares what the lacrosse player is doing.

"When they recruited me out of high school, reporters would ask me why I chose Arizona A&M over other schools. I just lied and said because of the rich tradition of the program and some other bull. Tradition, my ass! When these schools were established, black people were not even allowed to walk on the campuses unless they were cooking in the kitchen or cutting the grass. They only allowed us on their campus after they timed us in the 40. There goes their damn tradition."

Miles tried to get a word in, but was halted.

"But Mike...."

"Don't interrupt me. I'm not finished."

"The annual athletic department revenues generated by major universities nationwide from ticket sales, endorsements, television rights, team paraphernalia, and just about everything else the universities and the CAA make money from were over $9 billion a decade ago. Today, the football programs bring in that much alone.

Do you want to know how much they spent providing us these wonderful scholarships so we can get such a great education at these fine institutions? Try a little over $1 billion. Who are the criminals in this scenario? They didn't bring me here to make straight As. They brought me here to win a championship. Everybody knows it, but nobody ever says it. College football is only a minor league for the pros.

"We take all the risks that make all the money, and everybody else just sits back and waits on a check. So when an agent offered me five grand just to keep him in mind when I get ready to turn pro, I took it, and I'll do it all over again. I dare anyone to question what I'm willing to do to provide for my family. Everyone else provides for their family from what I do every Saturday, so why can't I? So you better wake up Superman and recognize what time it is."

Miles struggled to find a response that made sense. He just went with the first thing that came to his mind. "But we can't let all those things determine the risks we take. We can't risk everything. In a year, you will be rolling in money from a professional contract. One day players may actually get some decent money to survive on, but we have to obey the rules for now. We can't take risks."

Mike responded in a calmer voice. "You know, I remember reading an old article online back in high school about the field goal kicker for a school in Boise during the 2010 season. The school was undefeated and playing the last regular season game. Everyone predicted that with a win they would move up to a number two ranking to play in the national title game. Chase Daniels. I'll never forget his name. He missed a field goal that lost them the game. The article said the conference Boise was in would have received $8 million to play in the championship game. Instead, they got less than a million. He made a $7 million mistake. All that pressure on a student's shoulders. He hung himself in his apartment a week later after receiving so much national criticism. He couldn't live with making a mistake that big. They say we are student athletes, right? Seems to me that the world views us not as students, but just athletes."

Miles just stood there without saying a word. He could not argue with Mike while he relieved his frustration. Everything Mike said made complete sense. Miles remembered Mr. Somers telling him how backwards and unfair the college football world had become in this country. Mr. Somers shared several stories about how money had taken complete control over honor and integrity in college sports. He also told him about five Ohio players, including the starting quarterback, that violated CAA rules right before a bowl game in 2014. The players received a five-game suspension, but that didn't include the upcoming bowl game. They asked all the players to verbally agree to come back to play the following season so the suspension could take place then. All five players played in the bowl game and then turned pro without facing any CAA penalty for their actions. They received no punishment because it affected the money that would be made from the game if those critical players didn't play. It was all about the TV dollars and the sports betting world, according to Mr. Somers.

He also told Miles about a professional quarterback that was facing sexual assault charges one minute and the charges were dropped the next after he agreed to a financial arrangement with the victim. Another story came up about a professional football player who committed vehicular homicide while under the influence of alcohol, but he only received probation after writing a huge check to the victim's family. Miles remembered Mr. Somers getting really angry while just discussing it with him, and he never forgot what Somers said. Oddly enough, all those discretions never deterred Mr. Somers or the rest of the sports world from the most popular sport on the planet.

"If that had been you or me, we would both be sitting in jail right now, rotting away," said Mr. Somers. "The sports world is about what action can be taken to generate the most money. We, as fans, are just as guilty as the people who make those decisions. We want our teams to win. We want a win at all costs. We don't care if the players are good upstanding citizens or not. We don't care if the college players attend class or not. We don't care if the players are dirt poor and come from families that can barely afford to put food on the table. We just want the W. If the coach doesn't win, we demand he be fired. No one cares if he ran a legitimate program. So why wouldn't a coach be enticed to bend the rules to keep his job and the jobs of his staff?

"Everyone knows they should pay college football players, but they won't because that means they get less money in their pockets. They could put the money in a trust of some kind until after they leave school. They claim that paying players won't stop them from taking money and gifts. It's not supposed to stop it. You should pay them because it's fair for the sacrifices they are making. If they wanted to stop the players from receiving money and gifts, they would make it a felony to give it to them. They will never do that because the people giving the players money are the same ones who make millions of dollars in donations to the schools. They quite simply just want things to stay as is."

Miles remembered that conversation very vividly. Mr. Somers posed a question to Miles that still puzzled him to that day.

"Answer me this Miles. Why does the coach get a police escort after every game and not the players?"

"I don't know Mr. Somers."

"I mean...if fans wanted to try to hurt someone, wouldn't they go after the guy that threw the intercept, or fumbled the ball that ended up losing the game? Someday someone is going to go after a player, and I won't be the only one asking that question."

That day, on the eve of Miles' high school graduation, Mr. Somers made all his feelings known and appeared to get a little upset from his frustration with the whole system. While Mike and Mr. Somers held the same sentiment, Miles knew Mr. Somers wouldn't endorse taking money or gifts if it was prohibited. In fact he said, "Don't take anything from any team, agent, or booster claiming that it's only a gift. Take advantage of the free education and wait to make your money afterward because it's coming."

Miles could say nothing further to Mike. He was about to leave, but Mike wasn't finished speaking. "When I told you not to act all holy about this, I should have told you what I meant. There is a rumor going around that your mother took money."

Miles got so angry that he got within an inch of Mike's face and said, "We'll see." Miles would have sworn on his life that his mother would never use him like that, but it didn't stop him from wanting to hear it from her mouth. After hearing Mike's testimony, Miles wasn't sure about anything anymore. Normally, players were not allowed off campus the day before a game. Miles didn't care. He headed for his car and was off to question his mother. He had to be sure.

* * *

When he walked in the door, his mother and aunt were both sitting on the couch watching a television program in the living room. Miles turned off the television and stood in front of it staring directly at Melissa. She thought he was playing with them at first, but she quickly noticed the seriousness in his eyes. She questioned her son. "What's wrong, Miles? Did something happen? Is Sage alright? You're scaring me. Say something."

"Is it true? Did you take money from someone?"

Evelyn raised her eyebrows when she heard the question, but she didn't dare interrupt him.

"What on earth are you talking about? Did I take money from who? You're not making any sense."

"People are saying that you took money from someone for me to play football somewhere."

"Miles, that's simply not true. I didn't even want to you play such a violent game in the first place."

Melissa tried to convince her son that she would never go behind his back like that and do something so selfish. She was telling the truth. She loved her son more than anything else in her life, and she would never do anything to hurt him or to jeopardize his future.

Evelyn finally broke her silence. She couldn't take Miles not trusting his mother, something she had never witnessed. Evelyn interrupted their conversation in a low almost inaudible voice. "It was me. It was me."

Miles and Melissa both stopped speaking and looked at Evelyn. Melissa's mouth was wide open before she started to question her sister. "What did you do?"

"I didn't have to do anything. Almost a year ago, a man approached me one day after work in the parking deck of the hospital. He pulled out $5,000 cash and a business card and said all I had to do was contact him if I found out where Miles was going to school. He said there were no strings attached. He would give me another $5,000 when I contacted him. But Miles never told anyone where he was going, so I never heard from him again. The card didn't have a name, just a toll free number. I don't know who the man is."

"Do you realize how much trouble you could have gotten Miles in?" Melissa said.

"I didn't do anything wrong. It was around Christmas, and I needed the money to pay off some credit cards."

"What the hell were you thinking?" Melissa asked.

"Don't give me that crap, Melissa. When David died and you were pregnant, I never asked you for one thing then or since you've been living here. I make one little decision that benefited me for a change and now you act like I murdered someone. Give me a break."

"This is getting crazy. How could you do this Aunt Evelyn?" asked Miles. Miles had heard enough. He couldn't listen to anymore. He left and headed back toward his apartment. He knew people outside his home were making money from his talent, but he never thought his own family member would violate his trust in such a way.

It was dark enough for the streetlights in the complex to start cycling on when Miles returned to his apartment complex. Plagued with confusion, Miles exited his car and headed toward Shawn's apartment. Miles had to clear his head in order to get ready for the game the next day, and he knew Shawn would provide some type of humor to distract his thoughts, even if only momentarily. In addition, Miles wanted to find out if Shawn had heard anything about what was going on with Mike and possibly himself concerning the rumors.

CHAPTER 20
THE PAST FINALLY CAUGHT UP

November 2022

No one realized that Andrew and Teddy had been upstairs close to an hour at the frat house. No one paid any attention to them returning downstairs holding two folding chairs each. With an uneasy and nervous demeanor, Andrew looked rattled as if they had been upstairs watching porn or something. Teddy told Andrew to set his two chairs over in the corner out of the way while he made room for them. Andrew noticed that several dozen more male students had shown up since he first went upstairs with Teddy, who noticed the increase in attendance as well.

"We're going to need a lot more chairs," Teddy surmised. "I'll go ask Chase if we have some more outback somewhere. You wait here in the living room until I get back."

As Andrew agreed to wait, he found himself standing alone by the punch bowl where he originally met Teddy just an hour prior. After about five minutes Teddy hadn't returned; Andrew began feel slightly uncomfortable standing there alone. Just when he was about to start searching for his new acquaintance, Chase Fitzpatrick walked up and began what Andrew thought of as an odd conversation.

"Hey, I was wondering where you guys went. We are running a little low on ice, and the hors d'oeuvres are almost gone."

"I'm sorry, Mr. Fitzpatrick. My name is Andrew Myers. I'm here to hear more about all the wonderful opportunities at your fraternity and become a recruit."

"Then why in the hell have you been hanging out with the catering guy, Mitch, all afternoon?"

"Catering guy? That was your cousin Teddy, right?"

"I don't have a cousin named Teddy."

"He had one of your fraternity pins on his jacket."

"That's an old pin that we don't use anymore. I gave him that because he asked for it. We're getting rid of them anyway. He showed up one day and said he was starting a catering business and would host an open house for us for free to see if we liked his service. We said, 'Sure, why not?'"

Andrew stood there listening to every word, becoming more and more confused and worried about what he had just done. Before he could begin piecing the puzzle together, he looked up and saw Eugene Reynolds III, someone he never expected to see again. Andrew's eyes almost popped out of his head, and he began to get even more nervous. Two large, muscular men, who were apparently his bodyguards, towered over Eugene's half-sized body. Chase looked confused by the sudden appearance of three complete strangers who obviously had no interest in joining the fraternity.

"What's wrong, Andrew?" asked Eugene, who didn't settle Andrew's nerves with his phony concern. "You don't look so good. Could you be nervous about something? You have no idea how much planning went into this exact moment. I see you got really acquainted with Mitch."

"Who is Mitch?" Andrew asked.

"Oh, Mitch is just a little male escort I hired to help me settle a score with an old friend. I've got to hand it to you. You did a good job of covering up your secret all through high school, but it's time to let the cat out of the bag. And I can't think of a better audience for the occasion than the group of people who you aspire to be a part of the most."

When Eugene said "male escort," Andrew nearly swallowed his tongue. He knew that the situation could only grow worse for him at this point, so he tried to make a run for the front door. However, the two brutes accompanying Eugene grabbed Andrew before he took his second step. They held each of Andrew's arms and prevented him from leaving. Somewhat gangly and frail, Andrew struggled to release himself from the large men to no avail.

Chase didn't know what was going on, and he didn't care. He wanted all four of them out of the frat house. "Get the hell out now or I'll call the cops," he shouted.

Eugene had no intention of staying there any longer, but he had just one more thing to do before he could leave. He pulled out his satellite phone from his pocket and pointed it at the 80-inch monitor on the wall in the living room. The monitor came on and played a video of what took place upstairs between Andrew and Teddy, otherwise known as Mitch.

By that time, everyone in the frat house had gathered in the living room to see what all the commotion was about. The reason for the clamor was Eugene's video, which showed Andrew and Mitch kissing and fondling each other in one of the rooms upstairs. Most all the members and potential members looked disgusted and made derogatory remarks about Andrew, who began sobbing in the arms of the large men and held his head down. Only five or six of the nearly 50 students showed any sympathy for Andrew. None came to his aid. Meanwhile, Eugene just stood there with an evil grin on his face as he gloated about his sweet revenge.

After allowing the video to play for a minute and realizing the damage he sought had been delivered, he ordered the large men to release Andrew from their grasp. The teary-eyed Andrew ran out the front door, jumped in his car, and left.

While a tearful Andrew drove away from the frat house, a tearful Sage was just arriving at Shawn's apartment. When Shawn opened the door for her he wasn't wearing a shirt, which was common for him while he relaxed at home. Sage walked in the apartment to witness a mess of massive proportion. Shawn and Anthony's apartment was probably the filthiest of all the players. Empty pizza boxes covered the countertops and the coffee table, were an army of red disposable cups and old soda bottles added to the clutter. Shawn, accustomed to someone cleaning up behind him at home, had not learned to clean up after himself yet. Anthony, on the other hand, was just untidy.

Shawn immediately noticed Sage's uncharacteristically disheveled appearance and red, swollen eyes. He told her she could have a seat on the couch and offered her something to drink. However, she was afraid to eat or drink anything from his filthy apartment.

When Sage sat down on the couch, she felt something wet on her bottom. She jumped back up and noticed a red stain all over her light brown shorts and on the bottom portion of her white blouse. Apparently, someone left a cup of red punch on the couch.

Sage tipped it over when she sat down. Shawn instantly apologized for the mishap.

"Damn, my bad. I'm sorry, Sage."

"Don't worry about it. I have a lot more on my mind than this."

Anthony emerged from his room, where he was entertaining a young lady, to get two bottled waters from the refrigerator for the "workout" he sought to begin in his bedroom with his female guest. He noticed the stain on Sage's clothes and remembered he left the cup on the couch when his guest knocked on door earlier. "That was the cup of juice I was drinking. I forgot to get it when my girl came to the door. I'm sorry, baby girl."

"I'm okay. I maybe need something to change into while I'm here."

"Shawn can handle that. I gotta help my girl change her clothes," said Anthony with a wink before he walked back into his room.

Shawn left the room, returned with a towel, and tried to clean up the mess before it completely soaked into the couch fabric.

"This whole ordeal actually took my mind off of the reason I came in the first place," she chuckled while starring at her soiled clothing.

"I can wash that stuff while we chat," said Shawn, who only recently learned how to use a washing machine.

"I don't have anything else to put on."

"I have a jersey you can wear for the next hour or so. It shouldn't take longer than that I think. I'm still trying to figure out this whole washing thing."

Shawn placed the jersey on his bed and called Sage into his room to change. He left her in the room alone and closed the door behind him. Sage emerged a couple of minutes later with her stained clothes in hand. Shawn took them into the utility room to wash them. He returned to the living room to find Sage sitting on the couch in his old Oakridge number 80 jersey, viewing pictures on her satellite phone of her and Miles together.

The jersey was as short as a miniskirt, exposing Sage's beautifully tanned, smooth legs. She was careful to keep the jersey pulled down to the max so as not to reveal the fact that she wasn't wearing any underwear. She had her legs crossed and the front bottom portion of the jersey pulled down over her knees. Shawn sat down on the opposite end of the couch from Sage and tried to figure out what was wrong.

"What happened today?"

"I think Miles is cheating on me."

"Hell no, not Miles. He is as straight as they come. Outside of my mother, there is no other person on this planet I trust more than him. He is straight up in love with you, like for real."

"I just can't keep wondering about which out-of-town game will roll around when some girl is going to be waiting on his bed naked in his hotel room."

"It is nice when that happens."

"What?" asked Sage, obviously distressed. She was hoping that he would be reassuring.

"So I've heard," said Shawn. He pretended to joke, but he experienced that twice so far during the season, ending his summer long drought.

"It's not funny Shawn."

"I'd bet my life that Miles is not checking for anyone but you. Do you remember when I tried to holler at you in the cafeteria back in school? Man, you shot me down so hard. I'm glad you did, though, because I can't think of a better couple than you and Miles. You guys were meant for each other."

With that affirmation, Sage began smiling. Shawn supplied the reassurance she sought, so she started feeling better and telling Shawn about the scenario with Candy that prompted her anger.

"Do you think I may have overreacted?"

"You have to know your man and don't let appearances fool you. Sometimes we have to take pictures with all types of women to keep the fans happy. That doesn't mean we're into them. We just need to keep them happy so they keep supporting us."

While Sage and Shawn continued their discussion, Miles was pulling his car up outside and noticed Sage's car in front of Shawn's apartment. Miles hurried toward Shawn's apartment, anxious to find out why Sage was there. Shawn opened the door wearing no shirt, and Miles saw Sage wearing Shawn's jersey and what appeared to be nothing else. Shawn watched Miles' face turn bright red and swell up in anger. Shawn looked back at Sage then looked at his topless body. He then realized how the situation might have appeared to Miles.

Before Shawn could say a word, Miles wrapped his hands around Shawn's neck and began choking him. Miles then pushed Shawn into the apartment with his hands still firmly around Shawn's neck.

"Miles, stop it!" Sage screamed repeatedly, but her pleas were ignored.

Shawn fell back onto the flimsy, particleboard coffee table. It crumbled into pieces beneath him. Miles released one hand from Shawn's neck to punch him in the face twice.

* * *

Wearing only a towel, Anthony peeped out his room door to investigate. He saw Miles on top of his roommate trying to line up a third punch. Anthony instantly ran over and pulled Miles off of Shawn. Anthony held Miles in a standing choke hold from behind until he calmed down. Shawn gathered himself and stood up to discover that he had a busted lower lip, which dripped blood on the carpet. Miles didn't have any injuries or bruises other than various red patches on his skin.

"What the hell is this about?" Anthony asked.

No one said a word, though. The only audible sound was panting. Sage was the first to move. When she saw Shawn bleeding, she retrieved some napkins from the kitchen. He took the napkins and held them to his bottom lip. Miles then shook himself free from Anthony's loosened grip. Sage started walking in Miles' direction, but he just walked out of the apartment and drove away.

"Miles, it's not what you think. Miles. Miles..." Sage called his name several times from the apartment doorway. He was gone. She wanted to run outside after him, but she wasn't wearing any underwear. It wouldn't have made a difference anyway.

* * *

Candy had been on her best behavior concerning Miles all season long and figured Sage had enjoyed Miles long enough. She felt it was time to see if she could capitalize on the connection she made with him during the photo shoot kiss. She put on one of her sexiest red miniskirts and favorite 5-inch heels before hopping in her red BMW headed toward Miles' apartment.

About 10 minutes later, she was driving up to the apartment complex just as Miles was speeding out of it. He almost wrecked while entering the busy street. Candy knew something had to be wrong with Miles for him to drive so recklessly. She made a U-turn in the middle of the street and followed him.

Miles drove until he met the freeway and then headed north in the dark Arizona night. He wasn't exactly sure where he was headed. His satellite phone rang; he didn't answer it. Miles figured it was Sage calling. He didn't want to talk to her or anyone, for that matter. After his phone cycled through five unanswered calls, he turned it off.

After driving for more than 30 minutes he found himself at the entrance of Echo Canyon, which was closed. Miles parked his car, got out, and leaned against the front of his automobile. The only available light was from the full moon hovering above his head. In the dimly lit parking lot, he stared up at the stars. Miles thought about the first time he hiked the canyon with Shawn and how Shawn saved his life. He also thought about his first date with Sage just over a year ago.

Miles noticed a vehicle with bright headlights moving up the entrance toward him. As the vehicle came closer, the headlights blinded Miles until the vehicle came to a stop behind his car and the lights disappeared. Miles saw Candy emerge from the driver's side wearing the tightest and shortest skirt he had ever seen. She walked right up and stood in front of him.

"Candy, what are you doing here?" Miles asked.

"Is everything okay, Miles? I saw you almost get into a wreck back at your apartment. I was worried about you, so I followed you."

"I'm fine."

Candy could tell he was lying, for the moonlight revealed the frozen frown lines on Miles' face.

"Miles, I can tell something is wrong with you, so you don't have to lie to me. I'm your friend. You can tell me anything. Did you and Sage get into a fight?"

"I don't want to talk about it."

"You know, she's using you. Her family is broke. Her father owes my father over $300,000, and she is just with you because she knows you are going to make millions one day."

"That's not true. Sage would never use me. She loves me."

"Miles, I'm telling you the truth. I have no reason to lie. I would never lie to you about something this serious." Candy moved closer to Miles and standing toe to toe with him. "Just let me show you that I wouldn't lie to you."

She leaned in and kissed Miles while caressing his head with her left hand and rubbing his chest with her right. Miles was confused and didn't resist for a few seconds, but he pushed her away once he came to his senses.

"You need to leave. This isn't right. I just need to figure some things out by myself." Miles struggled to resist the temptation of Candy's amazing body and soft lips.

"Miles, I...."

Miles cut her off before she could finish her sentence. "I can't do this right now. Just please leave Candy. I need to be alone right now."

Candy knew there was nothing left she could do at that moment. She didn't want to lose Miles for good by pushing too hard, so she relented and drove away.

After about two hours of thinking about trust, honor, and betrayal among his closest friends and family, Miles got back into his car and fell asleep in the driver's seat while still parked at the canyon entrance.

CHAPTER 21
GAME DAY: #1 VS. #2

November 2022

Miles woke up the next day at 7:18 a.m. He missed his nightly room check and morning game-day phone call from one of the assistant coaches, but he didn't care. Coach Banks' policy was to have all his players accounted for the night before and the morning of game day. A team breakfast was scheduled at 8 a.m., so Miles left Echo Canyon to go join the team. He didn't bother to turn his satellite phone back on, however.

He hadn't stepped two feet into the breakfast room before Coach Banks was in his face questioning him about his whereabouts last night. "Where the hell have you been, Miles?"

"I needed some time alone to focus on the game today."

"You were focusing on the game alright. If fooling around with some girl means the same thing as focusing on the game, then I guess you're right."

Coach Banks pulled out his satellite phone and showed Miles a picture on the home page of a tabloid Web site. It was a picture of Miles kissing Candy at the Echo Canyon park entrance. Candy wasn't the only person who followed Miles when he left his apartment complex the day before. Apparently, a freelance photographer was waiting to get a money shot of Miles, and that's exactly what he did while hiding in nearby bushes.

"I should bench your ass today," said Coach Banks to Miles, who was completely caught off guard by the image. "What you did was extremely irresponsible and very inconsiderate of the team, the coaching staff, and the university."

Most of the football staff who overheard Coach Banks thought, "Who was he kidding?"

One coached whispered to another, "Do you really think he'll bench boy wonder and throw away the season?"

Coach Banks continued his rant for about two minutes before allowing Miles to go get his meal. Miles had a totally organic, healthy meal prepared separately just for him. Making sure he had "special meals" was the agreement that Coach Banks made with Miles' mother during his recruiting visit.

Once Miles got his plate, he didn't sit with R'Kansas and the rest of the starting offense like he normally did. Instead, he found an empty table and sat alone. Shawn walked over to his table and tried to speak with him, but Miles pretended he didn't see Shawn.

"What gives, Miles? I know what you thought you saw, but I would never violate your trust like that. You're my boy. You have to believe me. I would never betray you like that."

* * *

His comments didn't move the meter with Miles. Still, Shawn kept trying to talk to Miles before Coach Copper would come over to review the offensive game plan with Miles one more time before the scheduled 1 p.m. game. After being shunned for several minutes, Shawn went back to his original seat with the starting offense.

Noticing the tension but remaining focused on the upcoming game, Coach Copper walked over to Miles and said, "Now remember what I said, if you have to audible, no routes across the middle in the direction of Demetrius."

Miles simply nodded in agreement.

* * *

The Rock Warriors went through their normal game day routine of walking the field, warm-ups, and so forth. Seemingly everything was normal except the level of response from Miles. He was normally playful on game day. Uncomfortable with his silence, his teammates tried to goad him using awkward gestures or calling him by the nickname that some fans and players called him. "Superman, you ready to fly today?" one player joked.

Still, Miles did not respond. He just nodded. While most of the players knew what had transpired between him and Shawn, they didn't mention it so as not to further ignite tensions, especially on game day.

Mike Jones was just as distant as Miles and more focused than anyone on the team due to the critical mistake he made against the same team a year ago. His performance in that game was the only thing that kept him from turning pro after the last season. For Mike, this game held more than national championship opportunities; it was his opportunity for redemption. Although for different reasons, he joined Miles in solemn focus, saying nothing and merely nodding in respond to any conversation with him.

Several players took notice that Shawn did not say his pregame prayer in the locker room before the game. He never played a game without saying his football version of the Lord's Prayer, which said, "Yea, though I walk on the field in the shadow of death. I shall fear no defender, for he cannot cover me."

Game time finally arrived and Miles could not have had a worse start. He ended his streak of 305 consecutive passes without an interception by throwing two during the first two drives. It was just like his first Oakridge game all over again. Mr. Somers watched the dreadful performance in the stands with his daughter like he did for most home games.

Miles' mechanics were all over the place. Coach Banks questioned Miles on the sideline while he was sitting on the bench, trying to get him to erase his mistakes up to that point.

When the coach walked off, Shawn went over and sat by his friend to try to explain things. "Nothing happened, man! I promise you that I would never violate your trust like that. Just ask Sage. She will tell you the same thing. Nothing happened."

"It's fine, Shawn. I know you better than that, and I know you got my back. You always have such honorable intensions when it comes to women."

Shawn didn't pick up on the obvious sarcasm in his voice. He must have heard what he wanted to hear. In his mind, Miles had indicated that it was all just one big misunderstanding.

Demetrius "The Terminator" Term was on the field, anxiously waiting to make one of his lethal hits, but Coach Copper had his number. As the game plan indicated, he wasn't sending in any offensive plays over the middle of the football field. The only tackles Demetrius made were on Mike Jones several yards past the line of scrimmage. Still, Mike was gaining 7, 10, 13 yards per carry. In fact, he was the only reason the score was still tied 14 to 14 with two minutes to go before halftime.

With 1:48 remaining before the half, the Rock Warriors fair caught an Archer punt. The Rock Warrior offense took possession of the football on their on 32-yard line with no timeouts left in the half. After Miles broke the huddle, the players lined up in a shotgun formation with Shawn spread wide to his right. Miles scanned the defense and his offensive formation from left to right. When Miles' eyes met Shawn's helmet and he saw the number 80 on his left sleeve, he started having flashes of Shawn and Sage making love. All he could see was Sage wearing Shawn's Oakridge number 80 jersey and nothing else. He had been trying to deflect the images all day, but they kept popping up in his head.

R'Kansas pitched the ball to Miles, and the defense rushed toward the Rock Warrior quarterback. Miles looked to his left and back to his right. Shawn had given his defender a juke move and was streaking up the sideline with a 5-yard advantage. Miles looked away from Shawn and found Anthony open on a 10-yard curl pattern. Miles threw a precise left-handed spiral to Anthony just before the Archer defenders were in his face. Anthony caught the pass and scrambled for a 28-yard gain. The clock stopped so the chain crew could set the markers at the new first down location.

Both Coach Banks and Copper were livid over Miles not getting the ball to Shawn for an obvious touchdown. One of the cameramen caught Coach Banks throwing his headset on the ground, which aired repeatedly on the USPN Network as a highlight that evening. The clock had dwindled to 1:32 left in the half. Miles received the upcoming play call from Coach Copper, who was sitting upstairs in a booth overlooking the field, through his helmet earpiece. He immediately started barking the call to the offense while they were setting up for the next play. Meanwhile, the chain crew was still scrambling to move the markers, and the officials were rushing to get the ball set so the clock could restart.

Miles scanned the defense for player blitzes, as images of Shawn and Sage crept into mind once again. He kept seeing them kissing and caressing each other. Even though it never happened, the images in his head were real enough to give them validity. Trying to focus instead on the game, Miles continued scanning the defense and his offensive. He looked over the heads of the Archer linebackers and fixed his eyes on Demetrius in the safety position shaded over to Shawn's side of the field. The Terminator could not stand still while he waited for the ball to be hiked. Demetrius was pacing from left to right just waiting for some action. He had not yet delivered a big hit he had become notorious for during his career.

Coach Banks didn't hear what play Miles audibled before the ball was hiked because of the noise in the stadium. The Rock Warrior fans were definitely too excited to be quiet for the final drive of the half. They had seen Miles operate the 2-minute drive many times during the course of the season, so they had no doubt that a touchdown was inevitable.

Shawn was still spread out to the far right when Miles audibled the play. Shawn motioned back toward the line of scrimmage. Coach Copper's eyes stretched with a puzzled look on his face when Shawn went into motion. A split second after R'Kansas snapped the ball to Miles, Coach Copper began to panic. He recognized the play and started to communicate to Coach Banks to a call time out before remembering that none were left. It was too late anyway. The ball had been snapped.

Miles grabbed the football out of the air and placed it in the middle of his chest, firmly glued with both hands. Shawn took off up the field on an inside post pattern that lead him straight in the direction of the Terminator. Coach Banks realized what was developing before his eyes, just as Coach Copper did, but they were powerless to stop it.

Miles held on to the football for three seconds before throwing a left-handed spiral over the middle in Shawn's direction. The ball seemed like it hung in the air for days. Shawn glided with tremendous speed in his route and turned back to look for the ball. Demetrius had an evident opportunity for an interception, but he settled on making a hit instead. Miles threw the pass 2 feet too high, which was unusual for him. Shawn saw Demetrius' position on him before he turned to look for the ball. He knew what everyone else knew about the Terminator. All that must have escaped Shawn, who leapt off of his left foot into the air and raised both hands to make the catch.

Was Shawn overconfident? Did he think he could make the catch and get to the ground before Demetrius arrived? Miles knew the answers, for he knew Shawn very well. Miles knew that Shawn would attempt to be the hero of the game. He knew that Shawn lived for moments like that, so he baited him.

As soon as Shawn's fingers touched the ball the Terminator's shoulder pads hit Shawn in the right thigh, which caused him to spin around in the air and to land on the top of his head. The entire stadium took a silent breath at the sight of such a vicious hit. Some people, including his teammates on the sidelines and the fans in the stands, were saying, "Get up, Shawn."

Shawn just lay still on the field motionless. The Rock Warrior and the Archer medical staffs both ran onto the field to assist Shawn. Coach Banks ran onto the field. All his teammates on the field except Miles ran toward Shawn to see if he was okay. Miles didn't even look concerned.

The medical team worked on Shawn for several minutes before someone drove the medical cart onto the field to carry him to an ambulance and then to the hospital. Until he saw the medical cart, Miles was numb to the situation. At that point, he started thinking, "What have I done? Shawn, get up, please."

Miles finally ran to Shawn's location on the field and joined the rest of the offense. He made his way through the large shoulder pads of his teammates and put his eyes on Shawn still lying on the turf. The medical staff secured Shawn's head to prevent any sudden shifts before gently rolling him onto a paramedic board. They were preparing Shawn to be lifted onto the medical cart. Shawn was conscious and even moved his hands a little.

After the paramedics lifted Shawn onto the medical cart, a loud round of applause erupted in the stadium from both the home and visiting fans and team. Shawn gave a thumbs up with his right hand as the medical cart rolled away. The image was captured on the jumbo screen at Rock Warrior Stadium. The small but satisfying acknowledgement from Shawn gave the crowd more enthusiasm, which led to even louder applause. Shortly after Shawn disappeared down a tunnel through the corner of the end zone, the game resumed. However, Coach Banks ordered Miles to take a knee.

At halftime, the score was still tied 14 to 14. The locker room was unusually quiet. It wasn't just one thing that had everyone, including the coaches, dispirited. It was more than lacking the lead at halftime for the first time all season. They were all thinking about Shawn. Coach Banks delivered an angry speech about all the players giving more effort and winning the second half. Miles, however, was only focused on Shawn's condition instead of his own emotional upheaval. He caught bits and pieces of Banks' speech, but he missed it for the most part.

After Coach Banks concluded his rant, the Rock Warriors headed back to the field. Miles was the last to leave, and Coach Banks stopped him at the locker room door. "We don't have time for a pity party or sorrow right now. What's done is done. You need to refocus and go out and win that game, Superman."

That was the first time Banks called Miles "Superman." He employed whatever psychology he could to get Miles to refocus. Banks didn't know whether it worked or not. He was about to find out.

Miles jogged back to the sideline and began warming up his arm for the start of the second half. Coach Copper changed his strategy so that Miles was less responsible for making decisions in the passing game on offense. Thus, Miles simply handed the ball off to Mike Jones most of the second half. Miles had become the primary offensive weapon for Arizona A&M. Miles did complete 10 short-yardage passes during the second half just to loosen the Archer defense back up when then started to focus on Mike.

The Rock Warriors performed well enough to squeeze out a 31 to 28 victory over the Archers. Paul, Cody, and the rest of the defense held the opposing team from converting a 4th and long when they made a last-minute attempt to get into field goal range. Furthermore, Paul ended their hopes with a critical interception with less than a minute in the game. Mike Jones finished with 258 rushing yards, 87 receiving yards, and three touchdowns. He helped his team win and garnered the redemption he sought.

* * *

After the game, several Rock Warrior football players crowded the hospital waiting area along with several reporters. Miles was among them. He chatted with R'Kansas, Anthony, Cody, Paul, and Mike while they waited with the coaching staff to get an update on Shawn. While Mark Wells was nowhere to be found, Shawn's mother arrived shortly after the players. Coach Banks, Copper, and Miles greeted her. Miles didn't say much to her because he felt terrible for what happened and the role he played.

Coach Copper pulled Miles off to the side down a hallway. He was smart enough to figure out what Miles had done. He remembered how distant Miles acted toward Shawn during the team breakfast. He also knew Miles was extremely intelligent and did not forget the game plan that was drilled into his head all week about not throwing in the direction of Demetrius.

"You better pray that Shawn is okay. I don't care what he did to piss you off, but he didn't deserve the punishment that you and you alone decided for him. You put your own selfish feelings over the team and the welfare of a fellow teammate."

Miles didn't say a word. He couldn't respond because everything Coach Copper said was true. He compromised his integrity and everything his mother and Mr. Somers had taught him. Coach Copper left Miles in the hallway to ponder his message and rejoined the team in the waiting area. After a few moments of soul searching, Miles swallowed his pride and rejoined his teammates.

At 10:15 p.m., the doctor emerged from Shawn's room with a disturbed expression. Shawn's mother was the only one allowed to speak directly with him. The coaches stood close enough to hear everything. Miles and his teammates stood too far back to hear the doctor. Based on Mrs. Wells' screams and eventual collapse into Coach Banks' arms, the prognosis was disturbing.

Shawn sustained spinal damage from the Terminator's hit and his subsequent fall. The doctor said several months or possibly even years would pass before Shawn would be able to walk on his own. Essentially, Shawn's football career was over.

Miles literally cringed when Coach Copper shared the news with him and the rest of the team. He delivered the sad news while making direct eye contact with Miles, who began to second-guess himself. He began to wonder if he did, indeed, exaggerate or misinterpret the significance of the incident between Sage and Shawn.

He wanted to be alone, so Miles left the group and took the elevator down to a different floor. He had no idea what floor he ended up on. When the elevator door opened, he found himself in another waiting area. Miles stepped out of the elevator and ran directly into Sage.

Because she was sobbing, he figured she must have learned of Shawn's condition. He thought, "News really travels fast." Miles grabbed her in his arms, burying her head into his chest.

"Everything is going to be alright. Don't cry. Shawn will be fine. No one is more physically tough than he is, and no one has a better chance of getting back to their old self again."

Confused, Sage wiped some of the tears from her eyes with her hands and lifted her head from Miles' chest to look up at his face. She stopped sobbing and attempted to clarify his comments. "What do you mean 'Shawn will be fine?' Of course he'll be fine, but Andrew is dead."

Miles' looked confused. He raised his voice at Sage because what she said was obviously a lie as far as Miles was concerned. "What are you talking about? Andrew isn't dead. Why would you say something so awful? That's not funny."

"Andrew tried to commit suicide last night by jumping off the law school building. He barely had a pulse when someone found him lying in the shrubs. He died on the way here. Your Aunt Evelyn called me over an hour ago when she couldn't reach you after they brought him to her emergency room. They won't let me see his body because I'm not family."

Miles stood silent for several long seconds. He could not believe what he heard. The person who had been his best friend for over four years was now gone. All Miles wanted to know was why he would do that?

"Can you take me home?" Sage asked Miles.

"Sure" was all Miles could muster for the moment. In complete silence, he walked Sage down to the parking area from the hospital to his car. He opened the passenger door for her and she got in. She noticed something under her foot as soon as she sat down. Sage reached down to the floorboard to retrieve the item. It was Miles' satellite phone. She noticed it was turned off, which explained why he hadn't returned the numerous voicemails she left him the night before and early that morning. Sage turned Miles' phone back on and noticed he had several unread text messages, missed calls, and voicemail messages.

"You have several messages on your phone," Sage informed him before handing it to him.

Miles checked his call history and saw several missed calls and text messages from Sage, Shawn, Coach Banks, Coach Copper, and Andrew. He immediately checked his voicemail. He skipped all the messages until he arrived at the messages that Andrew left.

"Miles, I really need to speak to you now," said Andrew. "Please call me back." Miles also listened to several other messages from Andrew urging him to call back. He then noticed he had a new email notification on his phone and opened it to read it aloud:

Dear Miles,

I know we haven't been as close as we once were since arriving at college. I regret that and wish we had the kind of time we had in high school when life was much simpler. Something happened to me today that I thought never would. I guess you can't run from who you are forever. There are going to be several rumors surrounding why I did what I did, but I wanted you to hear it from me. I owe you that much. You have always been a dear friend to me, but I kept one big secret about myself from you over the years. I am gay. I know this may be a shock to you, which is totally understandable. Sage is the only person I confided in with this secret. I made her swear not to tell anyone. I planned to tell you during our senior year at Oakridge, but then you became this international superstar and I didn't want any rumors to begin circulating about your sexual preference based on your friendship with me. I just wanted you to hear the truth from me. Tell Sage, Christine, and Shawn I said goodbye. You have always been my dearest friend, and for that, I was truly blessed to have known you.

Your friend always,
Andrew

Miles couldn't believe the words he read. He wondered how he could have been so clueless. He knew that if he had not over reacted to the incident with Shawn and Sage, he would have taken the call from Andrew and maybe he would still be alive. He began yelling in his car and beating on the steering wheel. Sage tried to calm him down, saying, "Miles, stop it. It's going to be okay. There's nothing you could have done."

She continued to plead with him for several minutes until he eventually stopped yelling and burst into tears. He didn't think he could feel any worse than he did after hearing the news about Shawn. He was wrong.

CHAPTER 22
THE AFTERMATH

December 2022

The news headlines the following day read: "Best Friend of Football Prodigy Commits Suicide." Sports analysts across the nation commented about how "The Prodigy" would handle the loss of his best friend and his teammate in the same week.

Andrew's family buried him the following Tuesday at Green Acres Cemetery, which was located next to a little league football field. Miles, Sage, Melissa, and Mr. Somers attended the funeral along with the rest of Andrew's family and friends. Everyone close to him was present with the exception of Christine, who didn't want her final memory of Andrew to be of him lifeless. The funeral home had to hire security to restrict the paparazzi from recording and taking pictures of Miles. The security detail missed a few sneaky photographers they later found cowering behind tombstones. Miles tossed a white rose on top of his friend's casket while the funeral home staff lowered it into the ground at the cemetery. This sentimental moment went viral over the Internet about two minutes after the funeral.

Melissa rode with her son to the funeral, so they were both headed toward Miles' car at the conclusion of the ceremony. Miles opened the door for his mother, closed it once she got in, and turned to walk around to the driver's side when Mark Wells appeared out of nowhere, startling him. Mark stood face to face with Miles, making him even more uncomfortable. Mark was only an inch shorter than the towering Miles, whose voice trembled as he greeted Shawn's father. "Hello, Mr. Wells," he stammered.

"I told you to call me Mark. You might as well get use to speaking with me on a regular basis. Since you are responsible for my son not being able to play again, I'm sure you won't mind continuing his legacy on the field for him now and in the future. I look forward to representing you in a year or so."

"I don't understand."

"You will my, boy. You will."

Mark confused and scared Miles at the same time. Miles knew what he did to Shawn and apparently so did at least two other people. He wondered how many others figured out the horrible act he so recklessly committed. It went against everything his mother and Mr. Somers taught him. Miles couldn't believe he lost his composure and it resulted in a dead best friend and a teammate who would never again play the game he loved.

Coach Banks had the athletic director add additional security for Miles due to an increase in media following him around to question him about Shawn's injury and his demeanor surrounding the death of his best friend. That was the last thing he wanted to talk about before getting ready for the upcoming conference championship game. His mother begged him not to play after what happened to Andrew and Shawn. Miles didn't listen.

The energy at practice that week was lethargic at best, which angered Coach Banks. All the players were still down because of the injury to their teammate. Enthusiasm was absent, along with Shawn. Coach Copper's tone was different when he spoke to Miles all week. He was curt and only spoke to Miles about football-related activities, which was different from his normal readily engaging demeanor. He typically asked Miles about Sage or his mother in an effort to build a rapport.

Coach Copper wanted to bench Miles for the conference championship rematch game against the Archers, which took place on December 3, but Coach Banks was not about to throw a national championship away just yet. The Archers had the best record in their regional conference and earned the right to a rematch against the Rock Warriors, who were unbeaten in their region of the same conference, to basically determine who would play in the national championship game in January 2023. The conference championship game took place at the Los Angeles Coliseum and was like a home game for the Archers. Everyone knew the crowd would be deafening and raucous.

Mr. Somers and his daughter planned on driving to Los Angeles to attend. Sage contacted Mr. Somers to ask if she could ride with them, and he agreed.

On game day, Miles' conscience still would not allow him peace until he set the record straight with Coach Copper after an awkward week of practice. He walked toward the office in the team's locker room area where the coach was making last-minute adjustments to his game plan. Miles knocked twice before Coach Copper invited him into the office. Miles closed the door behind him for a bit of privacy.

Miles sat and began his prepared speech. He said, "Well, first of all, I want to say I'm sorry for..."

"Just stop right there with that tired apology. You know, I have interviewed for several head coaching jobs over the years and haven't gotten one opportunity at a top-tier program even though I know I deserve one. Coach Banks is the reason I haven't gotten any of these jobs. That's right. I said Coach Banks. Some secrets are just too difficult to stay hidden. He is too worried about replacing me, so he uses his influence to deny me what should be mine. The average person would respond on instinct and just quit or beat the hell out of him or both. I can't do that. I know my opportunity will come eventually unless I do something to mess that up like beating Coach Banks' butt. I bring all this up because you didn't plan on doing what you did to Shawn. You simply reacted on impulse. Someone did you wrong, and you had to strike back. Miles, you did something horrible to another human being that you will have to live with for the rest of your life. If it was up to me, you would not play another down for this team no matter how gifted you are. I know you lost a close friend of yours last week and you may still be mourning that loss. With that said, you better do everything in your power to help your team win today. You owe your best performance to Shawn since you made sure he couldn't give his today. Now get the hell out of my sight."

The coach went back to scribbling on his note pad as if nothing had just happened. Miles knew there was nothing left to be said. He picked himself up and left the office, closing the door behind him. He went back to his locker to finish getting ready.

At kickoff, the Rock Warriors were on the 20-yard line after the opposing kicker sailed the football through the back of the end zone. Once Coach Copper gave Miles the play, he jogged to the huddle. Shawn's absence caused some uneasiness, but his teammates, namely Miles, were determined to prevail for his sake.

The first play was a simple handoff to Mike Jones up the middle. He was stuffed at the line of scrimmage, gaining no yardage. The Archers' defense had adjusted its game plan from the previous game against the Rock Warriors and was not about to let Mike Jones collapse them again.

On the next play, Miles ran a fake bootleg to the right and turned back to his left and opened up to a full sprint down the field. He juked and spun his way down the field for a 35-yard gain before being sandwiched on the opponent's 45-yard line. In reaction, both Sage and Squirt covered their mouths in shock. The hits were pretty brutal, and it took Miles three or four seconds to get up after the defenders rolled off him. Pain shot down Miles' right arm, but he didn't let on that anything was wrong other than taking a little longer to get up.

"What is he doing?" questioned Mr. Somers, who sat with Sage and his daughter in the nosebleed section of the stands at the 50-yard line.

"What's the matter, dad?" asked Squirt.

"Miles is supposed to slide down to avoid being hit or tackled, but he didn't slide."

Coach Banks communicated through his headset to Coach Copper to tell Miles to start sliding. Coach Copper didn't tell Miles a thing about sliding. He only communicated the next play to Miles, but Miles called his own play. It was the exact play they had just run but to the opposite side. Miles scrambled for 20 yards on that play before meeting another vicious hit from two more defenders down field. Miles jumped right back up after that play, but he was a marked man.

Furious at Miles' rebellion, Coach Banks thought about calling a timeout to yell at his star quarterback for taking unnecessary risks, but he didn't want to use a timeout with only two minutes into the first quarter. Coach Copper again communicated the next play, but Miles ran the bootleg play once again. The third time was different, however. Miles motioned like he was going to run again after he faked the ball to Mike, but he raised his left arm and completed a 25-yard touchdown pass to Anthony in the left back corner of the end zone.

The Rock Warrior fans went wild, including Mr. Somers, his daughter, and Sage. Miles didn't jog down to the end zone, as he normally did, to celebrate with his teammates. He didn't even raise both hands to acknowledge a score. He simply jogged back to his team's sideline, where an angry Coach Banks waited.

"What the hell are you doing out there? Get your shit together or you'll be on the bench quick, fast, and in a hurry."

Miles didn't say a word in response to Coach Banks. He merely looked him in the eyes while he spoke and waited for the chastising to end. Miles walked over to an empty area of the bench and sat alone.

The Archers didn't score as fast as the Rock Warriors did, but they evened the score up 7-7 before the end of the first quarter. Coach Copper called the play he wanted the offense to run, but Miles changed it once again in the huddle. Miles lined up in a shotgun position behind the center and received the hiked football. He dropped back as if to pass, but he immediately took off in a full sprint down the field, leaping over defenders and spinning away from tackles. Miles accumulated 15 yards worth of real estate and ran down the sideline before being knocked completely out of bounds near the opposing team's sideline by the Terminator. He was waiting to land a good hit on Miles, just like he did Shawn. Surrounded by his Archer teammates, Demetrius taunted Miles on the sideline.

"Tell Shawn I said hello. Did he get the flowers I sent him? I'll send you some too after the game is over."

Infuriated, Miles said, "I'll say hello to you instead." He jumped up off the ground and motioned toward Demetrius until an official stepped in front of him and ordered him back to the field.

Coach Banks had seen enough. He called a timeout and marched onto the field with the back-up quarterback Ryan Fletcher, who was told to start warming up after the stunt Miles pulled during the first drive toward the end zone. Coach Banks commanded Miles to the bench, where he sat the rest of the half.

"Dad, why isn't Miles playing anymore?" asked Squirt.

"Miles hurt his foot and needed to be out for a few plays," responded Mr. Somers although Sage noticed Miles was walking fine.

The Archers took advantage of the sidelined superstar and accumulated a 21-7 lead at the half. The Rock Warrior defense, led by Cody and Paul, could not handle the offensive strategy implemented by their opponent.

Coach Banks spoke to Miles alone during halftime and tried to get him to refocus. All Miles could think about were his dead friend and his injured teammate and the part he played in them ending up that way.

The Rock Warrior defense was first on the field to start the second half. Cody and the rest of the defense held the Archers to 9 yards on the first drive of the half and forced a punt. Miles jogged back on the field with the offense lined up to run the next play.

Miles handed the ball off to Mike Jones for 6-, 7-, and 8-yard gains, respectively. He completed passes to Anthony and other receivers during the third quarter. They managed to tie the game up going into the fourth quarter, 21-21. It appeared as if Miles was back to his old self again.

The momentum of the game began to shift. The Archers' defensive coordinator had to do something to mix things up a little in the last quarter of the game, so he put Demetrius in position to blitz Miles during passing situations. Miles read the blitz every time, and Demetrius always reacted a second too late to complete a sack on Miles.

On the next pass attempt Demetrius delivered a pounding late hit on Miles, sending him crashing to the ground. Demetrius added, "Stay down, punk, before I make sure you and Shawn are sharing a room together next week. Hell, I may even send you to share a plot with your gay friend Andrew. I saw the video. Is that what yall did together?"

The official immediately threw a yellow penalty flag and charged Demetrius with a second penalty after hearing him taunt Miles while he was on the ground. Although Miles was in great pain from the hit, he hopped back up and ordered the offense to the huddle. He was determined to repay Demetrius for what he said.

Coach Copper called a play. Once again, Miles changed it. Not only was Miles going to run the ball, he was going to run directly in the direction of Demetrius. Miles lined up in shotgun formation behind his center. Demetrius shifted back to his safety position to defend a pass. The ball was hiked. Miles held the ball in the pocket while his receivers sprinted into their routes. Coach Copper gritted his teeth in the upstairs booth after he realized Miles had changed the play again.

Miles tucked the ball in his left arm and began a dash down field in the direction of the Terminator. Demetrius realized Miles was running the ball and sprinted full speed in his direction. Miles' eyes locked in on Demetrius and accelerated his speed. Demetrius waited for Miles to change direction to avoid his tackle, but Miles never deviated from his route. Demetrius rushed toward Miles, expecting a big tackle. Everyone in the stadium expected Miles to slide, change directions, or do something to avoid a hit from the most revered defensive player in the country. Neither player changed his path by a degree.

Miles and Demetrius collided with an atomic helmet to helmet hit that caused all the fans to rise to their feet to get a better look at what the outcome would be. Immediately unconscious, both players fell to the ground. They lay on the field motionless along with the fumbled football, which Anthony recovered for a 20-yard run into the end zone.

The medical staff for both teams rushed to the field. Before long, two medical carts were on the field to collect Miles and Demetrius. Both of their heads were placed in stationary braces prior to transport off the field.

Miles woke up three hours later in a hospital bed in downtown Los Angeles. Mr. Somers was sitting in a chair on the right side of his bed.

"What happened? Where am I?" asked Miles.

Mr. Somers told him what happened and how he ended up where he was. "You both sustained pretty bad concussions from the collision. After a few days rest, the doctors think you both will be alright, aside from some headaches, temporary memory loss, and blurred vision. Don't worry. We won the game 35-34. The other team missed an extra point."

Miles refocused and remembered everything after a few moments. He especially recalled the death of Andrew and what he did to Shawn. Mr. Somers was the closest thing Miles had to a father. He had to share his awful secret with the one person he respected the most.

"Mr. Somers, what happened to Shawn was my fault. I threw that ball in the direction I did because I wanted Shawn to get hit hard and suffer the way he caused me to suffer, but I didn't want him to get hurt the way he did."

"Miles, that doesn't sound like you at all. What happened to you?" Mr. Somers asked.

"What do you mean what happened? I'm just as much as a victim here as everyone."

"What do you mean?"

"Everyone used me. Shawn used me to get to the pros. Andrew used me to make thousands of dollars. Sage used me because her family is broke, and even you used me."

"How did I use you, Miles?"

"You forgot that you use to tell me all those stories about how you never could make the varsity football team and that you wished you could've played back then. You said that was one of the biggest regrets of your life. You used me so that you could live your childhood dream through me. That's the reason you came in that locker room back at Oakridge when I injured my right arm. You wanted me to go back out on that field for your benefit, not mine."

"You're right. This is all my fault. I should've never coerced you into playing this damn game."

Miles looked up and saw Sage standing by the doorway holding two cups of coffee with her mouth open in shock. She could not believe what she just heard. She didn't understand how Miles could do something so horrible to another person. The fact that he did it to his friend made it even worse. She handed Mr. Somers one of the cups of coffee, and he walked out of the room to give them some time alone.

Sage walked over to Miles' bedside. When she gathered up enough strength to say what she had to say, tears began to flow. She grabbed his right hand and held it with both of hers. "When I met you, you were the sweetest, kindest person I had ever met. But now this game has become bigger than us. We can never have a normal life together. Photographers, journalists and everyone else who wants to say they had a moment with the famous Miles Starr or Superman will always follow you. Now I learn that you took away the one thing that Shawn loved the most, on purpose. Andrew is dead because he could not be who he really was because of how it may affect you. He would have done anything for you. And now you think that I'm with you because of some bad business decisions my father made. I just can't be with you knowing these things. It's over. I love you, but it's over."

"It's over, just like that, Sage? If who I am is too much for you, why did you wait till now? Why did you wait until I was in love with you, until I would do just about anything to be with you? Are you afraid now that I'm injured I won't make the kind of money you and your family need?"

She turned away and headed toward the doorway, but she stopped to make one final comment. "I fell in love with you before I found out about my parents' financial issues, but I guess that could be a lie too, huh," she said before bursting into tears.

Miles sat up in his bed yelling, "Sage. Sage. We just need to talk."

She ignored his pleas and never spoke to him again.

CHAPTER 23
LIFE AFTER FOOTBALL

December 2022

Because they had trouble securing a flight from Phoenix to L.A. at the last minute, Melissa and Evelyn arrived at the hospital about five hours after Miles' incident on the field. Melissa sobbed almost hysterically at the sight of her only child lying in a hospital bed. Evelyn, however, was more interested in reading his medical chart to make her own assessment based on the doctor's notes. The doctors saw no swelling or bleeding on the radiological scans, so they released Miles after two days of observation.

When Miles returned home, his mother and aunt tried to convince him to never play football again. Their words fell on deaf ears, however. Miles made up his mind that he was not only going to continue to playing football, but he was going to play in honor of Andrew and Shawn. He vowed to mention both of them during every postgame press conference as his inspiration.

His new career philosophy was winning, and that's exactly what he did. He never lost another game for the rest of his career. Miles played in the college national championship game that year and the following year, winning two championships back to back.

Miles was drafted as the number one overall pick in the professional football draft. As quarterback for the Atlanta Ravens, he led the team to a professional football championship as a rookie in February 2025. The most shocking part of his football career came after that win. The following day, he announced he was retiring from professional football and enrolling in medical school.

This news came as a surprise to everyone, especially Mark Wells, Miles' agent. Mark was standing off to the side of the podium with Miles' publicist when the announcement was made. He waited for Miles to complete his speech before he ushered him to a back hallway for a private conversation.

"What the hell are you doing?" Mark asked, trying not to sound too agitated.

"You heard the speech just like everyone else. I'm done."

As Miles turned to walk away, Mark grabbed his shoulder.

"Oh, no, you're not done. You just get your behind back out there and tell everyone this was all a joke. Remember, you owe me. You owe my son!"

"You won Sports Agent of the Year, didn't you? So you got your notoriety. You got to represent a championship quarterback. You made millions. And as far as me owing you, you're a lawyer and now I'm a retired athlete. Show me in writing exactly what I owe you." Miles paused before continuing, "As far as Shawn, you owe him more than I ever will. We both never had a father."

Frozen with anger and shame, Mark hung his head as Miles walked past him and out the exit.

The media and fans devised all types of stories and rumors about his motives for retirement. He was questioned many times but never gave an answer that would adequately satisfy their curiosity and angst.

Miles breezed through medical school and became a neurologist after four years. Ten years after his last professional game, patients finally stopped recognizing him and asking for an autograph. Specializing in autism, Miles worked at a research hospital in Decatur, Georgia.

One day, Miles was reviewing a new patient chart and recognized the name Austin McCormick. He could not believe it and thought it couldn't be the same person he had known years ago. Miles had to see for himself, so he walked into the patient waiting area. He was immediately taken aback by the image of his long lost love Sage sitting with her now 26-year-old brother Austin. He was no longer a little boy, but, in fact, an average-size grown man. Sage was looking down, engrossed in an article on her satellite phone and didn't see Miles. However, Austin looked up, saw Miles, and uttered a very familiar phrase. "Go, Miles. Go."

Sage then looked up and almost dropped her phone in disbelief. She didn't want to appear too excited, but she could not resist the urge to walk up and give him a warm embrace.

"How the heck are you?" asked Sage smiling.

"Great, and you look great, by the way."

"Thank you. I see you have been staying in shape yourself."

"I have to get back to my patients, but we should meet some-time and really catch up."

Sage almost lost her composure, but maintained a straight face. She was overly excited by the gesture. "I'm not doing anything to-night," Sage added.

"I get done here at five. Here is my card. Text me your informa-tion and availability, and we'll see what happens."

"Consider it a date."

A few other patients in the waiting area kept staring at Sage even after Miles walked back inside the office. One elderly lady, Rebecca, got up the nerve to ask, "How did you get him to ask you out? I've been trying to get him to notice my daughter, who's a real beauty, by the way. I bring her in here with me all the time, and he's always real polite to her but nothing else."

"Miles is kinda different," replied Sage. "He usually already has in his mind what he wants. I pray that it's still me."

"I almost thought he simply didn't like women, but turns out that he's a real man after all. Sweetie, they're all the same, so don't get your hopes up too high. "

Another woman with a 6-year-old autistic child said to Rebecca, "I guess you can tell your daughter that *he* wasn't the problem." She then winked at Sage, who chuckled and then went back to reading her article.

* * *

When they met for dinner that night, they informed each other of the events that shaped the last 10 years of their lives. Sage told Miles that she went to school to become a nurse and was taking care of Austin by herself. She was more interested in learning about Miles than talking about her life, though, so she started ask-ing some calculated questions.

"Are you married?"

"No, I couldn't ever find your replacement."

"Do you have any kids?"

"No, do you?"

"No, Austin is enough for me."

They both looked relieved after learning the marital status of the other. It took less than a year before the two were seriously dating and eventually married. They bought a beautiful home in Alpharetta, Georgia, and Austin lived with them too. Sage was pregnant within two years with their first child.

During the week of Miles' 32nd birthday, he had been trying to get Sage to hint what his present would be. The only thing she told him was that it was going to be better than the gift she gave him on prom night for his 18th birthday. That made Miles even more anxious. He thought nothing would ever top their first intimate night of passion.

The doorbell rang on the Saturday morning of his birthday.

"Miles, can you get the door please?" Sage asked her husband in a kind voice from the future baby room she was decorating.

Without looking through the peephole to see who it was, he opened the door. His eyes widened in disbelief. Shawn was standing at his front door with an attractive athletic woman and a set of boy and girl twins.

"Hello, Superman!" said Shawn, flashing his famous million-dollar smile. He appeared to still be in amazing shape.

Miles stepped toward Shawn and hugged him firmly. Sage lingered a few feet behind Miles and smiled because she was the one who invited Shawn and his family. It was his birthday present.

Shawn, his wife, and their kids sat in the living room for the long-awaited reunion. Shawn told Miles about how his life changed since his injury over 10 years ago and how he went to a holistic rehabilitation clinic to recover from his injury. That's where he met his wife, Kia, who was a rehabilitative therapist. He said, with her help, it took him a year to recover to get back to walking independently. Over that period, he fell in love with his wife.

Kia was the one who motivated him to open up a fitness facility in Phoenix. Shawn was an expert in fitness back in high school, so Kia told him to put those skills to good use. She said, "No one knows more about keeping the body in tip top shape than you do. Why don't use that knowledge to start a business of your own?"

Shawn's first fitness center eventually became part of a national chain he created known as Wells Fitness. Miles had heard of it because he passed one on the way to the hospital every day. He just never knew Shawn owned it and had more than 150 fitness facilities nationwide.

Sage and Kia took the twins in the kitchen for a snack so Miles and Shawn could have a private talk.

"Shawn, I hope you can forgive me for what I did to you."

"That's why I'm here. I wanted to say thank you for setting me free. When I found out that I couldn't play football again, it was like a major weight being lifted from my shoulders. I didn't have to worry about living up to my father's standards anymore. I no longer live for his approval. I live for the approval of my wife and kids. You did me a favor when you threw that ball. I saw Demetrius running toward me, and I could've not tried to catch that ball. I made the decision. Thank you, Miles. Thank you."

A tear rolled down Miles' face. Shawn lifted a big weight off of Miles' shoulders too because Miles had carried the burden of injuring his friend from the moment it happened until that moment.

"I know you married the woman of your dreams, but what kind of big things have you done, Superman?

"I always hated that name."

"I know. Just thought I'd get one in for old times sake."

"Well, because of how well my athletic training went, Virtual Tech has succeeded in revolutionizing how athletes are trained around the globe today. They used me as a poster child for what the machine is capable of doing and made billions. I did a couple of endorsements for Virtual Tech the year I played with the Ravens. After I stopped playing, that was it for endorsement deals. Anyway, Holographic Simulation Chambers are now part of almost every successful sports organization – high school, college and the pros."

"I know because we have a chamber in every one of our fitness centers. And we have at least one Virtual Tech poster with Miles Starr using the chamber. They're old, but I won't allow anyone to take them down."

"Wow! I don't even have any of those posters anymore."

"Well, if you sign a few, I might give you one. Might even frame it for your kid's room."

"No football for any kid of mine."

"Remember, that's what your mother use to say before she knew your skills."

"Yeah, I remember."

"Who would have ever dreamed what you and I accomplished out there on the football field. I bet it won't ever be done again. You were the first and probably last player to be called 'The Prodigy'."

"I'll take that bet," Miles replied.

E P I L O G U E

August 2051

Right about the time I finished telling the story of Miles Starr to Tyler, his parents arrived to pick him up. It was after 10 p.m. Tyler had been with me over 12 hours, but he did not want to leave when my daughter, Michelle, rang the doorbell. Ironically, earlier that day, he didn't want to stay.

Tyler reluctantly gathered his backpack and headed outside to the car with his mother in tow. "Thanks, Dad. We had a great time. We'll see you tomorrow for lunch."

"Looking forward to it." I watched my daughter's family drive away before going back into my house.

Because he was so excited about the story I told him, Tyler asked his mother in the car on his way home if he could borrow her satellite phone. She didn't think much of it because he used it sometimes to play games online when they traveled. She handed Tyler the device in the back seat.

Tyler was quiet for a few minutes, but then no more. "Mom, is something wrong with your Web service?" he asked.

"What do you mean, dear?" she asked.

"I can't find him."

"Find who?"

"Miles Starr. Grandpa said he won two college championships and a professional championship, but I don't see any mention of him in the database I searched."

Michelle flinched when she heard the name Miles Starr. She struggled to come up with a reasonable response that wouldn't cause Tyler to get too suspicious.

"You're right, dear. The service provider was doing some testing on the network, so all the Web access on our phones and at home have been acting weird all day long."

Her response silenced Tyler for the time being, but she knew that wouldn't be the end of that conversation. Tyler wasn't going to give up that easily with his search for answers.

On the next day, Michelle and her family traveled back to my home to pick me up, so we could go out and have Sunday brunch. I saw them through the curtains when they pulled in my driveway, right on time as usual. I was getting my coat out of the closet when Michelle marched through the front door alone with an angry expression.

"Three championships, dad? Seriously, I thought it was five the last time or was it six? Did he marry Sage or Christine in your most recent fairytale? You promised me you wouldn't tell Tyler those stories. You drove mom away because she couldn't take you feeling sorry for yourself anymore. She should've died with her husband and not alone in an apartment."

I knew I was in trouble when she said those words. I thought, "What can I do? Everything she said is the truth."

"I don't care what you tell the kids in the neighborhood, but you promised me you weren't going to fill Tyler's head with things that are simply not true. You know how inquisitive he is. If you tell him something, he's going to look it up. I told you that.

"People are starting to question your sanity. They think you're losing it. Carlos called me last week and said your stories are getting more and more outlandish. I know you miss him and so do I, but you have to let go. It's not your fault."

I started crying again like I always do when I am forced to come to reality about Miles. I yelled at her before I knew it, saying, "It *is* my fault! It's your fault! We are all to blame! Every sports fan is to blame. We don't give a damn about the athletes or their well-being. We just want a win. We want a win at all costs. We don't care if players are beating their girlfriends or getting paid under the table or come from a poor family that can barely pay its rent as long as they show up to play on Saturday and Sunday, and win of course. We don't want coaches with ethics. We want coaches that produce wins. Miles would be alive and well today if I hadn't gone into that locker room at half time back at Oakridge. But I did. I went in that locker room because I knew what he could do. He could win the game and put on a show the world had never seen before, and that's exactly what he did. We all got what we wanted. We got a few cheers and a few stories to tell, but Andrew and Miles are dead because of it, because of me."

"Just stop it. Miles died in the hospital after the conference championship game in Los Angeles in December 2022 from a sub-dural hematoma he got from a hit during the game. You were there when the doctor told me, you, and Sage what happened. You just need to deal with it. It's been 30 years. It's time to bury this guilt with Miles and Andrew."

I continued the rant and feeling sorry for myself as I walked toward the door. My daughter felt sorry for me. I could see it in her watery eyes. She saw her tired old father whimpering like a schoolgirl because I refused to forgive myself for a series of actions that I never could have predicted.

I dried my tears with a Kleenex I pulled from a box on the end table in my living room. I accidentally knocked over a framed picture and my 8-inch little league football trophy. I stared at the picture as I placed it back in place. We took that picture 30 years ago while standing in the Oakridge stadium parking lot after the fifth football game of the season. I remember the final score to this day: Wildcats 56 and Broncos 28. It was a picture of Michelle, or "Squirt," when she was much younger, Melissa, Shawn, Andrew, Sage, Christine, Miles, and me.

CPSIA information can be obtained at www.ICGtesting.com
Printed in the USA
LVOW080013130312

272689LV00002B/6/P